A PENNY FOR YOUR MURDER

Caleb Lott

authorHOUSE

AuthorHouse™ UK
1663 Liberty Drive
Bloomington, IN 47403 USA
www.authorhouse.co.uk
Phone: 0800.197.4150

Published by AuthorHouse 12/29/2015

ISBN: 978-1-5049-7122-5 (sc)
ISBN: 978-1-5049-7123-2 (e)

Print information available on the last page.

This book is printed on acid-free paper.

To Julia

Truth will come to light; murder cannot be hid long;

The Merchant of Venice
Act 2, Scene 2

PROLOGUE

1983

A young man sat quietly on a wicker trash basket turned upside down just inside the door of a large walk-in closet. The light was off and the room was cool, yet his palms were sweaty, owing to his nerves and not to his environment.

The sixty square foot space, just off the master bedroom, had been a selling point when the house was purchased some ten years earlier, and was full of mostly women's clothes. The young man inhaled deeply through his nose and could identify a combination of scented detergent, sweat, and moth balls.

He was an average-looking man; white, about five foot seven, with a thin build and sandy blonde hair. He wore blue jeans and a light blue, pullover t-shirt that somewhat matched his gray eyes. His shoes were dirty, white canvas, Converse brand high tops.

His twenty five year old face was clean shaven and had kind of a boyish quality; by that it is meant that he had few if any lines or folds in the skin, and his cheeks puffed out slightly. His nose was smaller than average, and his lips were thin.

It was three o'clock in the afternoon, and though the three thousand square foot home was well air conditioned, the atmosphere in the small space was getting stale. Once, the young man had to stifle a sneeze.

The closet door was slightly ajar and from his vantage point the young man could see when anyone entered the adjoining bedroom. The opening cast a small shard of light into the room, and he could observe multi-colored dresses, many short, but some floor length; at least one full length fur; as well as various other blouses and pants on wooden hangars. Next to him was a metal rack full of shoes – pairs and pairs of women's shoes: heels, flats, sandals, and boots. As he looked further, he could barely make out a few men's suits in the far corner.

The bedroom was opulently furnished with a king sized, four poster bed; a large dresser with a four foot mirror; and a huge bureau, or as the young man's countrified mother would have called it, a 'chester drawers.'

His car was parked about a quarter of a mile away, in a shopping center parking lot, near a Rexall drug store and an A&P. After walking through a wooded area to the rear of the property, he climbed a short chain link fence and found the bedroom window on the west side of the lot, away from the swimming pool; just exactly where he was told it would be.

The home's rear windows were well concealed by large Azalea bushes that had long since shed their blooms. Azaleas flower only in the spring, for about two weeks, and afterwards turn into ordinary shrubbery suitable for hiding a burglar's point of entry.

He had entered the home via a bedroom window approximately twenty minutes earlier. After wrapping his right elbow in an old t-shirt, he had struck the middle pane twice, hard, before it broke. The glass had fallen onto the carpeted floor, and, just as he had planned, it had made little if any noise.

The young man laid a Smith and Wesson, model 10, blue steel revolver on the floor next to him and wiped both his hands on his jeans. A K-Bar knife was in a brown leather scabbard on his belt, over his left hip.

He held his left wrist up to the light and noted the time on his watch. It was three ten. He shut his eyes and tried to picture what he was about to do and how he was going to do it, but when he did, all he could see was his mother's face. He had not been a good son by his own measure, and this was only going to make things worse. He rubbed his own face hard and tried to scrub her image from his brain.

The young man was a hunter, and no stranger to killing. He had killed many deer, raccoons, and opossums while growing up in rural, north Mississippi. He told himself that this would be no different, but even as he took deep breaths in an effort to calm himself, his heart was beating so hard he was sure that it was audible. The adrenalin rush that he felt was familiar; he had felt it many times in the past when he looked at animals through the telescopic sight on his rifle. But this time it was different, much more potent. He wished he had taken a touch of something hard before coming to the house.

His concentration was broken by the noise of a door opening and closing. He couldn't tell if it was in the front or the back of the house, but he picked up the revolver and held it in his right hand as he slid off the trash basket, down onto one knee.

Three minutes later, a woman walked into the room. She was middle aged, with well-coiffed brown hair and a full figure. Her Mediterranean features and dark suntan helped identify her. She wore a long sleeved, white, oxford blouse, jeans, and pristine, white, US Keds tennis shoes.

The woman stood in front of the mirror on the opposite side of the room and pulled earrings from the lobes of her ears. Her back was to the closet door. She turned her head from side to side and admired her hair, then leaned in closely to the glass to massage the skin on both her cheeks and under her eyes.

Whether she saw him in the mirror or not, it didn't matter. He was through the closet door and at her back before she could move. He stood four feet away, pointed the revolver at her, and said nothing.

The woman's eyes widened as she turned toward him and pulled her arms to her chest in the pugilistic stance. Her voice shook, and as she spoke, she began to back away from the mirror toward the bed.

"Wh, what do you want?"

The young man said nothing. He was finding it harder to do what he had to do than what he thought it would be. His heart was racing, and his respirations were full and rapid.

"Here. There's jewelry on the dresser." She nodded toward the two obviously expensive earrings, both encrusted with diamonds.

Her breathing increased as well, and she continued to back away from the young man until her legs hit the side of the bed.

"Please, don't hurt me." Her voice was now a whimper.

The young man lifted the revolver to eye level, turned his head down and slightly to the left, and after shutting his eyes tightly, he made a face of disgust and squeezed the trigger.

CHAPTER 1

Six months later

A man calling himself John Edge sat in a nineteen fifties-era, green, vinyl-upholstered chair along the side of the first floor hall of the Public Safety building in Montgomery, Alabama, and waited. His right leg was crossed over his left and his chin rested on his left palm.

The venerable, white-washed, stone structure was located on the southwest corner of South Bainbridge Street and Dexter Avenue, and was one of seven or eight similar appearing government office buildings scattered around the State Capitol complex. The high ceilings, long hallways, and checkerboard tile floors inside were also typical.

Edge looked directly ahead toward the west entrance where the State Police had turned the

1

vestibule into a makeshift museum. It featured a vintage motorcycle; three or four uniforms on mannequins; and a marked, 1972 AMC Javelin patrol car, an experimental model used for highway patrol duty in the early part of that decade.

As he waited, Edge could hear the sounds of telephones and typewriters in the offices on either side of him. He had been waiting for thirty minutes and the gentle hum of the work had already relaxed him to the point that his chin had twice fallen off of his hand.

The noise of heels clicking on the tile floor roused him back to full consciousness, and he looked up to find a woman walking his direction. She was fifty, with graying hair and a dumpy figure, and a large smile appeared on her face as she neared him.

"Mr. Edge? I'm Margaret Collins. Can you step into my office?" she said with her southern accent.

He nodded, but said nothing.

Edge rose and followed the woman two doors down to a twelve by twelve room. She took a seat at her desk and smoothed out her print dress. He sat down on one of twin wooden chairs across from her, and crossed his legs.

"I'm with the Office of Professional Responsibility, and as you know, we're in charge of issuing private investigators licenses here in the state. Now, I've been looking over your application, and there are a couple of things that I wanted to clear up."

Edge said nothing.

"I see your Mississippi birth certificate is in order; a copy of your Alabama driver's license; and a Social Security card." She lifted up two pages fastened to a manila folder that sat on the desk in front of her.

"You were born in Starkville, Mississippi, is that correct?" she said.

"Yes."

"I have a personal work history here that lists 'out of the country' for the past eight years. What were you doing?"

"I was in the French Foreign Legion."

Her brows went up. "Oh. Well, that certainly is unusual. Do you have your passport?"

"No." He paused. "I wasn't aware I needed it."

She shook her head. "You don't. I was just curious." She paused and looked at the file. "We'll have to check that."

"You can try, but the French embassy won't confirm nor deny my service record."

She raised her brows. "Why not?"

"They just won't. It's part of the deal."

"Oh. Okay."

Her smile was gone now, and she studied the file closely looking for something that would enable her to refuse him a license.

"Have you ever been arrested?"

"No."

"Ever been discharged from a job?"

"No." He paused. "That wasn't one of the questions on the form."

"I know it wasn't."

"Are you looking for a reason to deny me this license, ma'am?"

Collins licked her lips. Her experience told her that Edge was hiding something. What, she didn't know.

The Public Safety Department had recently taken over the issuance of private detective licenses – a responsibility formerly held by the state Department of Revenue – in order to more closely monitor who was getting pseudo-investigative powers in the state. She had found reasons to reject a half dozen applicants within the past month, and while there was no concrete reason to do the same for Edge, there were just too many gaps in his history for her to feel comfortable.

She was wise to be suspicious. The real John Edge had been a soldier in the US Army's 23rd Infantry Division – the old Americal Division – who had died in Vietnam in 1968.

"No. I'm not," she said. "It's just that there seem to be some questions about your past."

"Ask me anything you like."

She studied his file. Collins would love to ask him some questions, but, frankly, she didn't know where to begin. This man had a clean criminal history and his driving record was spotless.

The real John Edge had died as a result of wounds sustained in a firefight with the Viet Cong. Fragments from an RPG (rocket propelled grenade) had struck him in the head and chest, and he had died in a helicopter on the way to a US Army field hospital.

It had only cost this man a hundred dollars to procure a copy of Edge's birth certificate from the state of Mississippi. Then, in order to get a new one in Edge's name, he had persuaded a clerk at the State Trooper post in Mobile that his Mississippi driver's license had been stolen; and the Social Security Administration was only too willing to issue him another card with John Edge's number, for the same reason.

Oh, whatever, Collins thought. So what if he was shady. Most of them were anyway. If they were all on the up and up, they'd be police officers. She looked up from the file, picked up a rubber stamp, and pounded the top page with the word, 'APPROVED.'

"No. It all seems to be in order," she said with a tone of resignation.

Then she handed him the folder across the desk. "Stop at the last office on the right at the end of the hall. They'll make your photograph and process your ID card." She rose, smiled weakly, and extended her hand. "Good luck in your new business."

The new John Edge stood and shook her hand. He took the file and nodded at Collins.

"Thank you, ma'am. You've been very helpful," he said.

In the hall, Edge took a deep breath. Getting the license had been the last step in his plan to relocate to Mobile, Alabama, on the coast, and open his own business. Frankly, it had been easier than he thought. He was silently thankful for the greed, the inherent willingness to cooperate, the laziness, and/or just the simple incompetence of civil servants who were more than eager to do what was expedient rather than what was right. He looked down at the file, and at the word, 'APPROVED,' and knew that the government was functioning on its last leg.

As he walked to the west end of the hall, a self-satisfied kind of peace overtook him. He took a long, deep breath and resolved to smile on his ID photograph.

CHAPTER 2

Two weeks later

T Bob's Saloon was as close to a neighborhood bar as there was in downtown Mobile. It sat on the northeast corner of Washington Avenue and Conti Streets and was a cross between an English pub and a red neck beer joint.

Its clientele included, on weekdays, the out of work, the alcoholic, and those recently released from incarceration; and on weeknights, professionals, financiers, civil servants, and merchants who worked at the government offices, banks, and shops downtown, and who thought it somehow chic to pretend they were slumming it in what they believed was a classic 'juke joint.' Every now and then a blues band performed live, and ladies' night was a weekly attraction that ensured that there was an adequate supply of young women to dress up the place.

The interior was mostly wood, around an easy to mop tile floor. There were two pool tables, a long mahogany bar, and metal tables and chairs broadcast about the interior. Outside, in the rear patio, lights hung from two spreading oaks within the confines of a board fence, and wooden picnic tables provided seating for those who enjoyed the cool sea breeze and the night air more than the thick smoke that hung like a fog in the interior.

John Edge sat at the end of the bar on a Tuesday afternoon at one o'clock and stared at a high ball glass half full of a new drink, something called Diet Coke; in Edge's estimation, a thoroughly reprehensible liquid that tasted like shoe polish, but which contained no sugar and therefore no calories.

Standing two inches over six feet, he had a slim build but large bones. His hands, at the end of thick forearms, featured long fingers that created a span that was close to eleven inches across from thumb to little finger. His hair was brown, cut short, and parted on the right side. Four, inch-long scars, visible souvenirs of a beating by West German pornographers in what he called his 'previous life,' sat on top of the prominent bones of his face: across his forehead, on his right cheek, the brow of his left eye, and the point of his chin. The retired Army doctor who stitched him up had assured him that the scars would eventually stretch out and become invisible, but as yet they had not.

Somehow, though, they seemed to compliment nicely his almost flat nose.

He wore a starched, white, short sleeved shirt, khaki pants, and chukka boots – soft leather shoes with thick soles; comfortable, yet sturdy enough for running. He carried a Colt Detective Special, a .38 caliber revolver in a holster on his left ankle, and a switchblade knife in his right front pants pocket.

The bar was quiet but for the low hum of the juke box playing country music, and the occasional 'click' of billiard balls striking one another. Two young men were playing pool on one of the tables behind him, and their sporadic paroxysms told him that one of them, at least, was drunk. Edge ignored them and took an occasional sip of his drink.

"Hey, buddy," one of the pool players, the obviously drunk one, said.

He was twenty-something with brown hair, a tooth missing in front, and a dirty t-shirt. His jeans were dirty also, and the only thing that belied his station was an obnoxiously large, gold pinky ring on his left hand.

"You see that shot?" His accent was heavily southern.

Edge looked over his shoulder but ignored him.

"Hey. Hey, you see that shot? A two cushion bank." He touched the pool cue to Edge's shoulder. Edge looked back at him.

"Get lost."

"Hey," the drunk said. "Hey. I said did you see that shot?"

His tone bordered on belligerence, and he struck the cue on Edge's shoulder, again, harder.

"Come on, Tommy. Leave him alone. Let's play," the drunk's opponent said.

"Hey, I'm talkin' to you."

Edge reached and grabbed the tip end of the cue. He took it in both hands but froze when he heard Josh the bartender speak.

"That cue's from off the wall, John. Don't break it."

Edge looked back at him, then slid off the bar stool, turned, and began to walk toward Tommy. He took his end of the cue and forced the grip end into the young drunk's abdomen. Then he pulled back hard on the stick thereby wrenching it free from Tommy's hands. Edge threw the cue on the table and then, as the drunk bent double, he seized him by his right arm and twisted the limb causing Tommy to cry out.

"Owwww!"

"Boy, you're gonna learn not to bother people."

"Don't hurt him, John," Josh said.

"If you can't," Edge said, "then maybe this'll help you remember."

Edge continued to twist his arm while he bent back his wrist. Then he walked the drunk to the front door, pushed him outside, and kicked him in the butt. The boy fell onto Conti Street and rolled twice. Edge turned and walked back to his place at the bar.

"Thanks, man," Josh said.

"For what?"

"For not tearin' up nothin' and not hurtin' him. Tommy's not a bad dude. He just gets a little carried away sometimes when he's had too much."

"I hate drunks," Edge said while frowning at Josh.

Back on his barstool, Edge intermittently pulled on the straw in his drink until about fifteen minutes later when a woman walked in the front door. She was dressed in a short-sleeved Oxford shirt and jeans, and she looked as out of place as Edge. After stopping just inside the threshold, she looked around then walked purposefully toward the bar.

"Mr. Edge?"

Edge nodded.

"Shelia Waltham. I'm the one that called."

Edge nodded again. "Let's go over here."

He picked up his drink, and the two walked to a metal table in the corner farthest from the bar and sat down. Edge studied her carefully.

She was in her mid-thirties, about five and a half feet tall. Her sandy hair was cut in a wedge cut, but shorter, with her ears visible, and her face was devoid of makeup. She wore no jewelry except a wristwatch.

Waltham took the measure of the room with a sour expression on her face.

"This is some place." She paused. "You don't have an office?" Her voice was an alto, and smooth.

"Not yet. I'm still finalizing the details. You don't mind meeting here, do you?"

"No, I guess not."

"Besides, I'd rather not meet people in my office. I . . . well, in the past, I've had trouble in my office. Undesirables seem to want to visit me there."

"I hope that won't be true in this case."

"That remains to be seen. Anyway, I haven't been in business very long. I'm still putting things together."

"I know."

He looked at her closely. Another place, another time, and Edge might have found her attractive. She had kind of an earthy quality, clean, and low maintenance. But at that place, and at that time, he put the thought out of his mind after he noticed the bottom portion of a large tattoo on her upper right arm.

"I've tried seven other agencies: four large corporations, and three independents such as yourself. The businesses don't handle anything but large settlement divorces, civil trial work, and disability cases."

"What about my direct competitors?"

"Well, one's black, and this case looks to be all white. I don't think he'd fit in very well. The other two are retired police officers." She paused. "Frankly, I don't think they're hungry; not hungry like you."

She was right. Any investigator living off a pension wouldn't give her case a thousand per cent. He wouldn't need to.

"What exactly is this case about?"

She reached in her right hip pocket, pulled out a business card, and slid it toward him.

"As I said over the phone, I represent the claims division of Manhattan Mutual Insurance. I work out of our Atlanta office. The wife of one of our policy holders, a Dorothy Wyatt, was murdered. The police haven't been able to come up with anything, and the policy is large enough to justify sending someone to make an attempt at figuring out what happened to her."

"How big's the policy?"

"Two million dollars."

Edge said nothing but raised an eyebrow. "I take it the husband is the beneficiary."

"He is."

"You think he's involved?"

She shrugged. "Well, we don't know. One would expect him to be, but the police have yet to come up with anything, and it's my understanding that he's alibied out."

Edge had worked cases like this before. They were conspiracies, and conspiracies had to be worked from the outside in. You had to find out who did the actual killing before you could implicate those with the most to gain from the death.

"Tell me about it."

Waltham shrugged again. "Not much to tell, really. I've seen the police report and all the evidence indicates that it was a burglary gone bad. It looks like she surprised a thief in her bedroom. There was a broken window, jewelry missing from the dresser, and some money was taken from her purse."

"How much?"

"Thirty seven dollars."

Well, people've been killed for less, he thought. "How was she killed?"

She paused and swallowed. "She was shot and her throat was slashed."

Edge was silent. He didn't want to contradict his new employer right off, but this was not a burglary gone bad. People generally weren't killed with two different types of weapons unless they were the object of the attack. Besides, most burglars did not, as a rule, kill. They ran out, they ran around, they ran over, they even hid, but they didn't kill.

"Wyatt, hunh." He paused. "Rich?"

"Yes. Well, a little."

"How'd they make their money?"

"The husband owns a local chain of coffee and pastry shops, the 'Bean and Dream.' They sell all of those high-end, exotic blends of tea and coffee, as well as upscale French pastries. They're also doing something new."

Edge raised his brows.

"Drive through coffee sales."

"Drive through?"

"Yes. Just like the hamburger chains."

Edge nodded then looked away. Sensational death, prominent local family, and a female victim; it sounded like what he was looking for. He needed the case, it sounded like a big spender, and it had the potential to be a publicity cow.

He smiled to himself, for just then a John Wayne line ran through his head. 'A man will never work for a woman unless he's got clabber for brains.'

"So, what's the deal?" he said.

She swallowed. "I give you a week's trial at five hundred dollars. You do your work. If I like the results, I'll sign a contract and you're on your way."

"If you don't?"

"You keep the money, and I look for another investigator."

Edge snorted. "Well, Ms Waltham. I don't audition. You either want me or you don't. For something like this, I get a one thousand dollar non-refundable retainer. I charge twenty five an hour, and you've got the right to pull the plug whenever you please. You'll get a bill from me every month, just like the phone company, and I'll fill you in on what I've found out whenever you call."

Waltham, obviously a woman not used to being told how to run her business, snorted also. She said nothing, but a feeling of respect came over her. She admired his confidence. What she didn't know was how much he wanted the case. She decided to find out.

"Okay. You've got a deal . . . but on one condition."

Edge raised his brows again.

"I've got an associate I want to send along with you, to keep an eye on you and report back to me."

He shook his head. "I work alone."

"You take my girl, or not at all."

Edge smirked. He wanted the case, but he had spent too much time in the past wet nursing female investigators through cases. They didn't always come out unscathed.

He took a deep breath and exhaled. "So, who is this girl? Somebody's wife or daughter? A project?" He paused. "A girlfriend?"

Waltham said nothing.

Edge looked at her. Her face told him that he might very well have hit the nail on the head. Finally, he looked away.

"Alright." He reached in his pocket and pulled out a business card. "Have her call me."

She took the card. "I'll send the file over tomorrow."

CHAPTER 3

It was Edge's first major case in Mobile, but in order to ingratiate himself with local law enforcement and get the information that he would have to have to be successful, he needed a sponsor, a rabbi; someone who'd let them know that he was okay, that they could trust him, that they could work with him. He knew only one professional person in town who came close to fitting that description.

Edge had met J. Hunter Floyd in a very detective-like way. The two had been eating lunch, separately, at a downtown restaurant. Edge had been alone, and Floyd was with a young woman.

They both finished their meals at about the same time and then made their way to the counter to pay their checks. Edge watched closely as the lawyer dropped his business card into one of those large glass bowls out of which the restaurant would draw the winner of a free meal each week.

He spied the name on the card and after paying his own tab, caught up with Floyd and the attractive blonde outside. When Edge noted that Floyd was wearing a wedding band, and that he was holding hands with the young woman, his mind went to work.

"Mr. Floyd, could I speak with you?"

"What? Yes? Who are you? How did you know my name?"

"My name is Edge. I'm a private detective. I saw your card in the contest bowl. I hope you and Mrs. Floyd don't mind stopping to talk," he said looking at the young woman who was wearing a short skirt and showing a lavish amount of cleavage.

Floyd looked down and quickly let go of the woman's hand. He cleared his throat.

"Oh, uh, well, yes, uh, sure, uh," he said looking at the young woman. He cleared his throat again, and Edge knew he had him.

"I'm just getting started in town, and I wanted to let you know that if you need any investigative help, I'm your man." Edge handed him a business card.

"Well, sure, sure," the older man said. He looked at the card and then from side to side. "And if I can help you, just let me know."

Edge nodded, turned away, and filed the man's name and address for future reference.

Edge left his meeting with Waltham and an hour later stopped in at the law offices of Floyd and Nealon. He found the early twentieth-century, Greek revival-styled building that had formerly been the residence of a wealthy commercial banker, on Dauphin Street, three blocks off Broad. The residence had been tastefully converted to office space for Floyd and about a dozen other attorneys.

Edge parked in the rear and announced himself to the middle aged receptionist just inside the back door. She called upstairs and in a minute Edge was seated across from Floyd, a rotund man with a mustache, glasses, and a bald head.

"What can I do for you, mister, uh, Edge, is it?" His voice was deep and distinguished.

"Yes, sir. We met at Domino's downtown, a couple of weeks ago. Do you remember?"

"Oh, right, right. You saw my name on a business card in that contest bowl."

"That's right. Well, you said if you could help me to let you know."

Floyd looked hard at him and said nothing. The scars on Edge's face and the long one on his left forearm told a story; one that troubled him.

"Just relax," Edge said. "I know people say things like that never thinking they'll have to pay off. Don't worry. I don't want anything big."

Floyd cleared his throat. "Well, how can I help you?"

"A letter."

"A letter?"

"Just write a letter for me."

"To whom?"

"To whom it may concern. Just tell'em: he's new, he's okay, and they should extend him every courtesy."

He cleared his throat again. "Well, I don't know. How do I know you're okay?"

Edge looked away toward the outer office where the same blonde woman he had seen at the restaurant was typing. "Well, you'll just have to take my word for it." He paused. "By the way, is your secretary out there the same person you were having lunch with the day I met you?"

Floyd chuckled and looked toward the young woman who was busy tapping away.

"Well, I guess you really are a detective, aren't you, Mr. Edge; and a smarmy one at that."

He picked up the phone and called the young woman into his office. Floyd dictated a short letter introducing Edge and asking that everyone take care of him.

"I don't know how much good this is going to do you," Floyd said as he signed the paper.

"You let me worry about that," Edge said taking the page that the young secretary had just finished typing. "I did some checking and you're a pretty big cheese in this town; former DA, hot liability lawyer."

He nodded slowly. "Well, I guess I do have sort of a reputation. We've had some things roll our way."

Edge nodded. "Well, my offer still stands. If I can help you, let me know."

Floyd chuckled again. "Mr. Edge . . . I never want to see you again. This ends it with us."

Edge rose, put the folded letter in his pocket and nodded. "I understand."

He walked out of the office a little sad knowing that he had walked over a bridge and then burned it. But, he had what he wanted. Now, he just hoped it would open the most important door that he needed to open.

It took twenty minutes in afternoon traffic to reach the Mobile Police Department's Detective Division office on Church Street. Edge found a parking space for his navy blue, 1982 Impala a half a block east, in front of Spanish Plaza.

He presented himself to the gray haired receptionist on the ground floor of the two story building and then sat down to wait. He had the letter from Floyd in his pocket, but he hoped he wouldn't need it.

In ten minutes, the older woman answered a telephone call and then directed Edge to the upstairs, on the east side of the building.

He knocked on the open door of the office of Lieutenant Victor Riley of the Homicide Squad. Riley was on the phone, but he looked up, over the top of his half-moon glasses, and beckoned him inside. Edge took a seat, and very shortly Riley hung up.

"What can I do for you, Mr. Edge?" Riley said.

He was at least fifty, a short, squatty man with a widow's peak and hanging jowls. His white, short sleeved shirt was wrinkled, and his tie had a stain on it.

"Yes, sir, well, I'm a private investigator, and I've been contracted by an insurance company with a financial interest in the murder of Dorothy Wyatt."

"A PI?" He paused. "I haven't heard of you, and I know most of the guys around town."

"Well, I'm new. Hunter Floyd knows me."

Riley laughed out loud. "You know Hunter Floyd? Well, you're either a drunk or you pimp the cheapest whores in town."

Edge just then realized that he might have gone to the wrong man to vouch for his character. He wondered what to do to save his self.

"Well, you know; any port in a storm."

"Oh, hey. I'm just joshin' ya. Floyd's okay. He's just got a reputation, that's all." He paused. "You licensed by the state?"

"Yes, sir." Edge showed him his credentials.

Riley looked at the license and handed it back to him. "You in police work before?"

"I've been out of the country for a few years. Before that, I was in Army Intelligence."

Riley leaned back and clasped his hands over his protruding abdomen. He took a deep breath and exhaled.

"Bootsie."

"Bootsie?" Edge raised his brows.

"That's what her family called her. 'Bootsie.' As bloody a scene as I've witnessed in quite a while." He paused. "Who did you say is interested in this thing?"

"Manhattan Mutual."

"Oh, the life insurance people. I get calls from some broad . . ."

"Waltham,"

"Waltham, right, every couple'a weeks. I tell her what I'm gonna tell you. We haven't got anything on it . . . yet."

"I know your guys are swamped. I heard you had sixty-six murders last year."

"And we're on pace to exceed it this year." He looked away as if the weight of each one was on him.

Edge recognized the telltale red nose of an alcoholic. It was clear that Riley was under a lot of pressure.

"And I've only got four men to handle'em." He paused. "I guess you want to take a run at this thing, hunh?" Riley leaned forward.

"I'm going to, but, I'd like to have your blessing."

He took a deep breath and exhaled. "Well, James Vaughn has the case assigned to him. I'll let him know. I've only got one condition: you get evidence, you bring it to me first. Got it?"

"I understand."

"You walk in one day with somebody in handcuffs, and I'm gonna take'em off him and put'em on you."

Edge said nothing.

"And if I hear about you breakin' doors or breakin' heads, I'm gonna put you in jail. I'm lookin' at this thing from a whole different perspective than you are. Understand?"

Edge sat stonefaced. Riley was responsible for making a case for court. Edge's job was to keep ManMut Insurance from paying Bootsie's old man two million dollars that he didn't deserve. Edge understood, but he didn't like the lieutenant's tone.

"Come on Lieutenant, can't we be friends?"

"I mean it, Edge. I don't have time to be fielding a lot of complaints about you hurricaning the town while you're horning in on one of my cases." He paused. "If you break it, you better be able to pay for it – or get away with it."

Edge chuckled. "I understand. You're a busy man with a lot on your plate."

"That's not the point. You find somebody good for this, I gotta get'em convicted," Riley said.

"Don't worry." He paused. "You think I could get a look at the file?"

"I gave some of it to that insurance lady; the police report and the autopsy results. They're both public record. The rest is confidential."

Edge nodded. He hadn't expected a lot of help.

Riley looked at him. "Anything else?"

"Nothing." Edge rose from his chair.

"Oh, Edge."

Edge stopped.

"Be careful. This is one mean son of a bitch."

Edge nodded. "So am I."

CHAPTER 4

Early the next morning, the insurance case file and a one thousand dollar money order arrived by special messenger at Edge's apartment, a one bedroom at the rear of a two story, brick, Creole-style home on North Joachim Street just off Adams.

It had a private entrance and a covered garage in the rear to keep the Chevy out of sight, and Edge had been living there since he moved to town. It was out of the way, quiet, and the large number of oaks spread about the property kept the place reasonably cool, even during the hottest days of the summer.

Edge settled into a beat up recliner with a cup of coffee and opened the file. There wasn't much to it, but what was there mattered.

The autopsy report described Dorothy Lizette Anderson 'Bootsie' Wyatt's injuries. There was a gunshot wound right in the middle of her forehead;

three long lacerations across her throat; and one stab wound, in the heart.

The gunshot was from close range; the doctor's estimate being three to five feet. The knife wounds appeared to be one through each carotid and one across the trachea. The stab wound was in the left ventricle. There was an old saying amongst hitmen and assassins: always kill'em twice. In this case, whoever had done this job must have been a novice, because he had killed this woman three times.

Edge used a magnifying glass to look closely at a couple of the autopsy photos. The wounds on her neck were smooth; the gunshot wound, a round hole with an abrasion collar, was just as described; and the stab wound to the heart was vertical, in the left ventricle. The body had been identified by the victim's sister, one Angela Anderson Lloyd. It listed her name and address.

There were also Xerox copies of two or three of the police department's scene photos stapled to the police report. They depicted the bedroom from the vantage point of a hallway door. The woman was lying half on, half off of a four poster bed that was prominent in the middle of the room. The dresser was to the right. Shards of glass lying on the floor next to a window by the bed pointed to the obvious point of entry. A closet door was near the window, and the bathroom door was next to the dresser. The photos were a poor substitute for the visit to the house he would have to convince the husband to allow him to make. Thankfully, Edge had the leverage to get that visit. Wyatt's husband would have two million reasons to cooperate.

The police narrative said that, according to her husband, the victim had left home at about ten AM to run errands. Robert Louis 'Bobby' Wyatt – Edge chuckled, 'Bobby' and 'Bootsie' – wasn't sure, but he thought that she was going to the dry cleaners, to a nearby pharmacy, to get her hair done, and then to a supermarket about a mile away. Edge felt that the stop at the market would have been her last.

More interesting was the lack of specificity regarding where Bobby Wyatt was while his wife was out. The police report said only that he was running errands also, with the couple's teenaged children.

The home was located in a fashionable neighborhood on the corner of Sunflower and Cottage Hill Roads called Sun Meadow. There was also a short list of the missing property obtained from the homeowner's insurance company: diamond earrings, a large diamond engagement stone, some pearls, and cash. It was a completely unimpressive haul.

Edge wiped his eyes and laid the file down. Up to that point, he didn't have a feel for anything except that the husband stood to gain two million dollars from his wife's death.

But assuming that was just a coincidence, Edge began to think of alternate suspects. The first was that the killer was just a random daytime burglar. This theory was highly unlikely. As he had wanted to point out to Waltham, burglars rarely kill. They certainly didn't kill three times.

The second theory was that the victim was followed home by a rapist or molester. But once again, Edge thought, why was murder necessary? Just put on a ski mask and do what you want to do.

That left the old standbys: a jealous lover, some unknown revenge motive, or just someone looking for something – in the bedroom.

Edge leaned back in his chair. The most logical place to start was with the husband, but he wanted to wait and deal with him when the woman from the insurance company was with him.

That was something else. Having a partner around his neck, while nothing new to him, was certainly going to slow things down. Any other time and he'd have turned the opportunity down. But, it being his first case in a new city, he had to establish himself and his reputation. Edge closed his eyes and thought back to another city and another life, a life that he had left behind. In minutes, he was asleep.

At noon, Edge left home and drove to T-Bob's. He was in a new town, and he had no snitches, no informants, no door into the criminal element. He had to remedy that pretty quickly.

Josh was once again behind the bar. He was wiping dry a beer mug and rocking back and forth to a song on the juke box.

Josh Osburn was the part owner, manager, and main bartender at T-Bob's, a name that had carried over from the previous proprietor. He was tall, with a bald head, a round belly, and soul patch right under his bottom lip. Josh was an amiable man who had welcomed Edge to town with a free drink and an offer to help out when he could. Edge took that to mean he could be bought for information.

Edge slid onto a barstool and looked around. There was an old couple seated over in the corner and one biker-type playing pool. Josh walked over.

"What can I get ya', John?"

"Well, you can start out with one of those Diet Coke things like I had yesterday; on the rocks."

Josh smiled and removed a glass from under the bar. "I don't see how you can drink that shit. It tastes like motor oil to me."

"It grows on ya. The ice helps," Edge said as he put a straw into the glass and gave it a long pull.

Josh went back to his drying. Edge cleared his throat.

"Hey, Josh. You know that kid that was in here yesterday, that Tommy?"

"Yeah, why?"

"I need to talk to him. How can I find him?"

"Oh, I don't know, John. You shamed him pretty bad yesterday. I don't know . . ." He shook his head.

Edge pulled out his wallet, extracted a five, and laid it on the counter. Josh looked down at the bill, slid it over to his side and picked it up. He folded it quickly and put it into the pocket of his jeans, all in one motion. Edge could tell that he had done it before.

He took a deep breath and exhaled. "His name is Tommy Dickens. He lives in an apartment over to the eleven hundred block'a Government, near Rapier; number two oh six, I think."

Edge looked up and nodded. "One more thing. Say I got something a little warm I want to change into cash. Who could I call?"

"You mean . . ."

"I'm talkin' high end stuff; nice jewelry."

He cleared his throat. "Well, I don't know. That's gonna take a little time to find out; them guys come and go, you know. I don't know who's on deck this month."

"Just off the top of your head."

"I'd hate to say." He paused. "But you know who could say is Marty over at Lazy Man's Pawn. He usually only buys cheap stuff, but if somebody's got something else, he might know where to send'em."

"Will he talk?"

Josh patted his pocket and smiled. "For the right price."

Edge chuckled. They were all alike. Low life mercenaries, who thought, mistakenly so, that money made it all worthwhile. In some ways the thought irked him; in some ways he believed they were right.

At the door of apartment two oh six at the Azalea Arms Apartments, Edge rapped twice and stood aside. It was a forties-era, three-story, brick building with a small parking lot in the back. It was, almost, but not quite, a flophouse; maybe two steps up the ladder.

Edge heard movement inside, and waited. Then a voice sounded from within.

"Who is it?"

"Special delivery."

He heard the chain unhook from the frame, and he stepped over to the knob side of the door. It opened about six inches and an eye appeared.

Edge moved quickly to slide his foot into the cranny just before the occupant could close the door. He gave it a hard shove and pushed his way into the room. Tommy Dickens went sprawling backwards, onto the floor.

"Relax, Tommy. It's just me."

Edge walked completely into the room, closed the door, and held out his hand in a move to help Tommy to his feet.

"What do you want? Who are you?" Tommy said as he ignored the hand and slid backward on his butt toward the wall.

His visage was a mixture of fear and anger. He sat on his backside wearing only a pair of white boxer shorts. Edge noticed his mullet haircut and the contrast of his dark, three day old growth of beard on his pasty white complexion.

The apartment was small, about four or five hundred square feet at the most. Edge thought that the building was probably once a hotel that had been converted over to apartments. There was a great room that doubled as living and bedroom space. He could see through an open door into a kitchenette, and a bathroom. The place was filthy.

Edge looked around. "Sheesh, Tommy, when's the last time you had the maid over?"

"I said, what'chu want?"

Edge took a deep breath. "Look, I just came over to apologize. I know I was a little rough on you yesterday, but I had things on my mind; and, well, you gotta admit, you *were* a little annoying."

Tommy said nothing.

Edge cleared his throat. "Anyway, so, I'm sorry." He held out his hand again.

Tommy slid back toward him and reluctantly took his large hand. Edge lifted the young man to his feet after which Tommy walked over and cleared some papers off a chair and sat down next to a dining table. His expression hadn't softened. He looked at the table and said nothing.

Edge walked over next to him, but didn't sit down. He was looking for a weapon, but saw none.

"Tommy, my name is John."

Tommy looked at him disgustedly but said nothing.

"I'm a private detective, and this morning, it occurred to me that we might be of assistance to each other."

Apparently, Dickens had heard only the word 'detective,' because Edge noticed his eyes cut to the far corner of the room. Edge nonchalantly turned that way and saw a sandwich bag full of marijuana sitting on an end table next to a threadbare couch against the back wall. Next to the plastic bag was a revolver.

He turned back to Dickens. "You see, I'm new in town. I need to get to know some people who can help me in my work. Naturally, our relationship will remain strictly confidential."

"How'd you find me?"

"Gee whiz, Tommy, you know I can't tell you that." He paused. "See how I kept the name of my informant a secret?"

Tommy said nothing. Edge couldn't tell if he was thinking or if he was just too stupid to know what to say.

"Of course, I'd be willing to pay you for your trouble; not much, but it could add up."

"I ain't no snitch."

"Sure you're not. You're a businessman, and you're smart enough to see a way to make a buck."

Tommy cleared his throat. If he'd had the courage, he'd have spit on him. But, he knew enough to know that he wouldn't get away with it.

Edge said nothing, turned, and started walking toward the living area. He made as if he intended to look out of the window on that side of the room. He could see out of his peripheral vision that Tommy was fidgeting noticeably.

"Tommy, I came over here to apologize and offer you a proposition. If you're too dumb to take advantage of it, well, I'll just have to show you the wisdom in my offer."

Quickly, Edge took three steps to his right and picked up the baggie and the revolver. He turned back toward the table to see Tommy walking toward him.

It was a six inch by nine inch plastic sandwich bag of what looked like a terrible grade of marijuana; brown instead of green leaves, with lots of stems and seeds. The revolver was a blue steel Saturday night special, rusted in places.

"Now, you put that down." His voice was angry.

Edge now knew. Tommy was dumb, or maybe slow.

"That's too much dope for one man to smoke, Tommy. You've got to be in distribution."

Edge set the bag back down on the table and proceeded to unload the revolver. He took out five rounds and slid them into his pocket. Tommy had stopped six feet away.

"You need to take better care of your piece, Tommy. It's gettin' rusty." He laid the gun back down also.

"What do you want?" Tommy said.

"Information. Who killed Dorothy Wyatt?"

"Who?"

"It's been in all the papers, Tommy; the rich broad on the west side. Her old man owns that coffee shop, the 'Bean and Dream.'"

The look on his face told Edge that Tommy didn't have the slightest idea of what he was talking about. It also told him that Tommy didn't read.

"I'm lookin' for the names of the burglars that operate on the west side; and I need to know who fences high end property out that way."

"What makes you think I know all that?"

Edge debated on whether or not to tell him. The fact was that Tommy was drunk and playing pool rather than working in the middle of the day on a Tuesday. That meant that he was either living off the government or he didn't get his money honestly. In addition, there was the gold pinky ring on his hand. It appeared expensive, but Tommy had no doubt gotten it cheap. That meant that he had either stolen it or he knew where to buy goods at a discount.

"Let's just say, I know things about people, Tommy. And, I know that the police would certainly like to talk to you."

His eyes got wide. Edge found it hard to believe that Tommy Dickens had lived as long as he had without any dealings with the cops.

"My guess is that they'd certainly be interested in this dope and that gun." Edge nodded toward the table and a nearby phone. "All it takes is a call. Your best bet is to work with me."

Tommy swallowed hard. He looked away then back at Edge. He took a deep breath, exhaled, and sat down on the couch.

"Varon. Alex Varon. He hits houses on the west side."

"Where can I find him?"

"In the phone book. His mama's name's Alice."

Edge knew that the name was of someone who was very inconsequential, but he didn't want to press. He turned toward the dope and the gun and picked up the weapon only.

"I'll leave the dope," he said.

Edge believed that the marijuana was how Tommy was going to make his next month's rent.

"But I'll take the gun. You don't need it, and it'll just get you killed."

He slipped the revolver into his pocket and pulled out a business card. It contained the number to his answering service. He dropped it on the table next to the dope.

"The next time I see you, I want to know the name of the fence that'll take high end jewelry. And I want a real name and not some two bit punk like that burglar you just gave me."

Edge started toward the door. He looked back at Tommy. The anger and fear were gone from his face. Now, he just looked whipped.

Edge walked out into the hall and started toward the staircase. He felt a heightened sense of satisfaction having confirmed to himself something he'd always believed: that every person you meet is a potential informant.

CHAPTER 5

After his talks with Josh the bartender and Tommy Dickens, Edge at least had a couple of names to work with. He was sure that this wasn't a random burglary gone bad, but he wanted to have something to report to Waltham next week; something to show that he had eliminated that particular possibility.

True to Tommy's word, Alice Varon's information was in the telephone book. Edge copied down the address that he found in the torn and damaged book in the booth on the corner of Government and George Streets.

The Varon residence was a small eleven hundred square foot house on Bonnie Lane in the Greenwich Hills subdivision off Cottage Hill Road, which was about two miles from the murder scene, according to the map that Edge had purchased shortly after he had moved to town. The house had a brick veneer and a carport, and while the neighborhood was probably once pretty nice, it was clear that it was beginning to deteriorate.

Edge found the house and parked down the street to watch for a while. He pulled out the day's paper and scanned the metro section for anything of interest. There was news of another homicide, a male slashed to death in an apartment off Azalea Road. Edge's mind drifted to Victor Riley.

In forty five minutes a late 70's Ford Thunderbird pulled into the driveway of the Varon home and a young man got out. He was short and pudgy, with sandy hair. If it *was* Varon, his slacks and white shirt struck Edge as slightly out of character. Maybe he's been to court, or to see his probation officer, Edge thought.

Edge watched as the young man walked purposefully through the front door and slammed it behind him. There was no other movement anywhere around the house.

While he contemplated his next move, the same young man exited the front door, got in the Ford, and backed it out into the street. Edge started his car and followed him.

They didn't go far, just down to Cottage Hill Road, to the food store at the Demetropolis Road intersection. Edge watched the young man park his car and enter the market. In ten minutes he was back with a grocery bag under his arm. Edge followed the young man back to his house.

If this person was Varon, making a move on him wasn't going to be easy. It would do no good to just walk up to him and accuse him of murder;

and asking him to implicate himself in a burglary, any burglary, was also going to be fruitless. And, Edge didn't want to start pounding on him in order to get the truth out of him. That was not how he wanted to begin his new life in Mobile. He thought about giving the name to James Vaughn, the PD investigator, but decided against it. Vaughn was too busy with other things to check him out. Edge was going to have to catch Varon in the middle of something; something that would give him leverage.

The Lazy Man's Pawn Shop on Halls Mill Road was a converted convenience store that stood alone at the Azalea Road intersection. Edge parked in front of it at three that afternoon. There were no other cars in the lot, and it looked like a good time to speak to Marty the pawnbroker.

The business was typical for its type. Behind burglar barred windows, there were glass showcases around the room in a three sided rectangle that served as a counter. Guitars and some larger merchandise hung on the walls, and televisions and stereo equipment filled the rows of shelves in the middle of the room. Edge noticed that things hadn't been dusted in quite a while.

"You Marty?" Edge said as he walked up to the smiling man behind the counter.

"That's me." He was a middle aged man with graying hair and a mustache.

"My name's John." His tone was serious.

Marty's smile vanished. "Yeah?"

"I need some information."

"What kind of information?"

Edge looked both ways and patted his hip pocket. "Valuable information."

Marty looked down. "You got somethin' you want to sell?"

"Yeah."

"Like what?"

"Like some real nice rocks."

Marty rubbed his face. "I can give you a name, but . . . it's gonna cost you."

"For a name?"

"This man values his privacy."

"How much?"

"Five hundred."

Edge chuckled and shook his head. He reached into his back pocket, pulled out his wallet, and extracted a ten. He held it up.

Marty reached and took it. "His name is Lardy."

"Lardy? What kinda name is that?"

"It's short for lard ass."

"He's a fatty."

"Right. Close to four hundred pounds."

"Where can I find him?"

"Well, he don't like me to give out his address." He reached for a pad and pen. "But call him at this number. He'll tell you where to meet him."

Edge nodded. "Okay. Thanks." He turned and walked out the front door to the tinkling of a small bell attached to the frame.

On the street, Edge made it for the first phone booth and called his answering service. An older woman, Madge, who had the afternoon shift answered.

"Hey, Madge. This is John Edge. Anything for me?"

"Hey, Mr. Edge. Uh, hold on." She was silent for minute. "Just one thing. A Ms Waltham called. She said she didn't want to talk to you, just wanted to know if you got her package."

"Call her back and tell her, yeah, I got it."

"Okay. Will do." There was silence once again. "So, how are you likin' Mobile?"

It was an odd question for an answering service operator to ask. Edge chalked it up to curiosity. "It's fine, thanks. Anything else?"

"Nothing."

"Okay. I'll call you later."

He hung up thinking that he'd have to look into changing answering services if questions like that persisted.

Edge put another quarter in the phone. It was time to get it over with, he thought. During the course of this investigation he would need the police. It was time to make nice with this James Vaughn and find out what the overworked investigator thought about this interloper.

Vaughn answered on the third ring. "Homicide, Vaughn."

"Mr. Vaughn, my name is John Edge." He paused. "Did Lieutenant Riley mention me?"

"Edge? Oh, yeah. The private dick."

He said it with a sneer in his voice, and Edge knew that there would be no help coming from him.

"Right. I was wondering if I could get some help on this case, this Wyatt case?"

"I'm sorry. I'm afraid I'm up to my ass in alligators. I just don't have time." He paused. "Anything else?"

Edge paused. "No. That's it."

They both hung up without further comment. It looks like, Edge thought, that this thing is going to be my baby to raise.

If anything was going to happen with Alex Varon, it was most probably going to happen at night, so at nine that evening Edge parked on Bonnie Lane and began watching from his car, with field glasses, the Varon residence, and the Thunderbird.

At eleven fifteen, the same male as earlier came out of the house, got in the Ford, and backed out of the driveway. It turned toward the Impala. Edge ducked down and, after the car passed, he started the engine and began to follow it.

The Ford stopped at a small lounge on Airport Boulevard, just west of Azalea. 'Glitters' turned out to be a lower class topless bar in a building that was once a fast food restaurant. Edge parked and followed the driver inside.

He ordered a Diet Coke and watched the young man from the T-Bird slide onto a stool at the bar, next to one of the waitresses. The headliner was doing her thing on the main stage and had the attention of the ten or fifteen men and three progressive women in the audience.

It took only a few minutes of surveillance for Edge to see what he thought he was going to see. Another man, one with gold chains and a short Afro, sat down with the waitress and the young man thought to be Varon, and the unmistakable movements of a drug transaction ensued.

Edge had to sit through another hour of the smoke, the loud music, and the not too attractive scenery, until the young man got up to go to the restroom. Edge spotted his chance and followed.

Inside, Edge spoke first. The young man was up against the urinal with his fly down. Edge walked up and stood right behind him.

The young man looked over his shoulder. "Hey, dude," he said, "like, this one's taken."

"Your name Varon?"

"What?"

Edge shoved his face into the tile wall above the urinal and piss sprayed out the side.

"Owwww. Wait!"

"Are you Alex Varon or not?"

"Okay, okay. Yeah. Who are you?"

"I'm the jawbone of an ass."

Edge took him by the collar and the back of his belt and, as urine sprayed on the wall, Edge dragged him over inside the commode stall and closed the door. He put Varon on his knees and held him by the neck, face first, toward the toilet.

"Now, I need answers, and you better talk fast. I know who and what you are. You're a small time punk burglar. You steal and you make life miserable for working people. Nobody's gonna listen when you squall." He pushed on his neck. "Who hit the Wyatt house in Sun Meadow?"

"What? Hold on, now!"

Edge pushed his face into the bowl. In seconds he brought it up.

"Come on. Who hit the Wyatt house where the woman got murdered?"

Varon sputtered and spit. "I don't know, I don't know."

Edge pushed him down again. He believed him but he had to make it good.

"Come on Alex. Who did it?"

He sputtered again. "I don't know! Come on, now!"

Edge pushed him down again. Then he eased up, reached into Varon's hip pocket, and pulled out a plastic bag containing eight or ten pink pills. He pulled Varon out of the way and held the pills above the bowl in an implicit threat to pour them out.

Varon sputtered. "Hey, what are you doin'?!"

"Don't you know this stuff'll stunt your growth?"

Varon wiped his face and slumped to a seated position. He looked up, and when he spoke his voice was a whimper.

"Look, I don't who you are, and I don't know anything about this Wyatt lady. And I don't know who hit her house." He paused. "Just don't dump my goods."

"Do you know who killed her?"

"No, no."

Edge reached out and slapped him. "Come on. You're on the street. You hear things."

He rubbed his cheek. "Owwww! Okay, okay. Word is a outta towner done it."

"Who?"

"Some guy named 'Chuck.' And that's it. That's all I know, I swear it. Now, please, leave me alone."

His eyes pleaded his case. Edge looked at him and figured he'd gotten from him all he could. He poured the pills into the toilet and engaged the handle. Yellow liquid emptied out of the bowl, and it began to refill itself with clear water.

Edge nodded. "Okay, Alex. Okay."

Edge stood up straight and walked out of the stall leaving Varon seated right where he belonged: on the floor of the men's room in a bar – the dirtiest place on earth.

CHAPTER 6

The next morning Edge slept late. His late night with Varon had been at least somewhat productive. He now had the name of a suspect: 'Chuck.' He didn't know whether it was a good name or a made up one, and he had yet to eliminate every other possibility, but at least he had a name to drop when talking to people, especially Waltham.

In the meantime, he also had things to work on while waiting on his new partner to get to town. The first one was to visit the victim's sister, Angela Lloyd, the woman who had identified Bootsie Wyatt's body. And the first question he wanted to ask her was: Why didn't Bobby Wyatt identify her body?

He called first, and Angela Lloyd agreed to meet him at two that afternoon. Edge found the Lloyd home in a nice neighborhood off Cottage Hill Road near Sollie.

She was forty or so, with dyed blonde hair and a matronly figure. She wore plenty of make up to hide her flaws, and the slacks and semi sheer blouse, as well as the costume jewelry she wore, gave her a kind of a glamorous look. Her voice was somewhat gravelly and heavily accented.

Anderson ushered him into the living room and nodded toward the couch on the wall opposite a brick fireplace. She sat in a club chair near the hall door.

"Thank you for seeing me."

"Anything. Anything I can do. I just want you to find out who killed my sister."

"Ms Anderson, now, you understand that I represent the company that insured your sister's life. They're only trying to decide whether or not to pay her husband's claim. The police are responsible for arresting whomever it was that killed her."

She waved her arm. "Oh, I know all that. But, believe me, if you deny this claim, it'll be because you found out who killed her."

"How's that?" He knew what she was going to say, he just wanted her to say it.

"Because that son of a bitch Bobby Wyatt did it."

Her voice rose an octave, and she spoke loudly. She was sitting on the edge of her chair, and it looked as if she was about to attack him.

Edge took out his pad and pen. "Why don't we just start at the beginning. When and how did your sister and Bobby Wyatt meet?"

She took a deep breath and exhaled. "They met when he was in the Army. He was a helicopter pilot

47

and spent time in Vietnam. He did his training over at Fort Rucker in Ozark."

Edge knew the place. He'd been there many times.

"He was stationed there, and she worked in the base commander's office. They met and married before he went overseas."

"What brought them to Mobile?"

"Well, Bobby's originally from St Louis. Bootsie – uh, that's what we call her – grew up here. She went to college at Troy and just stayed over there when she graduated."

Edge wrote quickly. "When did they come back to town?"

"Oh, I don't know. The very late sixties, early seventies, I guess; about the time of the draw down overseas. Bobby always said he didn't want to go back to St Louis, not even to see his family." She paused. "I always wondered about that."

Anderson was relaxed now. She was sitting against the back of the crushed velvet upholstered club chair and had crossed her right leg over her left.

"How many children did she have?"

"Two, a boy and a girl."

"How old?"

"Mikey is nineteen, I think, and Victoria is fifteen."

"They both in town?"

"Yes, well, uh, no. Mikey's at the University of Alabama. Victoria's still in high school."

"What about Mikey? How is he? I mean, has he ever been in any trouble?"

"Oh, no, no. I mean, well, all teenaged boys have some troubles, don't they? I think he used some marijuana one time. But he straightened up."

"Do the kids get along with their parents?"

"Oh, sure."

Edge paused. "Tell me about Bobby and Bootsie. How was their relationship?"

She looked away. It was a sad look, one that said that the Wyatt's marriage was not a success.

"It was terrible. He went overseas in '66, and when he came back he was abusive, and . . ." she paused, "well, he just wasn't fit to live with."

"How do you know?"

"How do I know? She told me, that's how I know. And, there's the diary."

"The diary?"

"Her diary. I gave it to the police. It was the only thing of hers I got out of the house."

Fat chance me ever getting a look at that diary, Edge thought. The police letting go of it even for a short while, for any reason, was highly unlikely.

It sounded as if Bobby Wyatt's story was not unlike a lot of vets that came back from overseas. The things that Wyatt had seen, and maybe some that he had done, might have been too much for him. They were for a lot of people. Then again, Edge thought, Bobby Wyatt could just be a plain ole sociopath who came into his own after he got out of the service and there was no one around to tell him what to do anymore.

"So, he's okay, he goes to Vietnam, and when he comes back he's not fit to live with, right?"

"Right."

49

"How?"

"Well, he was verbally abusive, and physically abusive, too. Then he started runnin' around on her; he called her names; he told her she was fat; said he wished she was dead. He was just one 'grade A' ass."

"And all this was in her diary?"

"It was. That's why I don't understand why the police aren't doing more to try to find out about Bobby."

"Well, maybe they are." He stopped right there, unwilling to make excuses for the Police Department.

"Why didn't she just divorce him?" he said.

"She told me once that if she did, he threatened to take the kids away from her. And, if she left him, he might not have to pay her any alimony. Besides, she was very religious; she didn't believe in divorce."

"Catholic?"

"Very Catholic."

He paused. "By the way, you didn't happen to make a copy of that diary, did you? I mean, before you gave it to the police?" he said.

"Well, yes, a few pages. Just the ones she wrote right before she died."

Edge's eyes widened. "I'd like a copy of those pages, if you don't mind."

She nodded. "If you think it'll get Bobby, okay. I'll do it and call you."

He looked back at his notes. "Tell me, why was it that you were the one who identified your sister? You know, at the morgue, after she died."

"Bobby wouldn't do it. He said he 'couldn't bear to see her like that.' I knew he was full of it. He just wanted to hold up the investigation; to do something to hinder the police from catching him, for as long as he could."

"Where were you when you heard about your sister?"

"I was here. We were getting ready to go to a function at my son's school."

"Who called?"

"Victoria. She was the one who found her mother, in the bedroom." Angela Lloyd looked away. "She was close to hysterics."

"Did Bobby ever tell you where he was that afternoon?"

She nodded. "He said he was with the kids; said that they had gone shopping. They were planning to come to the same event that we were; a midwinter drama, over at St John the Baptist, where my son goes to school. Bobby had taken Victoria to get a new dress and Mikey a new suit."

"Mikey was home for college?"

"Right."

"What time did they leave the house?"

"Bobby said at ten. Vickie told me it was closer to eleven. They went to the mall and then to a couple of shops over on Dauphin Street."

Edge continued to walk her through everything she knew about Bobby Wyatt and her sister's family. The Wyatt's were very social. They were members of the country club, and they spent their summers vacationing in Destin, Florida. Bobby and Bootsie played golf, though rarely with each other, and she was on a club tennis team that traveled throughout the southeast. The kids attended private school and had never been in any trouble: no drugs, no alcohol abuse, and good grades; just all around good kids.

But as usual, the public face of a family never told the full story. Lloyd spent a considerable amount of time talking about Wyatt's sexual affairs – rumors mostly – with several prominent women in Mobile, all names that Edge did not recognize. There were two, though, that she claimed to have some knowledge of.

"There was Arianna Dixon, and Althea Baltimore." She paused. "The Baltimore woman is black."

"How do you know about them?"

"Their names were in the diary."

Interesting, Edge thought. Bootsie obviously had evidence to confirm these affairs, yet she still couldn't bring herself to file for divorce.

"At the risk of seeming indelicate, what about Bootsie? What did she have going on?"

"What do you mean?"

"Did she have a boyfriend?"

"No. I mean, she never said anything."

"Would she have confided in someone else?"

Edge knew there had to be someone else to whom Bootsie Wyatt talked. Family members, especially female family members, always think they're the special ones that are privy to everything; but they're often surprised when they find out that those they think are the closest to them have confided in others, usually, outside the family.

She paused to think. "I don't think so. I mean, we were very close." She paused again. "But, if she talked to anyone else at all, I guess it'd have to have been Margie."

"Margie?"

"Wilhelm, from the garden club. I'll get you her number."

"What about the jewelry? The jewelry on the police report?" Edge said.

"Well, the pearls he gave her on their anniversary; the earrings were an inheritance; and the diamond ring was a replacement for her engagement stone."

"Replacement? Did she lose her ring?"

"Oh, no. He just wanted her to have a bigger one, to show off, I guess."

"What were those things worth?"

"The insurance company should have the appraisals. All total, I guess, about ten or fifteen thousand, maybe twenty."

Edge wrote. "Do you know of anyone that had a business grudge with Bobby?"

She looked away and thought. "I, really, I wouldn't know anything about that. You're gonna talk to Bobby, right?"

"Yes, ma'am. How about personal grudges? Did Bobby or your sister gamble or use drugs, or have any other vices?"

"Not Bootsie. She was . . .," she shook her head, "no, not Bootsie. And not Bobby either, I don't think. He ran around. That was his vice."

Edge looked at his notes and around the room. He felt like he'd been there an hour, but it had really only been about thirty minutes. There was probably much more that he could ask, but right at that moment, he was dry.

If Bobby Wyatt was behind his wife's death, then he didn't do the actual killing. He made sure he was alibied and miles away when it happened. Wyatt would have had to hire someone to do it, or someone would have done it to repay a debt.

If he wasn't behind it, then the motive for her death might have been to gain a business advantage. This 'Bean and Dream' coffee shop might just figure in more prominently than he had thus far thought.

Edge said his goodbyes and left Angela Lloyd a business card and instructions to call as soon as she had copies of the pages of that diary.

He left with a little more than he had, but still not enough.

CHAPTER 7

At four that afternoon, Edge was in T-Bob's Saloon with another Diet Coke in front of him, listening to country music on the juke box. The case was rolling around in his head and there seemed to be so many different directions to go that he didn't know which one to choose.

He knew that he could interview the Wyatt family friends and peers all he wanted, but it might not get him any closer to finding out who killed Bootsie. If Bobby Wyatt was behind it, he wasn't going to hire someone from that circle, his circle of acquaintances, to do the job. He was going to seek out and pay, or compel, someone closer to the other players with whom Edge had come in contact; someone of the same ilk as an Alex Varon, a Tommy Dickens, a Marty the pawnbroker, or Lardy the fence.

Edge didn't believe that he had come in contact with the killer as of yet. The mysterious 'Chuck,' mentioned by Alex Varon, if he existed, was still in the shadows, as was the link, if any, between him and Wyatt.

By the same token, Edge had not yet completely discounted any other motive. Something that he had not as of yet explored was the business angle. Competitors in the coffee and pastry shop business were popping up all over the country and their desire to make inroads into the Mobile area might cause them to play hard ball with an already established business. But murder? At any rate, the only person who could shed any light on that notion would be Bobby Wyatt himself.

There was one thing that Angela Lloyd had mentioned that had intrigued him and that was the possible existence of Bobby Wyatt's black mistress. If this woman had a jealous boyfriend it might have led to Bootsie's murder. Edge ruminated over the idea but then discarded it. A jealous male would be more likely to kill his own lover rather than his rival, and he certainly would have no grudge against the other man's wife.

As the afternoon crowd of yuppie business people and the inevitable female hangers-on that followed them began to slowly trickle in, Edge decided to go ahead and take his leave from the barstool. He moved to a corner table, and with his back to the wall he watched them enter the front door; twenty and thirty-something, low and mid-level, male professionals shedding their ties and jackets and ordering their beer by the pitcher. They were loud, boisterous, and eager to impress the women with their bravado.

The morning crowd, the hard core drinkers, the thieves, and those generally lower in station, was already gone. The phenomenon of two different classes of patrons sharing a bar at different times of the day was unique and something that Edge had never before witnessed.

The next morning, Edge hit the street early trying for a meeting with Margie Wilhelm from the garden club. Angela Lloyd had supplied her number and promised to make an introductory call.

Edge found Wilhelm's home in Sun Meadow, two streets over from the Wyatt house. On his way to her home, he drove slowly down Marigold Place and looked at the now vacant Wyatt residence.

The murder house appeared to be nothing out of the ordinary. It was about a three thousand square foot ranch with a large, manicured front yard and a fenced backyard. He could see around a corner of the house at a swimming pool in the rear. It all looked idyllic, and typical of the nouveau riche in Mobile.

At the Wilhelm home, Edge parked on the street and walked up. As he neared the door, he could hear a small dog barking at the front bay window. A poodle scratched the glass with its front paws.

Margie Wilhelm was a slight woman with brown hair and a dark suntan. Glasses hung on a chain around her neck, and she smiled slightly.

"Mr. Edge? Come in." She stood aside and gestured to the living room.

Edge nodded assent and followed her. He took a seat in a club chair in the far corner of the living room. Wilhelm sat on the couch.

"I have a luncheon in an hour or so. We'll have to make this quick," she said. Her accent was not southern. It sounded more like northern Midwest.

"I'll be brief," Edge said. He explained to her who he was as well his purpose for coming.

"I'm just trying to get some insight into Dorothy Wyatt, and perhaps begin to identify someone who might want to do her harm."

"Sure. Well, I don't know that there's much I can tell you. We were friends, but not especially close, you understand."

"Certainly."

"I've wracked my brain, and I surely can't think of anyone. She seemed to be very well liked." She paused. "Bootsie, that's what we called her, was a quiet woman. She seemed, almost sad, really. She didn't smile much, except when it was expected, and I don't recall her ever laughing. She was just quietly pleasant." She paused. "Now, that husband of hers. He's a different matter."

"How so?"

"Well, he's loud, he's sarcastic, he was always finding fault with her. To tell you the truth, I don't know how she lived with him."

"Did Bootsie ever confide in you about her husband?"

She paused to think. "Look, I don't want this to leave this room."

"I understand."

"They had a bad relationship. I don't know how they stayed married, really. She told me that he hit her. He used to curse her and belittle her on a regular basis. She told me it was almost unbearable."

"Why didn't she divorce him?"

"Well, I don't really know. She said one time that he told her that if she ever tried to divorce him, he'd kill her."

Edge nodded as he wrote. "Did she ever mention Mr. Wyatt being unfaithful?"

"Well, she did. She said he was, but she never named any names. She always said she'd just as soon not know."

Edge nodded. "What about Ms Wyatt? Any infidelity on her part?"

She paused and looked at the floor. "Look, I don't want to speak ill of the dead."

Edge said nothing.

"Some things are better left unsaid."

Edge still didn't speak.

She looked him directly in the eye. "There was one man that she had run into. He was someone from her past."

Edge prepared to write. "What's his name?"

"Paul something, I don't know his last name. Bootsie knew him from back in Ozark, when Bobby was overseas."

"Do you know where I can find him?"

"I do not. It may have been long over. I just know she mentioned meeting him once, about a year ago, and they had struck up a conversation."

"Did she act as if it was serious?"

"With the way that Bobby treated her, I think she probably hoped it would become so."

Edge left without much. This Paul was just a name; a name amongst many. The mosaic of a homicide victim's life was the pattern out of which one tile must be selected that was the key to their death; and the bigger the picture, the harder it was to find that right piece.

Edge spent the rest of the afternoon at the law offices of Attenborough and Newton, on State Street, about three blocks from his apartment. He was finalizing a deal with Randy Attenborough to use a small office in the back of the wood frame shotgun building that earlier in the century had been a private residence. Edge would provide the law firm some free service of civil process and some light security work, such as answering the alarm, and in return he could have use of the office. He would be responsible for maintaining his own phone and policing up a small bathroom that adjoined the room.

It wasn't a huge space, just large enough for a desk and a couple of chairs. Edge liked the private entrance. He had plans to bring in a filing cabinet and a portable television set. It was out of the way, convenient to his home, and it was quiet. All he could hear was the tapping of typewriters in the main office and the rustling of the sea breeze in a couple of large oaks outside his window. Parking for the Impala was across the street in a vacant lot. Edge needed a place where he could go and think. He didn't intend to see clients there.

The next order of business was to look for the fence, Lardy. He'd do that tomorrow.

CHAPTER 8

The next day, a telephone was installed at the Edge's office. His new number spelled, GUMSHOE. He saw the exciting coincidence as a good omen.

Edge sat at his desk with his foot on the corner and thought. He had the phone number for Lardy the fence, but he didn't like going into a place blind. He had to get a location for that exchange.

One call to the public library's reference section yielded an address from the county cross reference street directory. The return was for a fish camp on Cedar Point Road, just south of Alabama Point in south Mobile County. The publication said that the proprietor's name was Wayne McLain. Edge checked it on his map and set out before lunch.

McLain's Fish Camp was two wood buildings that sat on the west side of Alabama Highway 193, about a half mile south of the Highway 188 intersection.

There was a shell parking lot, six or eight boat slips, and a pier that extended from the rear of the smallest building, out about two hundred feet into Heron Bay.

Edge parked his Chevy in front and got out. Before he left home, he ran a holster through his belt at the small of his back and filled it with a Colt .45 semi-automatic pistol. Then he slipped a safari vest on over his white shirt to cover the weapon. He wasn't expecting trouble, but he didn't know.

Dusty cans of Vienna sausages, potted meat, and sardines, along with packages of out of date soda crackers filled two aisles as Edge walked between them toward the back of the store where the cash register was located. Two large bins containing bait sat on either end of the rear counter and there was a glass exit to the boardwalk directly behind the man who was seated on a stool at the register.

"You, Lardy?" Edge said with a smile on his face.

"Shore am," he said smiling. He had a missing tooth and his face was sunburned.

Lardy was four hundred pounds if he was an ounce. It was no wonder he was a fence, because he was surely too fat to do any real work. He sat on the stool and played with the galluses of the faded overalls that he wore over a white t-shirt.

"I'm, John," Edge said. He paused and looked at the teenaged boy sitting down on another stool at the end of the counter. "I'd like to talk to you. Marty sent me."

Lardy looked at Edge and then at the boy. "Hey, Herky. Go outside and make sure the skiff's tied up."

"It is," the boy said. "I checked this morning."

"Just go outside and check it, boy."

The boy slid off a stool and walked disgustedly out of the glass door behind Lardy. He disappeared to the left, headed toward the pier.

Lardy watched him walk out then turned back toward Edge. "Young'uns," he said disgustedly. "Now, what can I do for ya', John?"

Edge looked both ways and leaned in. "I got some stuff to sell: a necklace, some earrings, and a diamond ring."

Lardy nodded. "Okay, let's see'em."

"Oh, I don't got'em on me. But I can lay hands on'em quick. It's real good stuff, I mean, high end, you know? I want to get a bunch for'em." He paused. "Chuck told me you paid top dollar."

Lardy froze for a fraction. Then he spoke.

"Well, John, I'll be glad to take a look at what'chu got, when you got it. And I don't know which Chuck you're a talkin' about, but, I am known as a fair man. Now, unless you want to rent a fishin' pole or buy some bait, I don't see that we got anything to talk about."

Edge nodded his head. McLain had confirmed that he was a fence and that he could move good quality merchandise. He also confirmed that he was at least familiar with the name 'Chuck.'

"Okay." Edge nodded and started backing up. "I'll get back to ya."

Lardy nodded. "You do that. Oh, and, John?"

Edge stopped. "Yeah, Lardy?"

"You better be who you say you are, ya hear?" McLain nodded toward a shotgun leaned against the wall in the corner.

Edge paused, and glanced at the weapon. "I don't know what you're talkin' about, Lardy. I'm just a businessman."

Out in the parking lot, it suddenly occurred to Edge that even a forty five caliber round wouldn't penetrate the fat around the middle of Lardy McLain. He'd have to be shot in the head – or gutted like a fish.

Edge left the camp thinking he had learned a little, but something told him that McLain could have told him a lot more. On second thought, he said to himself, McLain was probably not the type of man who could be turned as an informant. One would have to hold something over his head – or around his neck – in order to get information out of him.

At his office, Edge checked his answering service. Madge told him that a woman, a Lucy Lance, had called. She wanted to Edge to call her.

"Who is this Ms Lance?" Madge said.

"Oh, it's my sister. She's just checking up on me."

Edge had an idea of who the woman was, but it was none of the concern of the nosy phone operator.

"Oh, well, that's good. It's good to have family watchin' out for you."

"I'll call her straight away."

He hung up thinking that, on top of everything else he had to do, he'd also have to start looking for another answering service. He dialed the number Madge had given him and a female answered on the third ring.

The Lagoon was the name of the house bar that was located just off the lobby of the General Andrew Jackson Hotel, a one hundred and fifty room high rise located on Government Street, seven blocks south of Edge's office. He made the walk in fifteen minutes and stepped out of the bright lobby into the dark hideway shortly after five. Near the entrance, he stopped and looked around.

She was wearing a red shirt, just as she had said she would be, and was seated in the far back corner looking out of a window onto Joachim Street. From a distance, she looked sad.

As Edge neared the table, the young woman looked up and smiled. She stood and extended her hand.

"Are you, Mr. Edge?"

Edge nodded, shook her hand, and sank deep into a vinyl upholstered chair. "Ms Lance?"

"Right. Good to meet you."

They both sat and sized each other up for several seconds. To Edge, she didn't look like Shelia Waltham's girlfriend, as he had initially suspected.

Lucy Lance was barely over five feet tall, with shoulder-length, dark brown hair and almost black eyes under dark lashes and brows. She had a thin nose, a narrow chin, and high cheekbones. A narrow brown belt around her thin waist nicely accented her healthy breasts. She had a thin, feminine build and didn't strike Edge as someone who might have lesbian tendencies.

"You come from Atlanta, too?" he said.

"I'm out of the New Orleans office. It's cheaper to drive over here than to fly in from Atlanta." She cleared her throat. "I'm told that you were a little reticent to take on a partner."

He took a deep breath and looked her up and down. "Ms Lance, I'll be upfront with you. You look too slight to be able to take care of yourself; and if I have to spend my time watching after you, well, I just won't get much else done." He paused. "It's nothing personal." He paused again. "There, I've said my piece. Now, you know how I feel."

"Thank you for your candor." She looked away. "But, I assure you that I am quite capable of seeing to my safety."

He wanted to tell her that his last three female associates had felt the same way. One ended up almost losing her arm, one was nearly choked to death, and the other was shot. But he kept silent.

"I realize you believe you can, but the folks we're going to deal with play by a different set of rules."

"I understand that."

"I hope so."

"I do."

Edge said nothing but looked her in the eye. He was searching for a glint of aggression, a spark of conflict, some sign that she had some fight in her; something that would let him know that she was willing to inflict pain if she had to. He saw none.

Finally, he spoke. "I take it you have some experience in this kind of thing?"

"I've been an investigator for ManMut for three years." She paused. "But, isn't that a question that I should be asking you?"

"Fair enough. I spent the last eight years in the French Foreign Legion, and before that I served in an Intelligence company, in the Army, in Vietnam."

"I see. I'm sure you realize that gathering information about crimes is much different than gathering information about troop movements and such. Criminal cases require evidence."

"As do armies, ma'am. Look, it's my understanding that your company doesn't want to find the murderer, they just want to deny Bobby Wyatt's claim, isn't that right?"

She smiled. "Touche, Mr. Edge. If Mr. Wyatt is guilty of murder, we certainly don't want to pay him two million dollars. But, I hope you get my meaning."

"You and your company are looking for one thing. You want to know who *didn't* kill Dorothy Wyatt; rest assured, I'm on board."

"And I'll be there to help you."

He looked at her hard. "Just don't get in the way."

If she was insulted by his last remark, she didn't show it. Edge spent the next few minutes detailing what he had done so far and what was next on the agenda. Lance listened intently and asked appropriate questions.

"So, you don't know who this 'Chuck' is?"

Edge shook his head. "Not yet."

"What about Mr. Wyatt? Have you talked to him yet?"

"I was waiting on you."

"Let's do that tomorrow."

CHAPTER 9

The next morning, Edge picked up Lucy Lance in front of the hotel, and they set out to get an audience with Bobby Wyatt. Lance had the address of the corporate offices of Robatt (for Robert Wyatt) Enterprises, which Edge guessed was the back room of the largest of the 'Bean and Dream' shops in Mobile.

Lance looked smart in slacks and oxford shirt. Her hair was pulled back, and she wore penny loafers. Edge looked her over.

"By the way," he said, "you carry a piece?"

She looked at him with brows raised. "You mean a gun?"

He nodded. "Right."

"No. We're not allowed."

"Do you have any weapon at all?"

She looked down at her pocket, reached in, and pulled out a bottle of some kind of spray. She held it up.

"I've got this. It's something new, pepper spray."

"Cayenne pepper."

"Right."

He looked at her. "Can you shoot a revolver?"

"Well, yeah. There's nothing to it, right? Just pull the trigger?"

Edge took a deep breath and exhaled. It was going to be harder than he thought.

In twenty minutes, he was parking the Impala in front of the Bean and Dream Coffee Shop on Old Shell Road, right in the heart of Spring Hill. The Spring Hill community, arguably the most exclusive and supercilious neighborhood in Mobile, was the perfect location for this type of establishment. Residents of the neighborhood would forever be dying to try the newest and most exotic of the coffees and pastries, and would most assuredly want to try them before anyone else.

They walked in the front door. Edge looked around at Lance.

"Let me do the talking. That's what you're payin' me for."

She smirked but nodded assent.

At the counter, behind the register, Edge spoke to a fresh faced girl with a small brown hat on her head. She looked about eighteen.

"Is Mr. Wyatt in?"

Her face flushed, and she looked at both of them. From what Edge had learned, he guessed that Wyatt was no peach to work for.

"Mr. Wyatt? Well, I don't know, I'll have to check."

She turned away and picked up a phone. In less than a minute she looked back at them.

"He says, 'who is it?'"

"Tell him the people from Manhattan Mutual."

She turned back and spoke into to the phone. Then she hung up.

"He says go on back. It's through the door and to your right."

Edge and Lance walked through a swinging door on the north side of the room and found the office inside the second door on the right. Wyatt rose.

"Come in, come in. Glad to see ya."

He motioned toward two chairs, and Edge and Lance sat down. Wyatt was close to fifty, with a bit of a spread and silver hair combed straight back. His deeply tanned face was large, a little jowly, with a Roman nose and deep blue eyes. His shirt was starched and his suit pants tightly creased.

"I'm glad you guys are here. I'm hopin' you've got my check." Wyatt was smiling.

"Actually, no, Mr. Wyatt, we don't. My name is John Edge and this is Ms Lance, and as your girl told you, we represent Manhattan Mutual."

"So when do I get the money?" He was sitting again, yet looking as if he wanted to jump out of his chair.

"Well, right now, we're still looking into your wife's case. We just wouldn't feel comfortable paying a claim until someone had been arrested."

Wyatt heard the words and lost his smile. "Funny, that's not what the policy said."

"On the contrary," Lance spoke up. "The policy reads that all reasonable steps may be taken to insure that the claim is paid accurately."

"Well, the only thing that could lead you to believe that the claim could not be paid accurately would be if I killed my wife – which I did not."

Edge jumped back in. "Mr. Wyatt, no one is here to accuse you of anything. But I'm sure you want to find out who killed your wife and bring that person to justice."

Edge was stroking him, while at the same time he really wanted to slap the arrogance out of him. First things first, he thought.

"What we'd like to do is to take a look at the crime scene," Edge said.

He shook his head. "We've moved out of that house. I don't even have a key to it anymore. We're – my daughter and I, that is – are staying in an apartment, temporarily."

"Who does?"

"I don't know. The real estate lady, I guess; a Ms Pendleton at Sunburst Realty."

Edge looked at Lance. She got the hint, took out a pad and jotted the name down.

"Tell me, Mr. Wyatt, where were you when you found out you're your wife had died?" Edge said.

Wyatt exhaled disgustedly. "I've already told the police and your Ms Waltham a dozen times. I was with my kids on a shopping trip."

Edge looked away while noting that he hadn't answered the question. He had merely recited his alibi.

"Tell me about the jewelry that was stolen; the diamond earrings. How long had your wife had them?"

"They were her grandmother's. She inherited them when she was a little girl."

"And the pearls?"

"An anniversary present, from me."

"How about the diamond ring?"

He looked away. "I bought that for her five years ago. I got it at Arnstein's."

"What was the occasion?"

"What? Oh," he smirked, "just because."

Edge knew that was a lie. It was probably an attempt at heading off a divorce proceeding; probably Bootsie had caught him with another woman.

"Mr. Wyatt, do you know a man by the name of Wayne McLain?"

"McLain? No. Did he kill my wife?"

"Not that I know of. How about a man named Alex Varon?"

"No."

"Anyone named, 'Chuck'?"

"No, no. Look, how much longer is this going to take? I've got work to do."

"Just a couple more questions. How was your relationship with your wife?"

He smirked. "Perfect. We had no troubles at all."

"How about your children?"

"How about them what?"

"How was their relationship with your wife?"

"Oh, please. You don't seriously think one or both of them killed my wife, do you?"

"We'd like to talk to them."

He shook his head. "Absolutely not. The police have already taken their statements, and I refuse to let them be browbeaten by a couple of, of . . . amateurs."

Edge let his slight pass. "Can you think of anyone who has a grudge against you or maybe a business rival that might want to take it out on your wife?"

"That's the craziest thing I ever heard. Kill my wife over coffee and donuts? Look, when do I get my money?"

Edge looked at Lance, and they both rose.

"Well, that's all we have," he said. "If you think of anything that might be of help, give me a call." Edge handed him a business card.

Wyatt took the card and let it drop to his desk. "Just let me know when I can get my money."

Edge and Lance turned to walk out. Edge spoke under his breath.

"The check's in the mail."

CHAPTER 10

After using a payphone inside the business to call Eileen Pendleton at Sunburst Real Estate, they left Spring Hill. Lance made the appointment to meet her at the Wyatt's former residence that afternoon, after lunch.

"Have you had any dealings with the Police Department over here?" Edge said.

"No. You're the first person I've met in Mobile."

He drove in silence, heading for downtown. Finally, he spoke.

"So, you're staying at the hotel, hunh?"

"Yeah. It's pretty nice, and they've got weekly rates."

"I guess you know that this thing might take a lot longer than a week."

She nodded. "I know. I'm prepared."

He nodded also. "Look, if you don't mind me sayin' so, you looked a little sad last night, you know, when I met you at the lounge."

"Really? Well, I guess I've got a lot on my mind."

"Anything I can do?"

She shook her head. "No. I think I made it clear that I can take care of myself."

He smiled. "Right." He paused. "Well, if I can help, let me know."

"I will."

They drove another two miles in silence. Then Edge spoke again.

"So, what's a nice girl like you doing in a place like this?"

He didn't expect her to open up, but he thought he'd give it a try, nevertheless.

She smiled. "Oh, you know, things happen. I've been with the company three years. They've been good to me."

He nodded. "Well, you're the best-looking investigator I've ever seen." He said that trying to get a reaction.

She looked at him. "Mr. Edge, we'll be a lot better off if we keep this on a purely professional level. Besides, I'm married."

He nodded. "I understand," he said, and drove on.

Lance spoke. "And, you know I'm here to observe, right? Just to make sure the company's money is being spent wisely."

"I know." He looked at her. "How'm I doing?"

"So far, so good. We seem to have leads and things to work on. But, I would like for you to fill me in on your strategy."

"My strategy? Wow, I've never been asked that before." He paused. "Okay, well, operating on the assumption that Bobby Wyatt is behind his wife's death, yet trying not get tunnel vision, I intend to find out who did it and work my way back to him."

"And how will you do that?"

"My guess is that Wyatt spent anywhere between ten and fifty thousand dollars for a hit. My other guess is that the jewelry was part of the payoff. I hope to locate the pieces and then trace them back to the killer who can then lead me to Wyatt."

"And you think the killer is this 'Chuck'?"

"I have no idea. It's just the only name I have."

"How did you get that name?"

Edge looked ahead. "Is that part of what you're here to observe?"

"Well, no. But, I'm supposed to try to mitigate liability to the company."

Edge's voice was quietly serious. "Ms Lance, try to remember who we're dealing with."

She said nothing and looked straight ahead knowing that Edge had probably beaten the name out of someone.

At two o'clock sharp, Edge and Lance met Eileen Pendleton at 442 Marigold Place, in the Sun Meadow subdivision. She was a silver haired woman in a cotton dress standing on the porch, holding a large day planner and a key. She looked at her watch as they walked up the sidewalk toward the front door.

"How long are you two going to be?"

Edge spoke. "Ma'am, it shouldn't take more than just a few minutes."

"That's good." She smirked. "It's gonna be hard enough to sell this place as it is, what with what went on in there. I've got other properties, and I really need to spend most of my time on them."

They entered the front door and walked straight ahead past the living room to a large den that connected to the kitchen on the left side and a long hall on the right. Edge stopped.

"The furniture . . ."

"Yes," Pendleton said, "it goes with the house."

Edge nodded.

She paused and looked around. "In a case like this, I can understand why they wouldn't want any of what's in here."

Pendleton led the way down the hall to the master bedroom, the last room on the left. The door was closed. She opened it and motioned to the interior of the room. Edge stood in the threshold. Lance stood beside him and looked around his shoulder.

The furnishings looked the same as in the photographs that Edge had seen. He glanced quickly to the window. The broken glass was gone and the pane repaired. The bedspread, as well as the carpeting near the dresser and the bed, had also been cleaned, or replaced.

Edge looked around for something that he hadn't already seen. He walked into the room and toward the door next to the dresser. Inside, the bathroom sparkled. He walked back to the side of the bed.

He tried to imagine how the killer might have done his work. If he was there only to kill, and the thefts were at least a planned afterthought, he had to have a place to lay in wait for Dorothy Wyatt.

Edge walked to the window and stood. He looked outside and noticed that there was a direct path from the window, across the backyard, to the fence, and the wooded area beyond. From there, it was only a short walk to the food store on the corner Cottage Hill and Sunflower.

He turned back toward the interior of the room. To his right was a door. He opened it and found an empty closet; empty save for a small wicker trash basket. Edge turned on the light inside the large walk in space and looked around.

This is where he waited, he thought. It was close to the window, it afforded a good view of the room, and he could approach her from behind as she stood near the bed.

Edge walked out and stood. He stared at the bed and thought. Lance walked over and stood next to him.

"What are you thinking about?" she said.

"Just thinking."

"About what?"

"About how Bootsie Wyatt died." He paused and gestured toward the door. "When she first walked into the room, she probably stood and looked at the mirror, 'cause that's what women do; probably checking her hair, especially if she'd just come from the beauty parlor." He nodded toward the closet. "He came at her from behind. She backed away toward the wall and turned toward the bed. He shot her first. Then she fell, back onto the bed, and he stood over her and cut her throat. Then he stabbed her, just to be sure." He paused and shook his head. "It was a damnable thing."

Lance stared at him, transfixed as he told the story. She didn't know if he was right, but it all made sense. She felt flushed and a bit faint. It was merely the thought of death that made her queasy. She reached out and took his arm to steady herself, and waited while he continued looking. Finally, she spoke.

"Is this all you wanted to see?" Her voice shook.

"Yeah," he nodded.

Back in the car, neither of them spoke. It was as if they had just exited a church. Edge sat, looking straight ahead, and said nothing.

Lance didn't speak either. Edge could tell that there was a change in her. Her face was ashen, as if it had just occurred to her what this case was really all about.

He took a deep breath and put his key in the ignition. The engine roared to life.

"Not just about payin' out some money, is it."

She swallowed and shook her head. "No." She paused. "What do we do now?"

"We keep on lookin' for this son of a bitch."

Lance made a quick call to Waltham, and in ten minutes they had an address for Althea Baltimore, one of Bobby Wyatt's alleged mistresses. Her address put her in an apartment complex on Airport Boulevard, just west of Azalea Road.

The manager confirmed that she was in three oh four, and she also confirmed that Baltimore lived with a male. It was shaping up to be an interesting lead, Edge thought.

They walked up one flight of steps and stood on either side of the door. Edge knocked. Blues music – B.B. King – sounded from within.

The woman who opened the door was thirtyish, tall, big boned yet proportional, with a model's face and skin the color of molasses. She wore a print housecoat, and her flat feet were bare.

"Ms Baltimore?"

"Yes."

"My name is Edge. This is Ms Lance. We represent Manhattan Mutual Insurance. We were wondering if we could talk to you." Edge showed his state issued credentials.

"I don't need no insurance."

"That's not why we're here, ma'am. It's about something a bit more serious."

Baltimore looked them both up and down and then backed out of the doorway facilitating their entrance. She nodded toward the couch.

Edge and Lance walked past her into the living space. It was busily furnished with wall ornaments, a large television, and some wicker chairs opposite a velour loveseat. They sat down.

"What's this all about?" Baltimore said as she sat in one of the chairs.

"Bobby Wyatt, ma'am. We understand you had a personal relationship with him," Lance said. Edge was surprised.

"Bobby Wyatt, who's that?"

"We think you know, ma'am," Edge said. "We understand you two were lovers."

She swallowed hard and shook her head. "Not, me. No. Unh, unh."

"Ma'am, you're not in any trouble. We just want to know what he might have told you about his wife; about their relationship."

"Look, I don't know no Bobby Wyatt, and he ain't tole me nothin' about his wife."

That settled that, Edge thought. Her admission had confirmed their relationship.

"We're just tryin' to find out who killed his wife, ma'am," Lance said.

At that moment, a large man stepped into the doorway off the hall. He filled it out completely, and when they saw him, Edge rose immediately. Lance did also.

"She say, she don't know no Bobby Wyatt. Is you deaf?" His tone was gruff and angry.

He was over six feet tall, and, except for his rounded belly, appeared solid. He wore a pair of boxers and nothing else.

"She knows him," Lance said confidently.

Edge noticed an assuredness in her that he hadn't seen before. He hoped her willingness to engage with Baltimore and this boyfriend didn't become problematic.

"She say, she don't," the man said. His voice was deep, and he walked into the room. "So why don't ya'll just get the fuck outta here." His anger was increasing.

"Hush, Demetrius. I'll take care'a this," Baltimore said.

"Okay, okay," Edge said. "We'll go. We don't want no trouble." He took two steps toward the door.

"I'm not ready, yet," Lance said staying behind.

"Yes, you are. Let's go." Edge took her arm.

She jerked away. "If she knows anything about this case, I want to know it."

"Ya'll get outta here," Demetrius said.

With that, the man reached for Edge and grabbed his arm. Edge reacted quickly. He made a large circle with his limb thereby wrenching it free from the large man's grasp. Then he went into a crouch and punched him hard in the abdomen. Demetrius was slowed, and Edge stepped away.

The blow ultimately had little effect, and Edge made ready for another strike. But there was no need. Lance stepped up and delivered a side kick to Demetrius' head. The blow struck him in the jaw, and he dropped to the floor, like a stone, completely unconscious.

Althea Baltimore yelped and stepped back. Everyone stood and looked at everyone else. Edge's eyes were wide, but he said nothing.

"Now, we're gonna go, Althea, but not before you tell the truth," Lance said.

Baltimore was shaking as she slumped back into her chair. "Okay, okay, me'an Bobby had a thang, a'ight? But I wadn't the only one. He had a bunch'a womens."

"Where'd you meet him?"

"I used to work at his sto; the one on Old Shell. He seen me an' as' me out."

"Did he ever say anything about his wife?"

"Jus' that he wisht she wadn't around."

"He ever say anything about killing her?" Edge said.

Althea shook her head.

"What about Demetrius? How'd he feel about it?"

"Me and 'Metrius wadn't together then. He ain't know nothin' about it 'til ya'll come in."

"Who killed Bobby's wife?"

"I 'ont know." She shook her head and looked down.

Lance shrugged her shoulders and then turned toward the door. Edge opened it and stepped into the threshold. Lance looked back at Baltimore.

"Just pour some water on him. He'll wake up. I didn't hit him that hard."

Baltimore nodded as Edge and Lance walked out the door.

In the car, Lance spoke.

"You think she's involved?"

Edge shook his head. "Nope. I never did. I only wanted to talk to her to get that lead out of the way. Wyatt's other squeeze, the one I know about, Arianna Dixon, has got an old man that's a lawyer. I'm pretty sure she wouldn't admit to anything; she probably wouldn't even let us in the door." He paused. "No, this was a lead. We checked it. Now, we can move on."

He looked at her and smiled. "By the way, that was impressive."

She smirked. "I told you I could take care of myself."

He nodded. "You certainly did. But don't get the big head."

She looked at him.

"You can't outkick a .45."

Halfway back to town, Edge stopped at a phone booth and checked his service. It was the middle of the afternoon and Madge was already on duty.

"Yes, Mr. Edge. You've got one call, from a man named Tommy Dickens. He said he needed John to meet him at T-Bob's, at four."

"Okay."

"He a friend of yours?"

"That's my brother, Madge. He checks up on me, too."

"Oh, well, sounds like you come from a good family."

He hung up thinking that the games that he played with Madge were getting old. He'd have to do something about her.

"Let's go," he said starting the car.

"Where to?"

"To visit an informant."

It took thirty minutes in late afternoon traffic to get back downtown. Edge parked on Conti Street, a block east of T-Bob's front door, and they walked up.

Inside, they took seats at a table in the corner. Edge ordered a Diet Coke and Lance the same. It was twenty minutes before Tommy arrived.

"Hey," he said as he sat down. His wet hair was combed, and he was wearing clean jeans.

"Hey, Tommy." Edge nodded to Lance. "This is Lucy. She works with me." He nodded toward the bar. "You want something?"

"Yeah, I'd love a beer." His voice was slow and lazy, as if he didn't want to be there, but he needed money.

Edge signaled to the bartender who brought over a beer in a frosty mug. Tommy blew on the head then turned up the glass and drained about three quarters of its contents.

When he had finished, Dickens belched. Edge spoke.

"What'chu got?"

"Well, I been askin' around, and I heard a couple'a things."

Edge said nothing.

"Like I heard that a guy killed that woman; a guy named 'Chuck.'"

"'Chuck' who?"

He shook his head. "I don't know. I heard he was from outta town, though."

Edge looked away. "Come on, Tommy. I already know all that. Give me something I can use."

Tommy looked away nervously. He licked his lips and snorted. Lance said nothing.

"Okay, okay. Well, there's this guy named Lardy that knows what happened."

Edge nodded. His brows were down and his mouth was tight. He reached in his pocket and pulled out a coin. He held it up between two fingers.

"See this nickel, Tommy? Well, that's about all your information is worth. Now, get me something I can use, or that pistol that I got off you, which *has* been reported stolen by the way, walks its way into the Police Department. You dig?"

Tommy's eyes got wide, and then he looked down and nodded.

"Yeah."

"Now, get back out there get me something that I don't already know." Edge reached over and smacked him on the head.

Tommy stood up, turned, and walked slowly out the front door. Edge and Lance watched as he left.

"You took a gun away from him?" she said.

"Just a hunk a junk. I doubt it would even shoot."

"Was it stolen?"

"I don't know. I just told him that to get his attention. Tommy's not too bright."

They sat and sipped on their drinks while music played on the juke box. Edge spoke first.

"There's got to be a way to connect Bobby Wyatt to the underworld. The criminal element is just not going to be in his circle of friends."

"Are you sure?"

"Well, I haven't heard of anything yet. He doesn't do dope; he doesn't gamble, that I know of;

and though he's got women, he apparently doesn't run whores." He paused. "There's got to be a door."

Then he remembered something. "Ms Lance, we need to take a road trip."

CHAPTER 11

The next morning they were on the road early enroute to Tuscaloosa, Alabama, and a visit with Michael Wyatt. A phone call to Angela Lloyd provided them with his phone number, and young Wyatt agreed to meet them at a Jack's restaurant near McFarland Boulevard.

Before they left, Edge glanced at the paper and noticed that the Mobile PD was involved in another homicide investigation. A woman was strangled at her apartment on South Florida Street; the case detective was James Vaughn.

Edge and Lance were waiting for Wyatt when he arrived at the restaurant at noon. The young boy found them in a booth near the front glass.

"My dad told me not to talk to you guys," he said as he sat down next to Lance.

Wyatt was tall, thin, with brown hair and a large nose. He was dressed in jeans and a red pullover shirt, and he carried a spiral notebook and a math text. He looked like a million other college students.

"So, why are you?" Edge said.

He said nothing for a minute. "'Cause, well, maybe I think the whole story about my mother hasn't come out yet."

"You think?"

He nodded. "Yeah. I think, maybe, my dad knows something about it."

Lance looked at him, hard. "You think your father killed your mother?"

"No, well, not killed her, no. He was with us when it happened. But," he paused, "but he, it looked like it didn't bother him too much, you know. Then he brought that woman over to the house not too long after the funeral."

"What woman?" Edge said.

"Her name is Dixon. I don't know her first name. Dad said they were gettin' married just as soon as she got a divorce; and now she stays with him and Vickie."

"So, you've just got some doubts, right?"

"Yeah. I mean, when we were at the funeral, he told us not to cry. Not to cry. Now why would he say a thing like that?" Wyatt's voice broke as he spoke.

"I don't know, son," Edge said.

They sat in silence for a minute as Wyatt composed himself. Traffic moved swiftly by outside, and students came and went buying sandwiches and drinks. Finally, Edge spoke.

"Mike, I need to ask you some questions. I can't tell you why I'm askin'em right now, but just trust me when I tell you that it's possible that they might help to clear things up a bit. Okay?"

He nodded his head. "Yeah, okay."

"Is this your first year in college?"

"Yeah."

"Where'd you go to high school?"

"St John the Baptist Catholic."

Edge smiled inwardly at the irony.

"What we wanna talk to you about are your friends." He paused. "Is there anyone that you hung around with in high school that was maybe a little shady?"

"Shady?"

"You know, they did drugs real heavy, maybe they had some trouble with the police . . ."

He looked up and thought. "Well, there was Andy, Andy Allison. He used to sell dope."

"He ever sell any to you?"

"Yeah, some grass; once or twice."

"Your folks find out about it?"

"Yeah. Mom was pretty mad. Dad kinda blew it off."

"Him and Andy ever meet?"

Wyatt nodded. "Yeah, at school; at the headmaster's office."

"How can I find Andy?"

"His mom, I guess. Marion Allison. She's in the phone book."

"Anybody else?"

"Aaron, Aaron Wilkins. He got busted by the cops for coppin' some beer from a store across from school."

"Your mom and dad know about that?"

He thought for a minute. "I don't know. I don't think so."

"Anybody else?"

He looked up and shook his head. "No, that's all I can think of. Most of my friends were nerds, you know?"

"What about your sister?"

His brows went up. "My sister? Are you kiddin'? She's straight as an arrow. She's never been in any trouble and doesn't know anybody that has."

"You sure?"

"Call her."

Edge looked at Lance. She shook her head.

"Any idea what Andy's doin' now?"

"Well, he last got busted for shoplifting, and I think he got probation. Seems like the last thing I heard was that he was workin' at a bar somewheres."

"A bar? How old is he? Isn't he the same age as you?"

"Andy's, uh, no, he's twenty one, I think. He was at least a year ahead'a me, and I think he got left back a year in elementary school."

Edge nodded. "Not too bright, hunh?"

Mike Wyatt shook his head and looked toward Lance. "Dumb as a rock, but he can talk you outta your shorts."

It took four hours to make it back home to Mobile.

Edge dropped his passenger off the hotel and, the next day being Saturday, made preparations to pick her up late in the morning on Monday. Lance told him that, over the weekend, he should not make a move without her, a directive that he promptly ignored.

Edge spent the evening in his office brainstorming. His only lead was 'Chuck,' the unknown burglar from out of town. He'd heard it now from two different yet related sources. It had been established that Tommy Dickens and Alex Varon knew each other, and they could have colluded to pass the name along to him. But, there was the fact that Lardy McLain all but admitted to knowing the name himself.

What was missing was a link from Bobby Wyatt to the underworld; the world of burglars, fenced property, and hit men. He began to think back to Wyatt's biography. First, he was in St Louis; then he was in the Army, at Fort Rucker; then he was in Vietnam; then he was back in the world, and in Mobile. Could there be someone in the Army that he had called on to help him with his predicament?

It would take an act of Congress to very quickly get information about Bobby Wyatt and his service record – where he went, the operations he was involved in, his fellow soldiers – if he went through normal channels. Or, he could call Phil.

Phil Anspach was high up in the CIA. After their tour in the military, Phil had gone to work for the company and had quickly risen to a deputy directorship. If anyone could get the information that Edge needed, he could. Besides, Phil owed him. Edge used his rolodex to locate Anspach's home number and called him.

"At home on a Friday night?" Edge said. "So much for your exciting social life."

"Mark? Is that you? Wow. What's it been? Five years?"

"Yeah, about that. How goes it?"

"Man, it is hot up here in Washington. Where are you?"

"A place called Mobile, Alabama."

"Alabama? Man, how'd you wind up there?"

"Don't ask. It's a story so long and convoluted that you haven't got time to hear it. How are Jean and the kids?"

"Kids? They're not kids anymore. Wes is in Georgetown, and Arnold has – now, get this – he's decided to try to get into West Point. Can you believe it?"

"You must've done some sell job on the Army."

"Never said a word. He thought it up all on his own." He paused. "Well, I know you didn't call just to pass the time. What can I do for you?"

At that moment, Edge thought how great it would have been to tell him, 'yeah, I just called to say, hello.' What a relief it would be to say that things were peaceful and calm and he was retired and spending his time on the beach writing or fishing. But it wasn't great. He needed information.

"Look, Phil, I'm trying to get a line on a guy that was in the service back in Vietnam. He was a chopper pilot; name's Robert Louis Wyatt, hometown, St Louis. He was stationed at Rucker in '65."

Edge could tell he was writing. "This for a case or something? You still doin' that PI thing?"

"Yeah. I think this Wyatt guy had his ole lady croaked. I'm workin' for an insurance company."

"What do you need?"

"You know, just some background: his unit, where and when, maybe if he was disciplined for anything. Or, if there was anybody in his outfit that might have been off the straight and narrow. I'm just lookin' for a lead."

"Okay. Give me a couple'a days." He paused. "Whatever happened to that girl you told me about?"

"Oh, man. That didn't end well."

Edge paused and remembered a time long ago when he almost had what Phil had; a wife, a home, a family.

"I'll tell you about it some time," Edge said.

"Okay. Sorry, didn't mean to bring up an old wound."

"That's okay. I've got some new ones."

Edge hung up and tried to think. What else could he do before Monday to break this case?

CHAPTER 12

The next morning Edge was up early. He found the address for Marion Allison in the phone book and after slipping on a tie, drove out to her house, on North Georgia Street, off Old Shell Road, not far from St John the Baptist High School.

The woman that answered the front door was a mess. She was forty, but looked older. The lines on her face were pronounced and there were dark circles under her eyes. Her hair was unkempt and the robe that she wore was threadbare. Edge could smell beer on her as soon as she opened her mouth.

"Yeah?"

"Ms Allison?"

"Yeah." She reached and smoothed her hair back.

"My name is Etheridge, and I'm on the alumni fundraising committee at St John's, class of '62. We're trying to get an accurate data base for all the recent graduates, and I was trying to locate Andrew; or, uh, Andy, Andy Allison."

"Andy?"

"Yes, ma'am. We're updating our list. The school is just about to start a drive to build a new science lab, and well, we'd like to be able to count on everybody."

"Oh." Her voice sounded as if she was still on the drunk that she had no doubt begun last night.

Edge opened up a padfolio and poised his pen. "So, if I could just get some contact information: address, place of employment, phone number, that sort of thing."

"Oh, well, Andy don't like nobody to know his phone number or address. He always said that. But you can find him down at The Lunatic, over on Halls Mill at McVay."

"The Lunatic. What is that?"

"It's a lounge. Andy works there behind the bar on weekends."

Edge wrote the information down on his pad. "Well, that's great ma'am. You've been a really big help."

"Hey, you gonna send me one of them fundraisin' letters?"

"You finished at St John's too?"

"I sure did. Class of uh, of uh," she started to laugh. "Oh, well, I don't 'member, right now. It's been a while ago."

"Well, thank you for your help." Edge turned toward the street.

"Tell Andy, when you see him, to call me; tell him to call his mother."

"I will."

That evening at five, Edge parked in the shell parking lot at the side of a cinderblock building that was The Lunatic Lounge. The structure was painted a dark maroon and there was a pink neon sign on top. Six other cars were in the lot, one of which was a new-looking, red, Cadillac Coupe de Ville. As he scanned the area, Edge saw a tall man and a dumpy young woman walk through the double doors in the front of the building.

Inside, Edge took a seat in the corner and watched as a four piece band was setting up on the stand at the opposite end of the room. The musicians worked slowly and the drummer stopped twice to draw from a beer can.

Edge's eyes scanned the room looking for someone who might be Andy Allison. There appeared to be only one employee in the place, a thin male wiping down the bar. He had brown hair parted in the middle and a Roman nose. About that time a middle aged, blonde walked out from what was probably the kitchen and put on an apron. She picked up a tray and looked around. Her eyes fell on Edge, and she walked to him.

"What'll you have?"

"You got Diet Coke?"

"Sure do."

"Make it on the rocks with a twist."

She nodded and turned away. In five minutes she was back with a high ball glass full.

Edge handed her a five. "Keep it."

She smiled. "Thanks."

"By the way, that guy behind the bar. Is that Andy?"

She looked over her shoulder. "Yeah. Crazy Andy."

"Crazy Andy? At The Lunatic Lounge?"

She smiled. "Ironic, hunh."

Edge reached in his wallet and pulled out another five.

"When he gets a break, ask him to come over and see me."

"Really? Andy?" She made a face. Then she smiled. "I could be a whole lot more fun."

Edge chuckled and shook his head. "Not tonight. Just send Andy. I got a message from his mother."

"Oh, okay." She paused and smiled again. "But hold onto your ass."

"Why?"

"'Cause he'll try to talk you out of it."

Edge smirked.

The band began to tune up as another couple entered the front door. The first couple, the tall man and the dumpy woman, had taken seats near the bandstand and was drinking beer. The guitar player, apparently the leader, nodded to the drummer who gave them the down beat, and the combo broke into a mournful rendition of *Rose Colored Glasses*. After the first verse, the first couple stood up to dance on a small tile space in front of the platform. Their Mutt and Jeff appearance was humorous, and Edge sipped his drink while they swayed back and forth in time to the music. In a minute the woman hauled off and slapped the man in the face. Then she threw her head back and laughed hysterically

They had played three songs when Edge looked up and saw Crazy Andy walking toward his table. He was wiping his hands on a towel and there was a look of concern on his face.

"You want to talk to me?" he said.

Edge nodded to a chair. "Sit down." He took a sip on his drink. "My name's Edge. I work for an insurance company."

Andy took a seat on the opposite side of the table. He fidgeted nervously with the towel.

"I don't need no insurance."

"I'm not here to sell ya any." He paused. "I ran into a couple of people that you know. They wanted me to tell you, hey."

"Oh, yeah?"

"Yeah. Your mother wants you to call her."

He shook his head and leaned forward. "What's she want, beer money?"

"Pretty hard on your mama, aren't you?"

"She hadn't done nothing but embarrass me for fifteen years."

"Pretty bad drunk?"

He shook his head. "Her middle name is 'Thunderbird.'"

"Where's your dad?"

"Who knows. He's been gone for five years, and I don't blame him."

Edge paused. "Well, the other person is . . . Mike Wyatt."

Andy sat up straight and leaned away in his chair. "Mikey? What'd he want?"

"It's not what he wants, it's what I want."

Andy said nothing.

"When's the last time you talked to Bobby Wyatt?"

"Bobby Wyatt?"

"Yeah."

"What makes you think I've talked to him?"

Edge said nothing.

Allison looked away, but said nothing.

"I know you talked to him," Edge said.

Allison swallowed hard.

"What did he want?" Edge said.

He furrowed his brow. "Who are you, man?"

"I told you, I'm working for Manhattan Mutual Insurance."

He paused. "This is about Miz Wyatt, right?"

"Right."

"Well, uh, . . ."

Edge raised his hand. "If you're gonna tell it, Andy, tell the truth and tell it all."

Andy Allison looked straight ahead. "Okay, but this is just between us, right? I mean, I ain't testifyin' in no court."

Edge just stared at him.

"He called me; said he wanted to hire somebody to kill his ole lady, and could I do it, or did I know anybody."

"What'id you tell him?"

"I told him, no."

Edge didn't believe him. From what he'd heard about Allison, he wouldn't've let this opportunity pass without trying to make a buck.

"So, what did he say then?"

"He said, okay, that for me to call him if I changed my mind."

"Did he mention money?"

Allison shook his head. "We didn't get that far. I told him never to call me again."

Fat chance. "Okay. Is that it?"

"Well, yeah. I mean, I ain't into no murder."

Edge looked at him and nodded. That part might actually be true, he thought. But it was hard to believe that the conversation that he described had ended their dealings; maybe the first talk, but there had to have been others.

The band was into a song about whiskey and love, and now both couples were dancing directly in front of the bandstand. Edge looked back at Allison, hard.

"If I find out you're lyin', Andy, I'm gonna take it outta your hide."

"Look, I told you the truth." He rose from his seat. "I gotta go back to work."

Edge nodded and watched him walk back behind the bar. The waitress who had relieved him picked up her tray and started back out onto the floor. There were now fifteen or twenty people in the place and the music seemed to have gotten louder; loud enough to drown out the conversations of the patrons. It was time for Edge to leave.

Outside in the parking lot, he took a long look at the cars. There were old pickups, dirty sedans, and even one faded ragtop. But the car that stood out above all the others was the shiny, new Cadillac. As he left, on a whim, Edge swung by and copied down the license number.

CHAPTER 13

The next day, Edge spent his time in the office reading part of the diary of Bootsie Wyatt; the part copied by her sister Angela Lloyd and held back before the whole book was submitted to the Police Department.

The pages covered the period of the last two weeks of Bootsie's life. They painted a picture of a woman at the end of her rope; one who was looking for a way out. The entry just before her death detailed her plans to be at her nephew's school function the next evening, as well as her plans to have her hair styled the day of the event. Well, Edge thought, at least she went with a cut, curl, and a set.

It wasn't the bombshell that he thought it was going to be. So Bootsie had an obnoxious old man; a lot of women have lived with a lot worse. One entry told of how she had visited a local priest and asked about divorce. The clergyman had told her that the church couldn't sanction it, except for the cause of adultery. Afterwards, notations about Baltimore and Dixon started appearing and apparently Bootsie had resolved, on paper at least, to begin to try to prove her husband's infidelity.

After he finished reading, Edge decided to try to locate Aaron Wilkins. Wilkins was the other name supplied by Michael Wyatt as someone who had been crossways with the law and who might have had some contact with Bobby Wyatt. Edge didn't know where to start, so he began at the downtown library, a facility open every Sunday from 12 to five.

He found Wilkins in the cross reference directory, living with his family on Westwood, off Dauphin Street. The home turned out to be a fifties-era bungalow, brick with white trim. There was a small Toyota in the driveway.

The woman that answered the front door was not middle aged, but looked it. Her hair had gray streaks, and the dark circles under her eyes said that she didn't, as a rule, sleep very well. They talked on the porch. The woman took a seat in a metal chair.

"Yes, ma'am. My name is Edge, and I'm with Manhattan Mutual. Are you Mrs. Wilkins?"

"Yes."

The woman began to tear up. Edge didn't know what he'd said to upset her, but clearly he had.

"I'm sorry, did I say something wrong?"

She shook her head and wiped her eyes. "No, no. I'm sorry. We don't need any more insurance."

"No, ma'am. I'm not here to sell you a policy. I'm looking for Aaron Wilkins."

That set the woman off, and Edge knew immediately what was wrong. He waited for her to compose herself. When she had blown her nose and wiped her eyes, she looked up and spoke.

"Aaron's my son. He died in a car accident three months ago."

"My condolences. Was it here in Mobile?"

"No. He was on his way back from Nashville. Aaron played the guitar and was trying to break into the music business."

Edge nodded. It looked as if this lead was fizzling.

"I understand," he said.

"They said he was driving drunk, but there's no way he would do that. He was a good boy."

"I understand." He paused. "Tell me, did your son ever mention a man named Bobby Wyatt?"

"Bobby who?" She sniffed.

"Bobby Wyatt."

"I don't think so. Why? Did he know him?"

"That's what I'm trying to find out."

She shook her head. "What's this all about?"

"I believe that Mr. Wyatt might be trying to fraudulently collect on an insurance policy. We're trying to prevent that from happening."

She nodded. It was clear that her pain was all that she wanted to think about. This Bobby Wyatt could take care of himself.

"Could there be anything in your son's property that might indicate if he knew Mr. Wyatt?"

"I didn't notice anything. He hadn't been staying at home the last few months. Aaron had been out of town, on a tour, playing." She looked up in the air. "He really was a gifted musician."

"Any papers, anything that might indicate a windfall of some type?"

She looked at Edge with hard eyes. "You think my son was involved in something illegal?"

"No, ma'am. I just think that Mr. Wyatt might have approached him for some help."

Indignance fell over her face like a curtain. "My son was no criminal. He was a good boy." She stood up. "I'd like for you to leave now."

Edge nodded and turned to leave. He stopped and looked back.

"Once again, I'm sorry for your loss."

As he walked down the sidewalk toward his car, he heard her break into sobs, again, just like he knew she would; the sounds of grief.

After he left, Edge filled up his tank and started driving. He went north on Highway 43 to Red Fox Road, then turned west toward Citronelle. It was something he did to clear his mind; and as a way of getting to know Mobile County.

He drove past Searcy Hospital, then past the Mowa Choctaw Indian Reservation. As he drove, he thought of Bootsie Wyatt, her last days and her last minutes. Edge could see the person that killed her standing in front of her with a pistol pointed at her head and Bootsie backing up toward the bed. He could see her shaking and bringing her arms up to her chest. How did he know she didn't fight back? No defensive wounds and the first shot to the head. That was what killed her and anything after that was overkill.

It was at times like these that Edge had to fight the urge to become emotionally invested in a case. With as many dead bodies as he had seen, he always had to tell himself, they were just pieces of meat. They weren't what they were when they were alive. The spirit was gone; the soul, the whatever it was inside of them that made them who they are had left. Finding out who caused their death was more like a contest, where the prize was money on which to eat, to secure shelter, and to buy clothing. Homicide investigation had become to him to be some grand quest for personal survival. It seemed almost crass to make finding the killers of the dead a matter of money rather than something more noble like righting a divinely judged wrong.

Justice for the dead. He had heard that many times before at death scenes, when talking to families, and in court. But what did it mean? There's no justice for the dead. Justice would be if they'd never died, or if they came back from the dead. Justice would be if their killer died also. When people ask for justice, what they really mean is they want vengeance. Revenge, that's what it's really all about. And, absent a divine visitation, it isn't going to happen in this life.

Perhaps someday, sometime far ahead in the future, under the influence of alcohol or pills, he would sit on a psychiatrist's couch, or in front of a fireplace, or on a porch swing somewhere and ball his eyes out over all the Bootsie Wyatts that he had stood over, or seen in photographs, or heard tell of, and then he could grieve for them properly. But now, he couldn't.

CHAPTER 14

Monday morning, Edge got a call from Lance. She was back in town and at the General Jackson Hotel.

"What did you do over the weekend?"

"What? Nothing, really."

"You talked to Andy Allison, didn't you."

"Yeah."

"Well?"

"Well, what?"

"What did he say?"

"Just what I thought he'd say. He admitted to knowing Bobby Wyatt, and he said that Wyatt had asked him if knew of a hit man. Andy told him that he wanted no part of it. That was it."

"Do you believe him?"

"No. We'll have to take a run at him later, when we get a little more." It was then that he thought of the tag number. "And we just may have it."

"What?"

"Some leverage. You gotta pen?"

"Yeah, go ahead."

"See if you can get a registration on a license plate." He recited the number from the red Cadillac to her.

"Okay," she said. "Whose car is it?"

"I don't know. But if it's Andy Allison, we've got something to hang over his head."

"Bootsie's murder?"

"Maybe, maybe not."

"So, what do we do now?"

"We wait. When we get the registration back, if it belongs to Andy, we take closer look."

He paused and cleared his throat. What he was about to say needed to be said, and right then was as good a time as any.

"By the way, you need to know that my style is a bit unorthodox."

"How do you mean?"

"I mean, getting the truth is the most important thing, and how I get it is not really that important to me."

There was silence on the other end of the phone. "I see."

"So, if you can't live with that, then maybe we should plan our interviews accordingly."

"Did you explain all this to Shelia?"

"No. She expects results, and that's what I intend to give her."

Silence again. "Well, Mr. Edge, you need to know that I'm also on board for whatever gets us the truth about this case. I intend to satisfy the company by whatever means necessary."

It was a sentiment that caught Edge completely off guard. He cleared his throat again.

"Okay, well, so, we're completely clear about where we stand."

"Crystal."

"Once again, you surprise me."

"Pick me up at eleven."

At eleven ten, Edge and Lance were eating lunch at The Back Porch, the house restaurant at the General Jackson. It was a buffet style meal, and on Monday the featured entrée was mutton. They sat next to a picture window that overlooked Government Street. A waitress brought them iced tea and water.

They were half way through their meal when a woman walked up to their table. She was slim, with dark hair and Asian features.

"Mark, is that you?" she said looking right at Edge.

He looked up from his food into the face of JoAnn Ward. He had to work to keep from betraying the recognition on his face.

"Excuse me?" he said.

"Mark, it's me, JoAnn."

"I'm sorry, ma'am," he said, "I'm afraid you must have me confused with someone else. I don't know you."

"Come on, Mark; the scars, the vest. I'd know you anywhere."

Lance looked at Edge, then at the woman, as she forked another bite of meat into her mouth. Her amused expression was evident.

"Come on, Mark. What's the game?" Ward looked at Lance. "Oh, I'm sorry, are you two a couple?"

Edge stood and looked at her. "Miss, I don't know you, and we're trying to finish our lunch. So, if you could just . . ."

Ward looked at him hard. Her visage had gone from 'happy to see an old friend,' to befuddlement, to irritation all in a minute.

"I, I must be mistaken. I'm terribly sorry."

"That's quite alright." Edge reached in his pocket and pulled out a business card. "My name is Edge. John Edge. If you ever need a private investigator, feel free to call me."

Ward took the card and looked at it. She looked at Lance and then nodded.

"Sure. Sure," she said, nodding as she began to back up. "I will. Thanks. If you two will excuse me."

Edge sat back down. Lance was looking at him. A slight smile was crossing her lips.

"An old flame you don't want to remember?"

He shook his head. "Absolutely not. I've never seen that woman before. But," he paused and took a sip of water, "I wouldn't mind seeing her again."

At two that afternoon, they were sitting in Edge's Impala in the parking lot a hundred yards from the Section 8 apartment of Andy Allison, in a complex located off Azalea Road near Pleasant Valley. With field glasses, Edge could see his apartment on the second floor of Building G, in the far southwest corner of the community.

One quick call by Lance to Waltham revealed to them that the Cadillac Coupe de Ville that Edge had seen in the parking lot of The Lunatic Lounge was indeed registered to Andy Allison.

Edge peered through the glasses and then handed them to Lance. "Think a man with a part time bartender's salary, living in subsidized housing can afford a car like that?"

The Caddy was parked in front of the building in a handicapped spot near the breezeway that divided the two halves of the structure.

"Not unless he's doing something illegal."

"Or has done something illegal."

Lance lowered the glasses and nodded. "How do you want to play it?"

Edge looked around. "How about the direct approach?"

"You mean knock on the door?"

"You got it."

"Let's go."

Edge stood on one side of the portal and Lance on the other, as he rapped three times. After seeing Lance in action in Althea Baltimore's apartment, he was no longer worried about her ability to protect herself.

"Come on in," said a voice from behind the door.

Edge looked at Lance and smiled. "Could he be that stupid?"

"You heard him."

Edge opened the door and they entered to find Allison lying on a couch in the living room. He was wearing boxers and nothing else, and if Lance saw the dark hair and flaccid penis protruding from the front flap of his shorts, she pretended not to notice.

"It's me, Andy. John Edge. Wake up."

"Ohhhh, man. Shit. Don't holler so loud."

He opened his eyes and looked up at the two of them before rubbing his face. "Oh, uh, I thought you was Linda."

"Nope, too bad. Wake up."

Allison slowly swung his feet to the floor and sat back on the couch. He rubbed his eyes and ran his hands through his thick hair. Then he looked up at Edge and Lance.

"Who are you?"

"Edge, man. Don't you remember me from the club?"

"Man, I can't remember ten minutes ago."

Edge walked over and stood next the couch directly in front of him. "We don't have time for this, Andy."

Allison stopped and let his hands fall to his lap. He suddenly realized the seriousness of what Edge was saying.

"Oh, yeah, right. You're the guy that was askin' about Bobby Wyatt."

"Right. And, I've got reason to believe that you weren't completely straight with me."

"What?"

"You lied to me, Andy."

"What? No."

"Yeah, you did. You took money from Bobby Wyatt."

"Come on. No, no." He frowned.

"Yes, you did. And you used it to buy that Caddy down there."

Allison said nothing.

Edge drew back and backhanded the young man across the mouth as hard as he could. Allison fell against the arm of the sofa. Lance said nothing.

"You feel that, Andy? Well, it can get a lot harder. Now, I want the truth."

Andy sat up straight. "Look, I told you the truth. He called me, but I told him, no."

Edge looked at Lance. She raised her eyebrow. She certainly is cool, Edge thought.

"So, where'd that car come from?"

"What? The car?"

"See, now that's how I know you're lyin'. Where did you get the money for the car?"

"Uh, well, you know, I work real hard, and tips are good . . ."

Edge grabbed him by the hair and pulled his head up straight. "Now, I'm only gonna ask you one more time. I hate a liar, so you better talk fast."

Allison's wide eyes looked from Edge to Lance and back to Edge. He held up his arms.

"Okay, okay. Wait. Now, you guys ain't the cops, right? You're not gonna call'em and send me off, right?"

"The truth, Andy."

Edge looked around the room for some kind of contraband, some kind of leverage to hold over his head. But he needn't bothered. Right then, the front door opened and contraband walked in without knocking.

"Andy, I got . . ." said the young girl. She looked around and then froze.

She was thin and blonde, and she wore a man's shirt and little else. It was white and it hung down over her knees. She was holding two bottles of cola. She looked from Lance to Edge and then to Allison.

"What's going on?" Her voice was high and soft, and her eyes were wide.

Lance spoke first. "How old are you, sweetheart?"

"Fifteen," the girl said without hesitating.

"Well, there you go," Edge said waving his hand. "Look who's here, Lucy? It's the bus that's gonna take Andy to the big house. Statutory rape'll make a nice collar, Andy. You'll have to register as a sex offender and everything."

Edge looked at the girl. "What's your name, child?"

"Linda."

He paused and looked back at Allison. "Well, Andy. Won't your mama be proud. By the way, did you ever call her? Well, it don't matter, you can call her from the County Jail."

Edge let go of Allison's hair and smoothed it out. He sat down next to him and waited.

Lance looked at the two. "Come on, Linda," she said. "Let's see if we can find you some clothes."

When they were gone, Edge moved in close. He spoke in low tones and there was anger in his voice. He could see Lance standing in the bedroom door listening while the young girl found her jeans.

"Now, I want it, and I want it all, or I get on the phone to the police."

"Okay, okay." Allison took a deep breath and exhaled. "Bobby called me about six or seven months ago and said he had a job to do. He wanted to know if I was game for somethin' heavy. I told him that depended on what it was. He said he needed somebody to off his wife and did I want the job." He paused.

"What did you say?"

"I said, 'fuck no,' just like I told you the other night. So he says that, did I know anyone who'd do the job; that he'd pay me a finder's fee. And I said, yeah, I did."

"Who?"

"Nobody. See, I got the idea to tell him I was gonna get somebody, and get him to give me some money, but I was never gonna do it. I was just gonna get him to pay me and then just say the guy backed out."

"How much did he pay you?"

"Five grand."

"Did you ever get him somebody?"

"I, I, uh, well, not really."

Edge looked at him hard. "What's that supposed to mean?"

"Well, I called Bobby and told him it was gonna cost twenty-five thousand; five more for me to make the contact, and then ten more up front for the hitter."

"So, you've made ten thousand already and you haven't done a thing."

He shrugged. "Uh, well, yeah, I guess."

"So, you got the money, and then what happened."

"I got somebody to call and talk to him like he was a hit man."

"Who?"

Allison's face looked pained. "Look, now he ain't gonna like me gettin' him involved."

Edge reached and hit him on the back of the head. "He's already involved, genius. Now, tell me who he is."

Allison rubbed his face, and Edge could see tears beginning to well up. He rubbed his eyes and looked down.

"He's gonna kill me."

"You better worry about what I can do to you. Besides, I know a place where you'll be safe."

He looked toward the bedroom door. Lance was watching them both.

"You mean jail?"

Edge said nothing.

He exhaled again. "His name is Ricardo Gomez."

"Where can I find him?"

He paused. "I found him at a place called El Diablo. A guy named Tommy Dickens put me in touch with him."

Allison was obviously unafraid of Tommy, Edge thought. This Ricardo must be tougher.

"Did Tommy know what you wanted him for?"

"No."

"And you told Bobby that this Ricardo was the man that was gonna kill his wife. And Ricardo called him, right?"

He nodded.

"Were you there when he made the call?"

He nodded again.

"What was their deal?"

"Ricardo told Bobby he wanted to up the price. He said he wanted fifty grand. They argued back and forth, and Ricardo hung up. He said they agreed on twenty-five and that Bobby was supposed to pay him fifteen thousand now and ten after the job was finished."

"Did he pay him anything?"

"Yeah. But Bobby called me back later and said that Ricardo was out. He wanted me to find him somebody else."

"Did you?"

"I gave him a number I got from off the bathroom wall at work."

"You remember the number?"

"Are you kiddin'?"

"Who was the number for?"

"Just somebody; a queer, I think, named, Chuck."

"What makes you think he was queer?"

"'Cause on the bathroom wall it said, 'call Chuck, for a 12 inch dick.'"

CHAPTER 15

They took Linda home, letting her out at the corner down the street from her house in the ritzy Regency subdivision off Airport Boulevard. Lance was finally able to get her last name and date of birth out of her, but little else. Edge was glad he didn't have to call the police.

As they drove back to town, Edge and Lance discussed what they knew, and now, what they didn't. He did most of the talking.

"Can we agree that Wyatt paid to have his wife killed?" Edge said.

Lance nodded. "Yes, but we still don't have enough to deny his claim. We've got to keep working."

"So, Bobby calls Andy, Andy calls Tommy, and Tommy gives him Ricardo's name. Then, apparently, Andy copies down a random name from off the bathroom wall, and tells Bobby he's a hit man." He paused and snorted. "A man called 'Chuck.'" He paused again. "How big a joke would that be, that the killer of Bootsie Wyatt was hired off the bathroom wall of a bar."

At five o'clock, Edge let Lance off at the hotel and went back to his office. If she was having any problem with the way Edge had conducted his interrogations or the investigation in general, she had not said so. That was good.

At the office, he checked his messages. Nosy Madge told him to call a woman named Harriet. She left a number that Edge didn't recognize. Then it struck him who it must be.

"Hey," the woman said when she answered.

"Hey."

"Can we meet?"

Edge said nothing. He knew this call was coming, and he had debated whether or not to see her.

Finally, he said: "Yeah. Do you know where Bienville Square is?"

"If it's downtown, I can find it."

"I'll see you there at six thirty. Meet me at the benches on the southeast corner." He paused. "Come alone."

Edge took a seat on one of the wrought iron benches near Dauphin and St Joseph Street at six fifteen. It was still early and the late night party crowd had not yet arrived downtown. A breeze blew off the water and the only other people in the square were two winos; one, nodding off on a bench, and another who was laid out in the grass under a huge spreading oak.

She was ten minutes early. JoAnn Ward sat down on the bench next to him. She wore a long sleeved blouse and knit slacks over flat slippers. Her hair was pulled back, and she wore no make up; but then again she never did, he thought. Her hands were free. She looked good, much older and more mature than when he had first met her six years earlier at Walt's Diner in Mauvilla.

"I'm surprised you came," she said.

"Yeah, well, I'm a little surprised myself." He paused. "What are you doing here?"

"The District Attorneys Association yearly meeting, over at the hotel."

He nodded.

Neither of them spoke for a couple of minutes. Ward glanced over at him. She could see that the scars on his face had not healed the way he had hoped. His face had a rough appearance that gave him a hard edge; inwardly, she smiled at the irony.

"So, how are things?" he said.

"Good; still with the DA's office, obviously. You?"

"I'm beginning to build a little something here." He nodded toward the ring on her left hand. "I see you got married."

She smiled and held up her hand. "Yeah. I did."

"Sheen, the FBI agent?"

"Oh, no. He turned out to be a real jerk; and he got transferred up to Headquarters, in Washington. No, my husband is a doctor."

He raised his brows. "Impressive."

"Yeah, it was love at first sight. He's in my father's practice." She smiled broadly.

"Good. I'm happy for you." He looked off down the street toward the waterfront.

She paused. "Why'd you leave, Mark?"

"Please." He looked at her. "My name is John Edge. Get in the habit of using it." He looked away again. "There was nothing for me there, JoAnn. It was over. I was growing stale and people were beginning to hate me." He shook his head. "It was time to move on."

"But you were so good at what you did?"

"Who says? The DA despised me and wanted the throw me in jail; the SO never wanted to see me coming; and, well, I'd made a lot of enemies within the criminal element. I was going to be looking over my shoulder as long as I was there. Not only that . . ."

"What?"

"I was lonely," he said, embarrassed at the admission. "Things just weren't turning out the way I'd planned."

"Oh, baloney. I know for a fact that the Sheriff said that if you'd come back to work, he'd love to have you. And, my boss won't be in office forever." She looked away. "And, well, you'd've found someone eventually."

Edge thought back to a conversation with Teresa Southworth, the madam at the largest bordello in Mauvilla. She said that he would never have anyone; it was written on his face.

He shook his head. "It was just too depressing over there. It seemed as if every road I drove down had a bad memory."

"And that's not going to happen here?"

"If it does, I'll just move on from here, too."

She snorted. "Change yourself; then change your circumstances."

"Quaint. Where'd you hear that?"

"I don't know, one of those TV preachers, I think."

"I'll remember that." He looked at her. "Is this what you wanted to see me about?"

"Well, yes, and, no. I came to town for this convention, but now that I've run into you there is something that you ought to know. I've heard that organized crime is looking for Mark Hatchett."

"The mob? Which one?"

"The New York mob."

"Why?"

"We don't know. It came into our Intelligence office and they put it out in a memo."

"The DA's office has an Intelligence office?"

"I know, right? But you know Andrea. If she thinks she can get a headline with it, she's gonna do it." Ward paused. "She actually misses you, you know."

"Well, she had a funny way'a showin' it."

"She's come down to my office a couple of times and asked where you were and what you were doing. She mentioned a case she thought that you could be of help on."

Edge snorted.

"Hey, she's not all that bad. You just gotta remember not to get in between her and her politics."

He snorted again.

"So," she said. "You're here for the duration, right?"

"Sure. I have a new identity in a new city and a new start." He shook his head. "I'm not leaving." He paused. "Why should I?"

"I don't know. I can't think of a single reason. I was just wondering."

"Well, wonder no more." He looked her in the eye, hard. "JoAnn, don't tell anyone, and I mean anyone, that you saw me."

She nodded. "I won't."

He reached in his pocket and pulled out another business card. He wrote his direct home and office numbers on them and handed it to her.

"If you, and only you, ever need me, you may call." He rose from his bench, as did she. "Otherwise, I don't want to ever see you again."

She looked at the card and the numbers. "I understand."

He heard her voice break. She was getting emotional at the sense of loss that she felt. He had saved her life, and she would always have a scar on her right arm to remind her of it. He had been her first mentor; had taught her how to investigate, to question, and to get to the truth of a matter. She would miss him.

"What's this?" she said smiling. "2-5-1-GUMSHOE?"

"That's my office number. It's an easy way to remember it."

She smiled as a tear trickled down her cheek. "Clever."

"Good bye, JoAnn."

He turned and walked north toward the center of the square, and did not look back.

CHAPTER 16

The next day, Edge and Lance went to the Police Department's Detective Division. Victor Riley was in his office, rubbing his eyes when they walked in.

"Well, Edge. What brings you here?" His tone was slightly belligerent.

"I just wanted to update you on what we've found out so far with regards to the Wyatt case."

"We?"

Edge nodded at Lance. "Oh, I'm sorry. This is Ms Lance from the claims office of Manhattan Mutual. She's observing my work. And," he said, "she's been an enormous help."

Riley nodded at the two of them. "Sit down."

Edge opened a notebook that contained his case notes and looked up at Riley.

"You want it step by step, or do you want the abridged version?"

"Make it short and sweet."

"Okay. Here's what we think we know. Bootsie Wyatt was killed by a man named 'Chuck' that Bobby Wyatt apparently hired off the bathroom wall at The Lunatic Lounge. We think he was paid something like ten or fifteen thousand dollars."

"Any idea who this 'Chuck' is?"

"Not yet. We've got another couple of leads to run down. We're hoping to get an identity on him soon."

"What was that you said? He was 'hired off the bathroom wall?'"

"Yeah. One of our witnesses, Andy Allison, was apparently rippin' Bobby off for hit money; taking his money but never doing anything. When Bobby got wise, he wanted the name of the man who was going to do the killing so he could deal directly with him. Andy went into the bathroom at the lounge where he works, and copied down a name and number from the men's room wall."

"And you think this guy killed Bootsie? This guy off the bathroom wall?"

"Sounds stupid doesn't it."

Riley lifted his brows. "Well, stranger things have happened." He paused. "You got any evidence yet?"

Edge shook his head. "None, yet."

Riley nodded. "Okay. Thanks for the update. Call me when you get something."

Edge nodded. Lance said nothing throughout the whole conversation.

"I read where things are picking up for you guys?" Edge said.

"We had another one last night, and this thing that Vaughn is working has got two teams tied up."

"I understand. Well, we'll get outta your hair."

Edge and Lance rose. They were almost out of the door when Riley called back.

"Edge? Remember what I told you."

He nodded. "Yeah, Lieutenant. I remember."

In the car, Lance looked at him. "What was all that?"

"What?"

"That 'remember what I told ya' stuff."

"Oh, that was his obligatory threat to put me in jail if I started to knock a few heads."

"Well, I guess that ship has sailed."

Edge looked at her. "For the both of us."

It took over an hour for Lance to get a location on Ricardo Gomez. He had a driver's license, but that was all. They were just before going to the El Diablo bar on Airport Boulevard when she got a page from Waltham letting them know that Gomez had listed the address on a credit card application as an apartment complex in Theodore, Alabama, on Sperry Road, not far from the dog track.

They found the run down complex, a collection of sixteen wood frame buildings painted brown, laid out in a square around a playground – two sandboxes and two swing sets – right in the middle of the property.

Edge found Building M on the south side. There were three cars in the lot. They parked and walked up the sidewalk just as a dark skinned man opened the door and stepped outside of an apartment on the bottom floor in the rear. The unit, M-2, was the one they were looking for.

"Ricardo," Edge said.

The man froze, then turned and started to run, south, into the woods, away from the building and toward the track. Edge turned and tossed his keys to Lance.

"Bring the car," he yelled.

Edge started after him. As best as he could see, Gomez was a small man with dark hair. He wore only a pair of green gym shorts and was barefooted.

Keeping him in sight was going to be a problem for two reasons. One was the density of the woods, and the other was the smaller man's speed. Edge hoped for a miracle.

Gomez, who had no doubt received a heads up from Allison that they would be looking for him, was running hard toward the track. When he reached the chain link fence that surrounded the property, he turned east toward the corner. Edge followed about twenty yards behind.

With his good shoes, Edge made up ground rapidly, while Gomez had to step carefully on his bare feet. Edge was within ten yards when Gomez broke out of the woods onto the soft, landscaped grass near the parking lot and began to pick up speed. He looked over his shoulder at Edge who loped along at an easy pace. Gomez jumped over some concrete barriers and onto the parking lot and was looking back at his pursuer when he ran headlong into Lance and the Impala. He hit the front fender and fell back. Edge sprinted up and stood next to the small man who was lying face down and panting heavily.

Edge put his foot on Gomez's back, and Lance got out of the car and walked around to where he lay.

Edge panted also. "Gee whiz, Ricardo, why'd you have to go and take off running like that?"

Gomez looked at him and between breaths said, "No hablas."

Edge smiled and said, "Bullshit." Then he kicked Gomez hard, in the ribs.

Then he kicked him again. After that, he reached down and lifted him to his feet by the hair of his head. He walked him over to passenger back door, opened it, and slid the grimacing man inside. Edge got in next to him. Lance took her place behind the wheel, started the engine, and in seconds they were on the road.

"Where to?" she said.

Edge looked at Gomez. "Anybody at your place?"

Gomez looked at him then rubbed his ribs. "No."

Edge looked at Lance. "Take us back over to the apartment complex."

She drove slowly back around the corner, down Sperry Road, and to building M. When she parked, Edge opened the car door and pushed the bare chested man out. The three of them walked to the apartment door, and Edge shoved Gomez inside.

"Who lives here with you?" Edge said gruffly as the brown man fell onto the sofa.

"No one, senor."

"You stay here by yourself?"

"Si."

"You here illegally?"

"No. I am on a student visa."

The words made Edge mad. Here was a man, in his thirties, who had come across the border on a student visa, a visa that had long since expired.

Edge looked around the room as Lance explored the bedroom and the kitchen. He spotted Gomez's wallet on the counter next to a small bag of marijuana.

There was a hundred and forty dollars in twenties, two credit cards – both in the name of Albert Larison – a driver's license, and a social security card inside the brown leather billfold. Edge slipped the two credit cards into his pocket.

When Edge saw what else was on the counter, his anger only intensified, for there next to Gomez's car keys was a book of food stamps. He picked them up and walked toward the sofa.

"Where do you work, Ricardo?"

"I do odd jobs, senor."

"Odd jobs? Like killing people?"

"What? No, senor. I never killed anyone."

"No, you just defraud people who hire you to do it."

"Que?"

Edge reached out and slapped him on the side of the head. Gomez fell over and grabbed his ear.

"Ricardo, I'm only gonna say this one time. Speak English."

"Si, uh, yes." Ricardo sat up and rubbed his head.

"Okay, Andy Allison told us the biggest part of it. I just need you to fill in the blanks."

"Andy?"

"You heard me."

Gomez said nothing.

"Andy gave you a number, and you called a guy, and in a little while, both of you are in the pink, right?"

Still he said nothing.

Edge made a fist. "It can hurt a whole lot worse, Ricardo."

He took a deep breath and exhaled. When he spoke his accent vanished.

"Andy called me and said he had a way to make some money, and he wanted to know if I wanted to get involved. I said, how? And he said that all I had to do was call and pretend to be a hit man, set up a meet, and pick up some money."

"Who'd you call?"

"Bobby is all I know."

"Tell me how it went down."

He took another deep breath and exhaled. "I told him to leave his wife's picture, address, and ten thousand dollars in a plastic bag under the right cross at Three Crosses."

"Three Crosses?" Lance said.

"It's a cemetery on Airport Boulevard. It's Springhill Gardens, or something," Gomez said. "There are three crosses there, just like at Calvary, in the Bible." He genuflected.

"Did you get the money?" Edge said.

"Si, uh, yes. I picked it up later that night at about eleven o'clock."

"What happened then?"

"I split the money with Andy, and I never called this Bobby again."

"What'd you do with the picture and the address?"

"I threw them in the dumpster."

"Did he know who you were?" Lance said.

"Not my real name. I told him I was 'Pancho Villa.'"

"What happened after that?"

"Andy told me he called Bobby and told him that I left the country."

"Left the country? Where'd he tell him you went?"

"To Mexico."

Edge nodded. The more he heard and saw, the more disgusted he got; the overstayed visa, the pretend hit man, the stolen credit card, the food stamps.

Edge looked at him. "You make me wannna puke, Ricardo." He looked at Lance. "Would you walk out to the car and get me a business card?"

Lance looked at Edge, then at Gomez. She seemed to know that something was about to happen that she shouldn't see. She nodded, turned, and walked out the front door.

Edge waited until the door was closed then slipped a sapper out from the inside pocket of his vest. Then he stepped forward and went to work on Ricardo Gomez.

Back behind the wheel of the Impala, Edge drove them to the SoMoCo Restaurant for lunch.

Afterward, about halfway back to town, she looked at him.

"What happened in there? In Gomez's apartment, I mean."

"What are you talking about?"

"I mean, you send me out to the car for a business card, and before I can get back, you're out the door and we're on our way."

Edge took a deep breath and exhaled. "Mr. Gomez is breaking the law by being in this country; he's swindling – albeit a criminal – out of money; and, on top of that, and I guess, what's worse, he's gettin' food stamps. He has a lot of things wrong in his life. He needed to be convinced that he should change, that he should make himself a better person."

"You tuned him up."

"I didn't say that."

She nodded and smiled. "But that's what happened." She paused. "Hey, look, don't get me wrong, I'm not saying that I wouldn't do the same thing, if I could. Frankly, I don't have a problem with it. But, well, you know, the company."

"ManMut."

"Yeah, they don't like this kind of thing. What is it they call it? Exposure?"

Edge nodded. "I understand. Well, first of all, you didn't see a thing. Second, Ricardo Gomez isn't telling anybody anything. If he does, he has a lot of 'splaining to do his self." He paused. "And, I found this lying on the counter."

Edge held up the plastic baggy of marijuana. "And he knows if he talks, I pull this out, and we'll be in a cell together."

"Leverage."

"It's a beautiful thing."

Edge dropped Lance off at the hotel and then went back to his office. There was a note on his door to contact Randy Attenborough's secretary.

Gina was gorgeous. She was five two with blonde hair, blue eyes, and a turned up nose. She habitually wore short skirts, and her blouses were almost always sheer. Edge wondered if she and Attenborough were sleeping together.

"Hey, Gina," he said smiling as he walked into the main office.

She was on the phone but smiled back, broadly, and motioned for him to sit down.

When she hung up, she smiled again. "Where you been?"

"Oh, out. You know, private eye stuff."

"Sounds mysterious."

"Not so much. It's just like walking. You put one foot in front of another and sooner or later you get where you want to go."

She raised her brows. "You make it sound so poetic."

"I guess, in a way, it is. There's a certain symmetry about it; kind'a like a monkey swinging through the trees in the jungle. He moves from one vine to the next using first one arm, and then another, while rocking from side to side. The movements all have amplitude and frequency. I do the same thing. I move forward a little bit at a time, swinging back and forth, then, when I'm just about to lose all my energy, I get to where I want to go."

She chuckled and shook her head. "That's the biggest bunch of bull I ever heard."

"Not a good line, hunh."

"Keep trying."

"What do you want?" he said playfully.

"Randy's got some papers for you to deliver."

"To serve?"

"No. They're contracts. He just wants you to run'em out to the client's house."

She handed him a manila envelope with a note taped to the outside on which was written an address. Edge recognized it as being located off Japonica Lane in west Mobile, not far from where Bootsie Wyatt was killed.

"Just take'em out there? Nothing to sign?"

"Nope. Just ID him, hand him the papers, and that's it."

Edge nodded. "Okay." He held up the envelope. "He want this done today?"

"Yep," she said smiling. "Just swing on out there and swing on back."

Edge smiled also. "Smart ass."

CHAPTER 17

It took Edge thirty minutes in afternoon traffic to get to the house on Brighton Place. It was a brick Federal with a small balcony on the second floor right above the front door, and a driveway up the left side. He was surprised to see two city police cars and one detective car parked on the street in front.

Edge parked the Impala and walked up, manila envelope in hand. There were no officers visible, so when he reached the front door, he used the knocker to rap twice.

A uniformed officer, an older man with a gut, opened the heavy door and looked at him.

"Yeah?" he said. His voice had kind of a high tone to it; nothing like what Edge expected.

"I'm looking for Fred Keyes."

"And you are?"

"John Edge. I'm from Mr. Attenborough's office."

"Just a minute." The officer turned away and closed the front door.

Edge stood on the concrete porch and looked around. The neighborhood was peaceful, unusual for a late afternoon in the summertime. He even heard a mockingbird squawking at him from the large oak tree on the side of the yard.

In three minutes the door opened and a short, stubby man stood in front of him. He wore a t-shirt and suit pants, and his feet were bare. His bald head was shiny and the horn rimmed glasses that he wore fell about halfway down his nose. Disgust painted his face.

"Mr. Edge?"

"Yes."

"Mr. Attenborough said you'd be coming by. You have something for me?"

Edge held up the manila envelope. "Just need to see some ID."

Keyes, nodded, pulled out his wallet, and produced a driver's license. Edge looked closely at the name then handed the parcel to him.

"Everything okay?" Edge said looking past Keyes into the house.

Keyes took a deep breath and exhaled. "No. Someone broke in and took all my wife's jewelry." He looked over his shoulder. "She's gonna be mortified."

"How'd they get in?"

"A rear bedroom window."

"Alarm?"

"It's on the fritz. Can you imagine that? The one day when my alarm's out, and that's the day that I get hit."

A thought flashed through Edge's mind.

"Good stuff? The jewelry, I mean."

"A couple of heirlooms."

"Well, you know, I run the pawn shops pretty often. If you give me a list of what you're missing, I'll keep a lookout for you."

"Could you? That'd be a big help."

Keyes walked away from the door and came back with a pad and pen. He quickly sketched out likenesses of two pieces; one, a broach, and the other what looked to Edge like the setting of a cocktail ring.

"Oh, my wife's gonna go crazy." He handed the paper to Edge. "These are the two most valuable. They came from her grandmother." He smirked. "I gave her the rest. She can live without those."

Edge looked at the page. The broach looked like it was about two inches wide and had a large stone in the middle of a sunburst.

"What kind of stone is this?"

"It's an emerald. I've got pictures, but I'll have to give them to the police."

Keyes pointed at the ring setting. "This one's a two carat diamond with two half carat stones, one on either side." Keyes nodded at the drawing. "The ring isn't too awful distinctive, but the broach . . ."

Edge nodded. "Yeah. I can see that."

"Her grandmother brought it from Ireland. It was the only thing of value she had when she got off the boat." He looked wistful.

Edge nodded again. "Okay. Well, I'll be watching." He paused. "Oh, and by the way, make sure you tell the police to check the alarm company. They have a lot of shady guys that work as contractors to install and repair those things."

His brows went up. "You know, I hadn't thought'a that. Thanks."

Edge nodded, handed him a business card, and turned toward the street.

He didn't quite know where to start with the information about the Keyes burglary, but he almost did. Just maybe he had found a way to worm his way under Lardy McLain's fat façade.

As he rode to town, he thought about his case. Wyatt was the man, he was sure. But who he hired to do the job was almost too murky to be discerned. Was it this 'Chuck' from off the bathroom wall? Was it someone else, someone from his past? Was it someone to whom Edge had already talked?

At his office, Edge checked his messages. There was one from Phil Anspach. He called him back.

"Hey, Phil. Anything for me?"

"Well, I took a look at Robert Wyatt's personnel jacket. It was colorful, to say the least."

"How so?"

"Wyatt was a pilot in the 227th of the 1st Air Cav flyin' Hueys outta Da Nang. He did most of his time around the Pleiku province. His tour was unremarkable until '67 when he got into a little scrape. Apparently, he and another pilot, a Morton, Charles E., were caught running whores back and forth from Saigon to firebases in the Delta, for a fee, of course."

"For soldiers?"

"Right. The girls were part of a house run by a madam downtown. Anyway, Morton had one in his chopper on his way back to Saigon one morning when he came under fire from the VC; took an RPG in the side and had to limp back. Morton went kinda crazy and figured that the girl had tipped them off that he'd be coming that way, so he booted her out."

"Of the helicopter?"

"About a thousand feet up. Well, this chick was apparently the belle of the ball, you know, the best they had, in that particular part of the world, anyway. Word eventually got back to the madam about what had happened, so she filed a complaint with the embassy, and the whole thing blew up. Well, Madame Chang got paid off, Wyatt and Morton both got demoted, as well as some other administrative punishment. After that, their careers were pretty much toast."

"This Morton," Edge said as he wrote the name down. "Any idea where he is?"

"Well, his jacket says he's from Mississippi, somewhere called Winona, so I'd guess he's back there."

"Okay," he said. "Anything else?"

"Well, not really. Wyatt got grounded for marijuana use once, and twice for being drunk on duty. And he took a couple of unauthorized trips over to Thailand, which earned him a little more time off." Anspach paused. "Other than that, I don't see anything."

"Phil, you've been a huge help. Thanks."

He paused. "We had a time over there, didn't we? Just reading this file brought back some memories."

"And some nightmares?"

"Oh, no. Not me. How about you?"

"Fewer and fewer. But, it's still with me."

"Hey, if you ever want to talk, give me a call. It's the least I can do."

"I will, brother. Thanks."

Edge hung up wondering if it wouldn't be just the biggest coincidence in the world that 'Chuck' off the bathroom wall and Morton, Charles E., war hero and friend of Bobby Wyatt, were both now suspects in his wife's murder; and Andy Allison had referred Wyatt to some guy named 'Chuck,' but that Wyatt had instead opted to hire his old flyboy buddy to do the job.

He rubbed his eyes then called Lance at her hotel. He filled her in on what he'd found out, then told her to contact Shelia Waltham to get her started trying to locate Charles Morton.

"What a coincidence, right?" Lance said. Edge noticed her words were slurred, slightly.

"Pretty big one so far."

"How do you feel about it?"

"I don't know yet. I think this lead might have some growl, but . . . I really don't know."

She paused. When she resumed, she talked slow.

"So, like what are you gonna do the rest of the evening?"

Edge chuckled. "Why, Ms Lance. If I didn't know better, I'd say that sounded like an invitation."

She paused again, apparently embarrassed, a state in which he had never seen her.

"Do you know better?" There was a smile in her voice.

"I don't, I suppose. I've just made some assumptions."

"Well, don't. I'm probably not who you think I am." Her voice became playful. "I'm better." At that moment Edge was positive she was drunk.

He cleared his throat. "I was thinking of working a little more."

"All work and no play . . ."

"I'll stick with all work . . . for now."

In twenty minutes he was at The Lunatic Lounge and parking on the side, in the far corner. He looked around for Andy Allison's Cadillac but didn't see it.

There was a fair crowd there, including the country band that had performed the other night. There was one couple locked in a tight embrace on the dance floor. Edge looked the other direction to see who was behind the bar. It was a woman, young but worn. He decided to take a chance.

Edge took a seat on a stool near the end closest to the restrooms. The woman walked over and stood in front of him.

"What'll you have?" she said smiling.

She was in her twenties but with noticeable wrinkles on her face. She had a large nose, but dark eyes and brows. Her white tank top hung on her thin frame.

"Make it a Diet Coke, on the rocks, with a twist."

"Sure."

In a minute she was back. "You don't look like a guy that needs to lose weight."

"You'd be surprised . . ."

"Audrey."

"Audrey, yeah. I've been accused of having a fat head."

She laughed. "Your first time here?"

"No. I've been here once before. I came back hoping you'd gotten another band."

She smiled. "You mean, *The Potlickers*? Oh, they're not so bad."

"I've heard better."

"They'll grow on ya."

Edge nodded and sipped his drink.

"Where's Andy tonight?"

"He's off. He mainly works on weekends."

Edge nodded again. "You know a guy named 'Chuck'? Maybe hangs out here?"

She paused. "You a cop?"

He shook his head. "No. I just heard that Chuck could do a job."

The smile left her face, and she licked her lips.

"Well, there was a guy in here once or twice, said his name was Chuck. He was kind'a weird. He was in here with Andy, but I ain't seen him here in six or eight months."

"You remember his last name?"

She shook her head. "We don't deal a lot in last names here, uh, . . ."

He smiled. "John."

"John."

"Yeah, Smith. John Smith. What'd he look like?"

"About twenty five or so, sandy hair, gray eyes. Kinda looked like a country boy, sounded like it too."

"This Chuck say anything about himself?"

She shook her head again. "No. Just had a few drinks and shot some pool. Said he was down here to do a job. I don't know what he meant." She paused. "Say, are you sure you're not the fuzz?"

"Absolutely not." He took another sip. "Let me ask you something, did he look like he, you know, maybe batted from the other side of the plate?"

"What'chu mean?"

"You know. Was he a homosexual?"

"You mean, queer?"

Edge nodded.

"Well, if that's what you mean, come on out and say it. This ain't that kinda bar, so you ain't offendin' nobody in here."

"So?"

"Naw. He hit on me the whole night, and I 'bout had to fight him off."

"Not your cup'a tea?"

"No." It was clear she wanted to say more.

"Tell me."

"Well, I just kinda got a bad vibe from him, ya know? I mean, he didn't act like somebody that was a real gentle person. There was just somethin' about his eyes; like it wouldn't cause him much problem to hurt somebody."

"You haven't seen him since?"

"No."

"You know, if you did, it could be worth some dough."

"Really? What did he do?"

"Just call the police if you see him. Ask for Lieutenant Riley."

Edge nodded and then got up from his stool. He walked to the men's room and closed the door. Taking a small flashlight, he shined it on the walls of both of the stalls and above the urinals. It was obvious to Edge that the place had recently been painted.

Back at the bar, Edge paid his tab and left. Outside in the car, he made notes. Allison knew Chuck; Chuck wasn't homosexual; and, according to Audrey, at least, he had the look of a killer.

CHAPTER 18

The next morning Edge was in the office at nine to report to Gina that he had delivered the papers for Attenborough. He related the story of the burglary and the theft of the large emerald. Later, he called and shared the same information with Lance.

"We need to get Shelia on this. The man's name was Keyes, Fred Keyes. We need to get out an alert about this stolen jewelry and get some people on the lookout for it."

"Why is it so important?" Her voice was more precise, more alert than it had been the last time they talked.

"Because, the person that stole Keyes' jewelry might use the same fence that Bootsie's killer did. If we can find the rocks, we can trace it back to the fence and then we'll have . . ."

"Leverage."

"Now you're getting the hang of it."

"I've always had the hang of it."

"You didn't have it last night."

There was silence on the other end. "I was a little under the weather last night."

"That what they're callin' gettin' 'plastered' now? 'Under the weather?'" He paused.

"Smart ass."

"Are you better today?"

"Pick me up in ten minutes."

In thirty minutes Edge pulled up in front of the General Jackson Hotel and waited. In two, Lance walked out of the front door wearing sunglasses. She got in the front seat.

"You'll have to learn not to drink while you're working," he said.

She paused. "I, I hope I didn't embarrass myself."

"No. All you did was hit on me."

Her head snapped his direction.

"Oh, yeah. You all but invited me up to your room."

He was exaggerating, but he needed some also – some leverage.

"Well, just know," she said, "that our relationship is strictly professional, that what if anything I may have said was out of, of fatigue and frustration."

He smiled. "Well, okay. Let's just keep it professional, then."

She nodded. They rode in silence. Finally, she spoke.

"Where to now?" she said.

Edge looked at her. "Have you heard from Shelia about Charles Morton?"

She stopped and then she spoke. "Oh, right. I did, actually. She said the only information she had on him was that he was still in Mississippi."

"Any criminal record?"

"Mostly petty stuff was all she could find. He did do some time in the Lee County jail up in Tupelo."

"Where's his address?"

"Winona."

"Winona. I know it. It's right off I-55. We can be there in four hours."

She took a deep breath. "Let's go in the morning. Is there something else we can do today?"

He thought. "Let's see if we can find Andy Allison."

Allison's Cadillac was parked in front of the breezeway at his apartment when they drove into the complex off Azalea Road. They sat and watched for a few minutes to see if he would leave.

Their patience was rewarded when at ten thirty Allison walked down the steps and got into the Caddy. Edge started the car and when Allison left, they followed him.

He followed all the major routes to get to a restaurant on Airport Boulevard near the city's municipal airport. Andy Allison parked in the shell parking lot of a place called Alice's.

Edge put the Impala across the street, about two hundred yards away, in a school parking lot, and watched through field glasses as Allison sat down at a table near the front window with an older white man. At first, Edge didn't recognize him, but then, when the man turned toward the window and Edge focused the glasses on him, it was clear.

"You know who that is?"

Lance nodded. "Yeah. That's Bobby Wyatt."

Allison talked with Wyatt for about thirty minutes and they both ordered hamburgers. They ate and drank what looked like iced tea until eleven forty five.

Edge looked over at Lance who was yawning.

"Gettin' itchy?" Edge said to Lance.

"Sleepy."

"Liquor'll do it to ya."

"What do you think they're doing," she said changing the subject.

"I have no idea."

They did have an idea just shortly. Wyatt and Allison rose from their table and walked outside. Then Wyatt passed Allison an envelope that he got from his truck.

"What's that look like to you?" Edge said.

"Looks like a payoff to me."

They shook hands and then Wyatt got in his tricked out Chevy pickup, and Allison got into the Caddy. Allison left first.

"Who do we follow?" she said.

"Always follow the money."

"I wonder if Bobby minds that he bought Andy that car," Edge said.

They trailed the red Caddy down Schillinger's Road to Three Notch Road, and then to Tillman's

Corner. When he got on the Halls Mill Road, Edge had an idea where he was going. They were there in fifteen minutes.

Edge parked down the street from the Lazy Man's Pawn Shop and got out the glasses once again. In the lot next to a yellow Volkswagen there was a beat up Ford Ranger pickup with a 'For Sale' sign in the rear window.

Allison entered the store, then, in less than five minutes, he walked back outside to the Ranger and used a key to get inside. He sat in the truck for two, maybe three minutes, then got out and reentered the pawn shop. In thirty seconds he was in the Caddy and gone.

"Could you see what he was doing?"

Lance shook her head. "No. The sun was too bright."

"You think he dropped the envelope off in there?"

"Maybe."

"I guess we'll never know."

"We could sit and watch it."

"For how long?"

She had a point. If he'd left the money in the truck the drop could show up today, tomorrow, or next week. If he got something out of the truck, there'd be no reason to watch it.

Edge and Lance left and followed Allison back to the apartment complex. They watched his room and shortly afterward, a young girl exited an apartment across the breezeway and went into Allison's room.

"One in every port," Edge said.

"That's disgusting."

Edge smiled at her. "Let's go."

In thirty minutes, they were at Arnstein's Jewelry on Hillcrest Road, the location of the purchase of Bootsie Wyatt's diamond ring; the one bought for her by her husband as a gift. It was just before one o'clock.

"You take the lead on this one," Edge said as they walked in the front door.

Lance nodded, and at the glass counter, she asked to speak to the manager. They were directed to a desk in the far northeast corner where they found a conservatively dressed man with short brown hair. He rose and smiled.

"Levi Silverstein," he said. "Nice to meet you."

"Lucy Lance. This is John Edge. We represent Manhattan Mutual Insurance."

The smile left his face, but a frown did not replace it. "Sit down."

They took seats across from him. Edge took out a pad.

"How can I help you folks?" Silverstein folded his hands.

"This is a matter of some sensitivity, but we would certainly appreciate your help. We're looking into the murder of Dorothy Wyatt, and we wanted to ask you about her diamond ring; the one that was stolen."

Silverstein's brows went up. "Well, certainly, but I've already told the police all I know."

"Well, if you wouldn't mind going over it once more, I'd appreciate it."

She smiled at him, and it was just then that Edge realized that Lance was all woman, and knew it.

Silverstein smiled. "Okay, well, Mr. Wyatt came in and purchased the ring, oh, two, maybe three years ago. It was a two carat diamond, pear shaped, of a very high quality."

"How much was the appraisal?"

"Without looking at the paperwork, which the police have, by the way, I can't say for sure, but best as I remember it was close to fifteen thousand."

"I'm sure you'd know it if you saw it again, but is there any way for Mr. Edge or myself to recognize it?"

"Yes. Anyone could recognize it with the right tools. See, it was implanted with a chip; an identification chip. It's a new technology which allows us to identify our work."

"What if someone tries to cut it up?"

"Well, obviously, it doesn't work if the chip is found and discarded. But, of course, the diamond no longer carries the same value."

"Is there anyone else around here that knows about or uses this method?"

"As far as I know, we're the only ones in town that do it. And, it's not widely known; I mean, we don't publicize this service."

"So, what about Mr. Wyatt? Were you the person who sold him the ring?" Edge spoke wanting to get every last thing from Silverstein that he could.

"I was."

"Was he happy to buy it? Did he act like he hated to spend the money? Did he mention why he was doing it?"

"Well, as I said, he told me it was for his anniversary. But, well, I got the impression that there was something wrong and he needed a, a kind of a peace offering."

"Did he mention what was wrong?"

Silverstein shook his head. "No, but . . . it was a little obvious."

"How's that?"

"When he came to buy it,"

"Yeah?"

"He wasn't alone. The woman with him picked it out."

Edge said nothing.

"It wasn't Ms Wyatt."

Downtown, Edge dropped Lance off at the hotel with instructions to be ready to leave for Winona, Mississippi, the next morning. Also, she was to call when she heard back from Waltham about the Keyes jewelry.

Edge went back to his office and put his feet up on the desk. He rubbed his eyes and tried to think.

As he saw it, the suspects about which he knew were only possibles, not probables. There was Charles Morton, Bobby Wyatt's Army buddy who was known to have committed murder in the past, albeit a wartime incident that had been swept under the rug.

The other was 'Chuck' from The Lunatic Lounge. Audrey the bartender had said it: 'Chuck' had that look in his eye; a look that spelled trouble.

Edge was ambivalent about women's intuition. On the one hand, a hunch that couldn't be justified logically wasn't useful. On the other, he had read about a female's heightened sense of non-verbal communication, a sense that could potentially spot someone who was saying something without saying something.

He closed his eyes. There was Bobby Wyatt, connected to Andy Allison; Allison was connected to Marty at Lazy Man's Pawn, who was connected to Lardy McLain. Allison was also connected to 'Chuck,' as well as to Ricardo Gomez. And Wyatt was connected to Charles 'Chuck' Morton. He was beginning to think he would need one of those large bulletin boards in order to keep track of all the players.

There was no reason to believe that Morton had come from out of nowhere to kill Bootsie Wyatt. The only thing that made him believable was the bond that soldiers have in war; the bond that says that if you need help, I'll be there. After what Wyatt and Morton had been through, it wouldn't be a stretch.

After a few minutes, Edge was asleep. The next few days would be long ones.

CHAPTER 19

The next morning, Edge picked Lance up at the front door of the General Jackson at seven. She was carrying a small overnight bag and there was a somber look on her face, albeit somewhat obscured by sunglasses.

Edge drove to Highway 98 West, heading toward Hattiesburg, Mississippi, and very shortly they were on the open road with nothing to do but talk.

"So, you anxious to get back to New Orleans?" Edge said.

Lance nodded. "Yeah. I'm going home just as soon as we get back from up here."

"I don't like New Orleans myself; got a lotta bad memories over there."

"How so?"

"Oh, I spent some time there in the early sixties; lived on Montague Street. Man," he shook his head, "there was revolution in the air."

She snorted. "Oh, please. That's old Bob Dylan song."

Edge chuckled. "You caught me."

"Why so cryptic?"

"I could say the same about you."

"Well, I haven't said anything because I get the feeling that you think you know all about me already."

He smirked. "Okay, I confess. I don't."

She looked straight ahead, out the windshield. "Well, to start with, I'm not, as you seem to think, Shelia Waltham's lesbian lover." She looked at him. "I'm married. My husband is the Vice President in charge of claims for ManMut."

"Kids?"

"One. She's in boarding school in the northeast."

"Sounds very progressive."

"Is that supposed to insult me? She's away because she was a bit unruly growing up. We just felt that getting her away from a city like New Orleans, and into a more structured environment, would be better for her.

"I was a police officer in New Orleans before I came to work in the insurance business, so, yes, I know how to handle myself."

"So why aren't you investigating this case? Why come to me?"

"Because you know the people, the city, the layout."

"Why come along at all?"

"The truth? I just like to get out of the office. And, because, like Shelia said, you're new, and we don't want to throw our money away."

"Well?"

She looked at him. "Well, you stack up pretty good so far. I've been giving Shelia reports, and I told her I was pleased."

Edge nodded. He didn't accept compliments well, but neither did he turn them down.

"My being with you doesn't cramp your style does it?" she said.

"Well, yes and no. It does, but in a good way. Probably, some of the things I'd've done normally, I've held back on because you were there."

"You were an officer, too, somewhere, weren't you?"

"Well," he paused, "I read a couple'a Wambaugh novels."

"Okay, okay." She smiled and chuckled.

He drove on silently. They made several miles before she spoke.

"Do you think we've talked to the killer yet?"

He looked at her. "I don't think so. I think the key to this is the stolen jewelry. It'll lead us to a fence, and then maybe to whoever it was that got rid of Bootsie's jewelry."

"And you still believe that person connects to Bobby Wyatt."

"I don't see why not."

It took them four hours to get to Winona, Mississippi, a town of about four thousand located just off US 82, less than a mile east of Interstate

55. In town, Edge found the Police Department a couple of blocks off US 51, the town's main drag.

"Yes, ma'am," Edge said to the middle aged woman who doubled as a receptionist and a dispatcher. "My name is Edge, and this is my associate, Ms Lance." Edge showed his state-issued PI credentials. "We'd like to see the Chief, if possible. If not, then the investigator'll do."

The woman wore pants and a blouse, and she raised her glasses, a pair that hung around her neck by a chain, and stared closely at the credentials. Then she looked Lance up and down.

"Well, okay. I'll see if the Chief's in."

She picked up the phone and in seconds directed them down a short hall to the last office on the right, near an exit. Edge and Lance found the Chief behind his desk.

Arthur DeLaughter was a rotund man, in his fifties, with gray hair that was receding. His complexion was fair, which made for a red face around green eyes. He smiled broadly.

"Ya'll sit down, here." He nodded to chairs. "How can I hep ya?"

"Thank you, sir," Edge said. "My name's Edge and this is Ms Lance. We represent Manhattan Mutual Life Insurance, and we're working on a claim arising out of a murder case in Mobile, Alabama."

The chief leaned back and folded his arms. Not a good sign, Edge thought.

"We'd like to talk to a man from your town named Charles Morton. Do you know him?"

"Charlie? Sure. He lives, or lived, out off 51, about two miles outside'a town." He paused. "You think Charlie killed somebody?"

"Well, no. But he does know our suspect, and we were hoping to maybe get a little background information."

"Hm. I can't imagine him knowing somebody who's involved in a murder." He paused. "But, you know . . ."

"Yes?" Edge said.

"Well, Charlie did come back from the war kinda, well, not right, you know? He's had some troubles."

Edge nodded. "Do you think we could talk to him?"

"Oh, well, I ain't seen Charlie around here in two'a three years. He come home from the war and worked at the furniture plant 'til it closed, then he just did odd jobs until prob'ly '79 or '80."

"He ever get in any trouble?"

"You mean arrested? Well, yeah, a couple'a times; for drunk and fightin' mostly. He never did nothin' serious, though."

Edge thought a minute. "What about family? Anyone else around here that we can talk to?"

"Well, there's his Aunt Polly and Uncle John. John ain't doin' too well, but Aunt Polly'll be glad to talk to you. She just lives about two miles down the road."

"How about a wife, or ex-wife?"

"His ex moved away to Memphis a while ago, after he come back messed up. He does have a boy, though, Leon."

"Is he here?"

"I don't think so. I think Leon lives down in Eupora, about twenty miles east on 82."

Edge looked at Lance. She was engaged making notes and was silent.

"Well, okay. I guess all that's left for us is to stop by and talk to Aunt Polly."

"You want me to call her?"

"Would you? Just let her know that we're looking to talk to Charlie and, really, we're not the police."

He smiled. "Oh, she's not like that. She'll help ya, if she can."

DeLaughter picked up the phone and in seconds, in the way that only a small town police chief can, he had Polly Morton on the line and was telling her to talk to the two investigators from Mobile.

"They'll be by directly," he said before hanging up.

Edge rose as did Lance. "We thank you, Chief."

"Ya'll need help gettin' down there?"

"I think we can find it. Just go down 51 about two miles?"

"Right. Theirs is the house on the corner of 51 and Old Greensboro Road. It's a dirt road, but it's marked. You shouldn't have any trouble findin' it."

Fifteen minutes later, Edge drove the Impala into a grass yard on a tree covered hill on the southeast corner of US 51 and Old Greensboro Road. On top of the hill sat a well-kept, clapboard cottage that looked like it was built in the fifties. There was a small barn about a hundred yards to the south, but Edge saw no livestock. The scene was almost idyllic.

"Get out and come in," a heavy set woman said as she waddled through the front door. "Ya'll the insurance people from Mobile?"

"Yes, ma'am. How ya'll doin'?"

Edge knew it was a dangerous question. The woman was liable to begin talking about what all was wrong with her and never stop.

"Oh, I guess I'm doin' alright. My hip started actin' up on me last night, got me all stove up; but I took some as'prin and it feels a little better."

Edge and Lance walked up on the porch to meet Aunt Polly.

She was in her seventies and looked it. Her face was heavily lined, and while she tried to keep her gray hair pinned up, half of the strands had liberated themselves from the confines of the pins and were flying away in the breeze. Her print house dress was cotton, and she wore US Keds tennis shoes with no strings.

"Can we sit out here in the cool? Paw's asleep in yunder," she said.

They took seats in metal rocking chairs on the porch and sat back as the breeze blew through the trees. Edge wanted to get the conversation around to Charlie Morton quickly, but country people have a way of talking about everything else first, before they get to what you want them to talk about. You couldn't rush them, or they just thought you wanted something from them and didn't care about them, as people. Aunt Polly spoke first.

"We hadn't had much rain lately, so this breeze shore feels good. Paw, he don't get out here much to enjoy the outside. He's got the cough, and he has to stay as quiet as he can, all the time."

"That's too bad."

Aunt Polly nodded as she rocked. Thinking about her husband clearly depressed her.

"So, I hear ya'll lookin' for Charlie."

"Yes, ma'am."

"Well, I thank he's down in New Orleans. I got a card from him about a year ago. He said he was doin' alright and livin' with some boys uptown on some street; I don't 'member which one."

"You still got that card?"

"Well, I might. But I couldn't tell you where it is. I got so much junk in there." She nodded over her shoulder. "I don't git to clean up the house like I want. Paw, he stays sick most'a the time."

That was fine, he thought. The New Orleans PD and Lance's contacts would know where to find him.

"Tell me about Charlie. I heard he come back from Vietnam a little different. I was over there, myself. I know what it was like."

"Well, you're right, now, he wadn't the same when he come back. He was drankin' too much and couldn't hold no job; and you couldn't talk to'im."

"Did he ever mention a man named Bobby Wyatt? He would'a known him from the Army."

"Bobby Wyatt? No, I don't thank so. But he didn't talk too much about over there."

"I understand his wife left him."

"She did. She left'im about ten or so years ago. I don't blame her. He just got so bad you couldn't stand to be around'im." She paused. "He learned to fly helicopters in the service. I don't know why he didn't try to get in to that; but, I don't guess there's too much call for it around here."

Edge looked out over the front yard at the flowers and the green grass. He'd spent some time in the country, outside in the air and the space. He liked it.

"Tell me about his son?"

"Leon? Oh, well, when his mama and daddy got divorced, she took off to Memphis and o' course she took Leon with'er. I didn't see him too much for a few years. Then he come back down here to live, over in Eupora."

"What's he doin' over there?"

"He's workin' at a shirt factory." She nodded.

"He married?"

"No. He's gotta girl he runs around with, and I thank they might be engaged, but," she shook her head, "they ain't married."

Edge looked over at Lance who appeared bored. They'd found out where Morton was, she was ready to go.

"By the way, does anybody ever call Charlie, 'Chas,' or 'Chuck'?"

"Not as long as I've known him. Now, maybe in the service they did, but not around here."

Edge looked off toward the road. A car was coming toward them in the distance. He said nothing for a minute, until it arrived. The driver of the vehicle, a dusty, blue pickup, waved to Aunt Polly as he stopped at the stop sign. Then he turned north onto the blacktop, toward Winona, and he was gone.

"Albert Lee Watson. I guess he's gone to pick up Charlene from work," Aunt Polly said.

They all sat and said nothing. Edge looked at Lance who was leaned back in her chair with her eyes closed. Aunt Polly had her eyes closed also. Edge tried to think of anything that he had forgotten to ask.

Aunt Polly opened her eyes and sneezed. "Shew!"

"Bless you."

"Thank you. There's a lotta pollen in the air."

"Tell me, is Leon's last name Morton?"

"It is. His mama remarried. She's a Dozier, now, I thank."

Edge nodded. "Okay, well, look, we sure thank you for sittin' with us for a few minutes."

Lance opened her eyes and started to lean forward in her chair. She yawned.

"Well, ya'll don't have to rush off. We'll be startin' dinner in a little while."

"Well, thank ya, but we need to be gettin' on the road."

All three rose from their seats. Lance started down the steps of the front porch toward the cars.

"I hope Uncle John gets ta feelin' better."

"Well, thank ya, but I don't know if he ever will."

"Well, listen, if you should happen to hear from Charlie," he handed her a business card, "give him my number and ask him to call me."

She took the card. "I shore will."

Aunt Polly followed them out to the car, and Edge slid behind the wheel. Lance was already settling in. Edge rolled down the window.

"Thank you, ma'am."

"Ya'll come back."

He turned the car around in the yard and in seconds he was on 51 headed back toward town. He looked over at Lance.

"All this around here's a little too tame for you, hunh?"

She snorted. "Hunh. Old women and their lives; they're just so . . ."

"Tired?"

"No."

"Boring?"

"No."

Edge said nothing.

"I don't know, hopeless, I guess. They're gettin' to the end of their lives; nursing their sick husbands; looking forward to absolutely nothing. It's sad, really."

"You'll be there one day."

"I don't intend to."

"What, you're gonna kill yourself?"

"No."

"You're gonna kill your husband?"

"No. I'm just not gonna let life hold me down like that."

Edge chuckled. "Right."

"No, really."

"Look, nobody knows what kinda hand they're gonna be dealt. Your old man could get sick, too, and what are you gonna do? Abandon him? Run off? No, you'll stay there and take care of him, and he'll die slow, and you'll have to wait around, and it'll be painful, and nobody'll come around 'cause he's sick, and you'll get lonely." He paused. "It'll be your cross, and you'll just have to find something inside you that'll help you cope."

She snorted but said nothing.

When Edge got to Highway 82, he stopped. To the west was the interstate and Mobile, or New Orleans. To the east was Eupora and Leon Morton.

"Well, which way?" she said.

Edge looked both ways. "It's only twenty miles to Eupora. Why don't we see if we can find Leon. Maybe we can catch him before he gets off work."

Lance nodded. "Okay. Let's go."

It was forty minutes later when they found the Athlon Garment factory on State Highway 9, just off Roane Avenue. The personnel office was near the lobby.

They identified themselves to a pudgy young woman with blonde hair and a short skirt who told them that she would see about getting Leon Morton. She directed them to a break room down the hall. They sat down on plastic chairs around a metal table.

He arrived five minutes later. Leon Morton had sandy blonde hair and a slim build. His face was clean shaven and his gray eyes had a kind of distant look to them.

Edge extended his hand, and Morton took it. His grip was clammy. Edge identified himself and told him why they were there. Morton nodded at Lance, and they all sat down.

"We were just wondering if you know how to get in touch with your father," Edge said.

Morton looked suspicious. "How come?"

"We think he might have some information about an old Army buddy that we think committed murder."

"I don't think so. Daddy's been outta commission for a few years. He's kinda had trouble with drinkin' and stuff." Morton looked away.

"We've got reason to believe that he's had some contact with a man named Bobby Wyatt."

His brows went up, and he seemed to tense, just for a second. Edge looked at Lance. She saw it also and leaned forward in her chair.

"Uh, well, I think I've got a number here." Morton pulled out his wallet and thumbed through some scraps of paper. "Yeah, he's in New Orleans. Here's his phone number."

"Have you talked with him lately?"

"Not in about two years."

"How was he?"

"He was gettin' along. He was livin' at kind of a halfway house and goin' to AA. Said he was makin' some progress, but the night I talked to him, he sounded wasted."

"He say where the house was?"

"Just that it was uptown. Look, I gotta get back to work. Is there much more?"

Edge looked at Lance. She shook her head.

"No, I guess not. Okay, Leon, we really appreciate your help." Edge handed him a business card. "If you hear from your daddy, would you call me?"

"Sure."

"How can we get in touch with you?"

Morton provided them with a phone number in Eupora. Lance took out a notebook and copied it down.

They all rose. Edge looked at him hard.

"Be seein' ya, Leon."

In the car, Edge looked at Lance. She was rubbing her eyes.

"What'chu think of that guy?" he said.

"How do you mean?"

"I mean, I got a feeling about him."

"You think he's our man?"

Edge exhaled as he backed the car out onto Main Street. "I don't know. I just got a feelin' off him."

"Now, you're beginning to sound like a woman."

CHAPTER 20

Instead of going on to New Orleans, Lance suggested that they go back to Mobile, and she would go back home the next day and get a good address on Charlie Morton. When she had it, she'd call, and Edge could meet her in the Big Easy.

They rode silently for the two hundred and seventy miles back to Mobile, Edge thinking about Leon Morton. He couldn't put his finger on it, but there was something about the young man that just didn't sit right; the way he froze when Bobby Wyatt's name was mentioned; the way he had to get back to work quickly afterwards; the way he gave up his father's phone number so easily.

They arrived home about ten o'clock. Edge dropped Lance off at the hotel and then went on to his office. Inside, he checked his service. Madge was on duty.

"Hey, where have you been? I got a ton'a messages for you."

"I been workin', Madge." He readied his pen. "What'chu got?"

"Well, there was a call from Lieutenant Riley at the Police Department. He says to call him tomorrow. Do you need the number?"

"No, I got it."

"And there was a call from Shelia Waltham. She said to send her a bill so she could get you paid."

"I'll take care of it."

"Then there was a call from a guy named Josh. He said he had some information for you. You want his number?"

"No. I got it, too."

"Oh, and one last one. A woman called. She didn't leave her name, but she said one of the Parisi brothers was in town. She just said to tell you that and to tell you to be careful."

Edge swallowed. "She didn't say who she was? No number?"

"No. Just said to be careful."

"Okay. Thanks, Madge."

"Hey, Mr. Edge," she said.

"Yeah, Madge?"

"I took that call. The woman sounded kind'a scared." She paused. "Be careful, hunh?"

"Sure. Thanks, Madge."

He hung up the phone and wondered about the last call. By all rights, both Parisi brothers should be dead. This could be a long lost cousin or something. The call obviously came from JoAnn

Ward. No one else knew who he was or where he was. He wished she would lose his number.

The rest could wait for tomorrow. Edge went home and went to bed.

The next morning, Edge found a note on his door from Attenborough. He wanted Edge to serve a couple of papers. Fine, he thought. While Lance was out of town he could keep himself busy.

He called Victor Riley at the Police Department shortly after eight. Of all the people he had met in town, Riley was the one he seemed to have the most respect for and the one he most wanted respect from.

"Edge, I've been getting some complaints about you," he said gruffly.

"Lies, Lieutenant. All lies."

"Some wetback named Ricardo called and said you worked him over pretty good."

"He make a complaint?"

"Nope. He just said that you were investigatin' the Wyatt case, and he wanted me to have 'a talk' with you. Do I need to have a talk with you?"

"Absolutely not." He paused. "I spoke with Ricardo at his apartment, sure, but he was in good health when I left. As a matter of fact, on my way out, I picked up a bag'a dope and a couple'a stolen credit cards just so he wouldn't get his self into any trouble.

"Ricardo milked a few thousand dollars out of Bobby Wyatt making him believe that he was a hit man. He got him to pay him five grand or so, but then he didn't do the job. The payoff was made out at the Three Crosses Cemetery on Airport. Plus, he's an illegal and a thug; and, worst of all, the very worst thing of all is he's getting food stamps illegally. Believe him at your peril."

Riley said nothing for a beat. "Okay, okay. I get it. What did you do with the dope and the card?"

"I flushed the dope and mailed one of the cards off to the credit card company. I held onto the other." He paused. "Don't worry, Ricardo's got enough money to keep himself wired for a while."

Edge heard him snort on the other end. "You makin' any progress on this thing?"

"Well, yes and no. We're still lookin' for this 'Chuck' that was supposed to have done the actual killing. Other than that, we're gropin'."

"That reminds me, a woman named Audrey called. She wanted to know about the reward for a guy named 'Chuck' that killed somebody. I told her there wasn't one to my knowledge. Is that something you stirred up?"

"Money talks, bullshit walks, Lieutenant."

"Don't waste my time."

Edge hung up and walked around to the front of the building and sat down across the desk from Gina. She looked especially fetching in a yellow sundress and sandals.

"You look like you're ready for the beach," he said.

"I am. We're going' this weekend. I'm just tryin' to get in the mood." She smiled broadly.

"Well, that dress'll do it." He paused. "Who's we?"

"Me and my honey, Tim."

"Lawyer?"

"Are you kiddin'?"

Edge smiled.

"No. He's a guy I met at a golf tournament, when the ladies were playing out at the Country Club. He's an accountant."

"Imagine that, love on the green; a hole in one."

"That's dirty."

"Only in your head."

Smiling, she reached and picked up a couple of subpoenas and handed them to him. "Here, see if you can keep yourself out of trouble with those."

He nodded, silently disappointed at the thought of Tim and Gina, together.

At noon, he parked on the Washington Avenue side of T Bob's Saloon and went inside. He found a seat at the end of the bar next to the pool table.

Albert, the relief bartender was wiping down the bar. Edge walked over and took a seat.

"Hey, Albert. How ya doin?"

Albert wasn't the wisest owl in the parliament, but he was a tremendous bartender. Josh said he could make any kind of drink anyone wanted and had, in fact, won contests out of state and overseas making drinks that no one had ever heard of. He could make obscure drinks that were known only in Africa or the Soviet Union. Josh called him a mixological savant.

"Hey, Mr. Edge. What can I get for you?"

"Can you make me a Diet Coke, on the rocks?"

"Oooookay," Albert said.

Edge could tell he was confused. "A can'a Diet Coke in a glass over ice. Oh, and give it a twist'a lemon."

"Oh, yeah. Thanks." Albert turned away.

"Hey, Albert. Is Josh in?"

"Yeah, he's in the back."

"Could you get him?"

"Okay."

Albert walked through a door behind the bar and returned seconds later followed by Josh.

"Hey, John. I called you."

"Yeah, I got your message. What's up?"

Josh waited until Albert had served Edge his drink and walked away. Then he leaned forward.

"Look, Tommy said you was lookin' for the guy that killed the rich lady in West Mobile; somebody named 'Chuck' right?"

"Yep." He took a sip.

"Well, I don't know who did it, but you could take a look at Chuck Latimer."

"Chuck Latimer?"

"Yeah. He's done time and, you know, he thinks he's a badass."

"What'd he do time for?"

"Dope and burglary, I think."

"What's he look like?"

"He's got black hair; kinda short, with green eyes."

Edge could tell that Josh was fishing for money. He wasn't going to oblige him this time.

"Okay, Josh. I'll take a look at him. Thanks. If the information pans out, there'll be a little something for you."

Josh stood up straight with a disappointed look on his face. He smiled sheepishly and backed away from the bar.

"Sure, John. Well, let me know how it turns out."

"Right."

Edge laid a dollar on the bar for the drink and slid off the stool. In a minute he was gone.

CHAPTER 21

Edge spent the next three days on process service for Attenborough, his landlord. He served two notices of suit and three subpoenas, and he finished the last one and got back to his office in the early afternoon on Friday.

The phone was ringing when he sat down at his desk. Edge picked it up.

"Yeah," he said.

"Hatchett."

The speech was mush mouthed. It sounded like the speaker was lipless. He didn't know who it was, but he had a good idea.

"I'm afraid you've got the wrong number."

"I'm afraid I don't."

"Who is this?"

"I've got a friend of yours here."

The next voice he heard was familiar. "I'm sorry, Mark. He made me . . ."

"That's your buddy, JoAnn," the man said. "Well, maybe she ain't so great a buddy after all."

"This Parisi?"

"Now, here's how we're gonna play it. You come to the Crimson Tide Motel on Highway 90, in twenty minutes, and I may just let your little friend here live. Room 17. Come alone."

Parisi hung up without further comment. Edge sat and rubbed his eyes. He knew he was going to have to kill someone today.

In seventeen minutes Edge parked the Impala near the office of the Crimson Tide Motel. It was a collection of about thirty duplex style cabins, surrounded by old growth oak trees. The buildings were scattered about in a village setting, and the lane that drove through the middle of it was made of oyster shells. Each building was painted white and each had a crimson door.

Edge wore his safari vest over a short sleeved white shirt. He was ready. His forty five was in its holster in the small of his back, the Colt was on his ankle, and his knife was in his pants pocket.

He walked until he found room seventeen, at the east side of the lot. That side of the property backed up to a shopping center next door. He stood to the side of the door and tried to look through the only window in the room. The curtains were drawn tightly, and he heard nothing coming from the inside.

He reached and tried the knob. It was unlocked. Edge thought about busting in, but he wanted to get Parisi as close to him as possible. One of the ways that he could orchestrate that was if the fat Italian answered the door. The fact that another man could be in the room crossed his mind, but he knew he could only deal with one of them at the time.

Edge tapped lightly on the door. He heard movement toward the entrance.

The door swung open. "Get in."

Edge stepped inside the dark room to find Ralph Parisi standing behind the door with a revolver in his hand and an angry look on his face. Edge took two steps to his left and stopped in front of the window. Parisi closed the door.

"Hey, Ralph; or Sam. How's it goin'?" Edge said cheerfully.

Edge looked around. To his left was a queen sized bed. Beyond the bed, on the opposite side of the room, sat a worried- looking and bruised Jo Ann Ward in a hard chair, her hands restrained behind her back. Next to her was a closed door, presumably the bathroom.

Parisi reached and turned on the lamp on the desk across from the foot of the bed. It was then that Edge could see what he was angry about.

His face was heavily scarred. He was bald and the skin around his mouth and nose was flat. The fire had definitely done a job on him.

Parisi pointed the revolver at him and took two steps forward. He was within arm's length of Edge.

"Look. Look at me, Hatchett. Here's how it's goin' down. You killed my brother and the fag that worked for us. And you burnt me like toast.

Now, I'm gonna kill you and your little friend over there." He nodded to Ward.

His speech was distorted by the fact that his lips were all but missing, but his tone was clear. Edge had never seen a more angry man.

"Oh, come on, Ralph. Can't we discuss this? They're doing some great things with plastic surgery these days."

Parisi, incensed by Edge's levity, took another step forward and raised the revolver to pistol whip him. It was the break that Edge was waiting for.

Edge reached up and took Parisi's right wrist with his left hand. He bladed himself to the fat man and elbowed him twice in the abdomen and about ten or twelve times in the face. Parisi pulled the trigger and the weapon discharged through the wall into room sixteen. Edge stepped on his instep and continued to elbow him about the head while managing to get him turned with his back toward the bathroom door. The weapon discharged two more times. Edge felt the big man relax slightly.

At that point, JoAnn Ward started rocking her chair and eventually fell over onto her right side, effectively taking herself out of the line of fire. At the same time, the bathroom door opened and another man, armed with a snub nosed revolver, stepped out and took aim. He was short with greased hair and a mustache, and he was wearing a baby blue leisure suit.

Edge dropped to one knee behind the bed while holding onto Parisi's wrist. The fat man was out of breath and semi-conscious, and he began to fall forward.

Edge reached and slipped the .45 out of its holster. The man across the room was still trying to get a clear shot at him. Edge snuck a peak around Parisi and over the side of the bed. Then he fired one round and the accomplice across the room fell dead of a bullet wound to center mass.

That left only a mostly-incapacitated Ralph Parisi. Edge put the forty five to his heart and pulled the trigger. He slumped forward, and Edge just barely slipped out from under him before he hit the floor. The room fell quiet save for the echo of the pistol shot.

Edge took two deep breaths and stood. He walked over to the man in front of the bathroom and took the revolver from his hand. He slid it into his pocket and put the .45 back in his holster. Then he turned to Ward.

"You alright?"

"Yeah," she grunted. "Just help me up."

Edge, still deaf from the proximity of the gunshot, couldn't hear her, but he inferred from her position what she wanted. He lifted the chair upright and then looked at her hands. She was handcuffed. He reached into his pocket, took out his key ring, and used a handcuff key to free her wrists.

"Thanks," she said as tears began to fall from her eyes.

Neither of them spoke as they heard sirens in the background. Ward sat down on the bed and wiped her face.

Edge cleared his throat. "Look. We gotta get our stories straight, in a hurry."

Ward shook her head as she wiped her eyes. "Don't worry about this. I got it."

He nodded and threw the handcuffs on the bed. In two minutes they heard a knock. Edge opened it to find two uniformed officers standing on either side of the door with guns drawn. He held up his hands.

An hour later, Edge and Ward were in Victor Riley's office at the Detective Division. Ward was reciting for the third time what had happened at the Crimson Tide Motel.

"So, you're an assistant DA in Manipi County, right?" Riley said.

"Yes, sir. I was just on my way inside my office this morning when this guy Parisi walked up to me, put a gun in my side, and told me to go with him."

"Did he say why?"

"Yeah, he said he was looking for a man named Mark Hatchett. Hatchett used to be a private detective in Mauvilla. I knew him. We worked on a couple of cases together, but he left town, and I don't know where he is. Well, I tried to tell Parisi that, but he wouldn't listen.

"He put me in a car with that other dead guy and drove up to the lake on the west side of town. Do you know anything about Mauvilla, Lieutenant?"

"Not much."

"Well, it's where the kids go to park, but it's deserted in the daytime. Anyway, he slapped me and said he wanted Hatchett. I told him I didn't know where he was, but he didn't believe me. So he slapped me around some more."

Edge saw a tear in her eye. He didn't know if it was part of her act or if reliving the experience was bringing her emotions to the surface. In the light of the office, Edge could see the bruising through her olive complexion. There was dried blood around her mouth and swelling around her eyes; one was about to close. They did a number on her, he thought. But . . . they're dead now.

"What happened then?"

"I couldn't think of what to do, so I remembered Mr. Edge. We met in Mobile at the DA's convention a couple of weeks ago. We talked in the hotel restaurant. Do you remember?" she said turning to Edge, her brows upraised.

"I remember."

"You said if I ever needed any help, I should call." She paused and looked down. "I remembered your number, 251-GUMSHOE. So I gave it to him. I hope that was okay," she said as she looked at Edge.

"That's fine," Edge said. "You did the right thing."

"Anyway, I finally told them that Hatchett was in Mobile, and we drove down here. I said to let me go, but he said that he needed me to get Hatchett to come to where he was."

"How did you find the motel?" Riley said.

"We just ran up on it on the highway. It took about an hour and a half to get to Mobile. He said it looked like a good place, and so they took me inside and handcuffed me to a chair.

"He tried to call Mr. Edge several times before he finally got him. Then when he did, he shoved the phone in my face and told me to get him there."

"What did you say?"

"What could I say? I told Mr. Edge who I was and for him to come to the motel, that I needed help. I just didn't mention his name. Thank heavens he came." Ward looked at Edge with silent eyes of thanks.

"What happened when he got there?"

"Mr. Edge knocked on the door, and Parisi opened it. When Mr. Edge walked inside, Parisi saw he wasn't Hatchett and got angry. He threatened to kill us both. He asked Mr. Edge who he was and after that, I don't really remember. It was all kind of a blur. I rocked over onto the floor and shut my eyes when the shooting started."

Riley looked at Edge. "So?"

"So, I told him who I was, and I think I asked him how he got such an ugly mug as that. He stepped forward to pistol whip me, so I caught his wrist, turned sideways, and gave him about two dozen elbow strikes to the face and the belly. He fired off a couple'a rounds, but then he passed out, or came close to it. I pulled my piece and shot him.

"About that time his partner, the greaser with the bad suit came outta the bathroom and pointed his gun at me. I saw Ms Ward fall over in her chair, and I thought he'd killed her, so I dropped to my knees by the bed and plugged him." He paused. "That's it. Your people showed up and, well, here we are."

Riley wiped his mouth. He took a deep breath and exhaled, as he leaned back in his chair.

"There's somethin' fishy about all this," he said. "I can't lay my finger on it, but it just don't smell right."

"Come on, Vic," Edge said.

It was the first time Edge had called him 'Vic.' He felt the time was right and it would keep things in perspective.

"This lady's an officer of the court. You know *she's* tellin' the truth. Plus, she's got the bruises to prove it. And me, well, I was just defendin' myself."

Riley nodded. "A lawyer that lies? Well, we know that can't happen." He paused. "The only thing saving you guys from a hard look at this thing is the dead guys. They're both scum; hoods from New York. The Bureau says they were both in porn production." He paused and looked at Edge. "I guess you did us all a favor."

"You're welcome." Edge said as he wiped blood off of his shirt. There was quite a lot of it there.

"Lieutenant, could I please call my husband? It's getting late, and if I'm not home when he gets there, he'll be worried."

"Sure." Riley rose. "I'll give you some privacy." He walked out of the room.

Edge rose also. "I'll be in the hall."

"Wait," she said. "Sit back down."

He slumped into his chair, suddenly tired and overwhelmed with his afternoon's work. He looked at her battered face.

"I tried not to tell him," she said. "But, I don't know, it hurt when he hit me."

"Don't worry about it. It's over. They're gone, and you'll heal." He paused. "You did before."

She nodded. "Looks like you and I just can't stay outta hot water, can we."

"No, it doesn't."

They looked at each other.

"He told me that Mark Hatchett burned down his house and killed his brother. He didn't say how he knew."

Edge said nothing.

"That was Sam, by the way. Ralph was killed. He said he never met you, so he was really just acting when he saw you walk in the door. If you'd told him you weren't Mark Hatchett he'd've probably believed you."

"Then he would've killed you."

"That is a possibility."

He nodded. "So, how's your husband gonna take this?"

She smirked. "Well, he won't be happy." She paused. "I'm, I'm gonna have to tell him the truth, eventually. I made a promise: no secrets."

"I hope it's when I'm on my deathbed."

"Don't worry. He's not that kind'a guy. He's really a loving and sensitive man; a healer."

"Famous last words." He paused and shrugged his shoulders. "Look, you do what you have to do. I understand. I was just hoping that maybe . . ."

"It'll last, John. You've got a new life here, and it'll be okay. I won't mess it up."

"Well, I'm sure off to a rousing start to gettin' rid'a my old one."

CHAPTER 22

Edge spent the next two days recuperating. He took a short day trip to the beach in Pensacola and afterwards visited the Naval Aviation Museum. It was a diversion; something to get his mind off the red stream that had flowed from the chest of Sam Parisi onto his vest and white shirt; as well as the sight of the bruised and battered face of JoAnn Ward.

On Monday morning, Lucy Lance called Edge at his office. There was concern in her voice.

"You had some weekend," she said.

"How'd you know?"

"It was in the newspaper here." She paused. "How're you takin' it?"

"I'm fine."

There was silence on the phone. She didn't believe him.

"So, I got an address on Charles Morton. You wanna come over?"

"Sure. I can be there tomorrow morning. Where do you want me to meet you?"

"Just pick me up in front of the Police Department. You know where it is?"

Unfortunately he did. "Yeah. Say, around ten?"

"Great." She paused. "Edge?"

"Yeah."

"You had to do it, right? It was you or him?"

"What? Oh, yeah. Well, that's the way I saw it."

"Then don't worry about it. I worried and it nearly killed me." She paused. "It's the reason I don't carry a gun."

"Tell me about it."

"Just a robbery call downtown; he came out shooting, and I shot back. I wasn't the same for a long time. Pills, drinking; I even went to a psychic trying to get over it. I felt so guilty that I wanted to die myself. Then, one day, somebody told me it was okay to save my own life. That kind of snapped me out of it." She paused. "But I still have trouble with . . ."

"Death?"

"Yeah. It hits me hard."

"Wow, sounds like you went through the mill. But you're okay now, right?"

"I'm coping. It helps to have a family. They take your mind off it and put it on what's important."

"Sounds like you've had an eventful young life."

She chuckled. "I'm not so young."

"Well, good for you, anyway." His voice was not contemptuous.

"Just so you know," she said.

"Well, Lucy – can I call you Lucy?"

"Sure."

"Lucy, I appreciate the sentiment, but it's not necessary. This wasn't my first rodeo."

"Okay. Well, sure. I get it," she said.

"Look, I'll see you tomorrow morning, okay?"

"Ten sharp."

The next day, Edge pulled up in front of the Tulane Street side of the New Orleans Police Department and found an angled parking space at the foot of the concrete steps, right in front. He looked at his watch. It was three minutes of.

He sat adjusting the radio knob until he found WWL, the news and traffic station that he usually listened to when he was in town, and when he looked up again, he saw Lance walking down the steps. She had a coffee cup in her hand and sunglasses on her face.

Inside the car, he looked at her. "You got that address?"

"Yeah. Start headin' uptown."

He backed out of the parking space, got turned around and in a few minutes they were at the one thousand block of Telemachus, a lower middle class neighborhood not far from the park. The halfway house where Charlie Morton lived was midway down the block.

"Where'd this information come from?" he said.

"Off his last arrest report. The detectives recognized it as a drug and alcohol resident's home."

They got out, and Lance led the way to the front door of a wood frame house on the north side of the street. It was old and mildewed in some places, but it appeared sturdy.

A cur dog lying under a tree struggled to his feet and ambled over to investigate. Edge perceived its presence as a metaphor for the men inside; tired, barely able to move, beaten down by life, but willing to struggle to their feet in order to continue living.

Edge looked over his shoulder. "Must be some nice place, hunh," he said as he nodded toward the dog. "Got security and everything."

Lance smiled. Edge could see that she was more comfortable working in her own hometown. That was fine, he thought. Let her work. He had always hated New Orleans, and the quicker he got out of town the better.

"Yes, sir," Lance said to the fat man in a torn t-shirt that opened the front door. "We'd like to talk to Charlie Morton, please." She smiled.

"Who are you?" the fat man said.

"Tell him, Ms Lance and Mr. Edge. We're from Manhattan Mutual Insurance Company." She paused. "Tell him we have a message from his son."

The fat man's brows went up. "Is somethin' wrong?"

"No. We just need to talk to him."

He looked them up and down. "Wait here."

The fat man closed the door in their faces. In seconds it reopened.

A tall man stood in the threshold. He was thin and bony, and his thinning hair was combed over to the side. Edge pegged him at a worn out forty five. He wore a short-sleeved plaid shirt and faded jeans, but no shoes.

"Mr. Morton?"

The man nodded.

Lance looked around. "May we come in?"

"What's this about?"

"A friend of yours. Bobby Wyatt."

The surprise on his face was noticeable. Morton turned to the side and nodded toward a parlor on the right, off the foyer. They followed him in and took seats on a green velour couch that had seen much better days. Morton sat on a hard wooden chair with his back to a dormant fireplace.

Lance looked around. "Is this place court-ordered?"

Morton shook his head. "No. We're voluntary. It's kinda' of a, a commune, I guess. Everybody pitches in to make the bills, and we have meetin's every Thursday night where we all kinda encourage each other and talk things through."

She nodded and took a deep breath. "Mr. Morton, when's the last time you talked to Bobby Wyatt?" Lance said.

"Bobby? Shew, I don't know. But ya know, I kinda been out of it for a few years. I coulda' talked to him last week and not even remember it."

"Think hard, Mr. Morton. This is important."

He looked up and closed his eyes. Then he took a deep breath and exhaled.

"You know, it seems like it might'a been in the last year or so. I think he called me; asked me what I was doin' and how I was."

"What made him call?"

"He said he heard I was having a rough time of it, and he just wanted to check on me."

"How did he get your number?"

"My number? Oh, I don't know. I think he said he got it from my family up in Winona. I don't know who could'a give it to him, though."

"What did he want?"

"He, uh, he just wanted to see how I was doin'. He asked about my family, and he told me about his. He said he was married and had a couple'a kids; said they was doin' real good; said he had his own business."

"Did he ask you for anything? To do anything for him?"

"Do anything? No. He just wanted to talk."

"Did he say anything about his wife?"

"Well, yeah. He said he was married, and he complained about her a little; but, heck, you know, we all do that." He chuckled.

"Tell me about you and Bobby. What kind of relationship do you have?" Edge said.

"Wow, Bobby and me, we go way back; back to the war." He shook his head. "We had some hot times back in country, now. There ain't nothin' I wouldn't do for Bobby; ner him for me."

I bet, Edge thought.

"We flew choppers in the 1st Air Cav, that's the Air Cavalry Division."

"I'm familiar with it," Edge said.

"We was in a lotta scrapes together."

Edge looked at him hard. "Like runnin' whores to firebases?"

Morton looked shocked. "How'd you . . .?"

"It doesn't matter. What matters is what Bobby said to you when you talked."

Morton shook his head slowly. "Well, like I say, I don't 'member much. We just talked about family and old times, you know."

"Did you mention your son?"

"Sure. I told him about Leon."

"How 'bout your ex?"

He shook his head. "Naw. She's dead to me."

"You ever talk to her?"

He shook his head. "She used to call when she wanted somethin' for Leon, but I hadn't heard from her since he got outta the house."

"How long has it been since you've seen Leon?" Lance said.

"Well, now, we don't get to talk too often. He's busy and, you know, I'm down here, but, I guess I saw him about two or three Christmases ago."

A theory was forming in Edge's mind.

"Do you know if Bobby ever talked to your son?"

He shook his head. "Not that I know of."

Lance looked at Edge. "We saw Leon the other day," she said.

"Really?" Morton was suddenly animated. "Did he say anything about me? I mean, how'd he look? How was he?"

"Yeah. He looked good. He's working at a shirt factory in a little town called Eupora, Mississippi."

"Did he say anything about me?"

"Yeah, he told us you'd, you know, had your troubles, but that you were doing a whole lot better." She paused. "Are you?"

Morton looked away and shrugged. "I have my good days and bad days." He sighed. "I gotta a job, and I'm gettin' some help here, but still, you know, it's hard."

Edge looked closely at the man who apparently was fighting an addiction. To be in the clutches of chemicals that can kill you, but to whom you couldn't say 'no' had to be maddening. But something about this man told Edge that he wasn't as bad off as he made out like he was. His eyes were just a little too bright.

"Bobby Wyatt's wife is dead, Charlie," Lance said.

He froze. "Oh, no."

"Yeah. Do you know anything about it?"

"Now, how would I know anything about that?"

"Well, we just thought that with you guys bein' so close and goin' through so much and all, that maybe he might'a said something to you that could help us."

He shook his head. "No. He didn't say nothin' to me."

For a man who couldn't remember whether or not Bobby Wyatt had called in the past year, he certainly could remember a lot about what was said, and not said, Edge thought. Addicts have a way of using their drug abuse to conveniently forget things someone else wants them to remember.

"Charlie, Your name's Charles, right?" Edge said.

"Yeah. Charles Everett Morton."

"You ever been called 'Chuck'?"

He chuckled. "No. I been Charlie ever since I was two or three. My daddy's name was Charles, but mama called him Chuck. She always said that she didn't want him comin' when she called me, ner me comin' when she called him, so she just started callin' me Charlie; sometimes she called me, 'Chip.'"

Edge nodded. "When's the last time you were in Mobile?"

"Mobile? Well, let me see. I don't know that I ever been over there."

"Think, Charlie."

He looked up at the ceiling and shut his eyes hard. "Well, I growed up in Winona; I went in service in '62; I come home from overseas in '67, no '68, it was; then I come down here in about seventy five, I think." He shook his head. "No, I don't think I ever been to Mobile."

"But like you said, you been out of it for a few years and maybe you couldn't remember if you had."

"Well, now, you could be right about that."

"Where you workin', Charlie?" Lance said.

"Workin'?"

"Yeah. You said you were working. Where you workin'?"

"Oh, well, uh, I work down at the docks unloadin' and loadin' ships. It's just casual labor, but I usually get pulled in every day."

"I see. Well, hey, that sounds good."

Edge was skeptical. It sounded an awful lot like Morton was dealing drugs.

Lance looked at Edge and shook her head. They both rose and started toward the door.

"Well, Mr. Morton, thank you for talking with us," Edge said. "Here's my card. If you think of anything, call me."

"Yes, sir, I'll sure do it."

Outside in the Impala, Lance put her sunglasses back on and turned toward him.

"Well, what do you think?"

"About what?"

"About all that."

"Well, he lied an awful lot in there. He couldn't remember if they talked, but he remembered what they said; he never asked how she died or any particulars about the crime; and he has a job, but he doesn't have a job."

"You think he's involved."

"I didn't say that. He's too big a screw up to ever pull off anything as heavy as killin' Bootsie. He proved that back in Vietnam."

"So, you don't think he's involved."

"I didn't say that either. He's clearly covering up something. Bobby didn't strike me as the kind of person who'd just out of the blue pick up the phone and call to check on an old Army buddy – not unless he wanted something in return. He's too big a sociopath for that." He paused. "Charlie's involved, somehow."

Edge dropped Lance off at her office, a second story walkup over an independent insurance agency, downtown, a block from the Superdome. He went inside to check his messages.

His answering service told him that Shelia Waltham had called. He called back immediately.

"I think I have something for you on your stolen emerald. I called around to Birmingham, Montgomery, and Nashville, and checked with the police departments there. They've all got pawn shop details.

"Anyway, I found an emerald in Montgomery, at Zip's Pawn Gun and Jewelry on the North Boulevard. It came in last Friday, and he listed it as over a karat and a half. I called the police department, and they went and picked it up."

"They say who pawned it?"

"The name given was Andy Allison; ID'd by a driver's license."

What a stroke of luck, Edge thought. More leverage on Allison.

"Do you know him?" Waltham said.

"We've met."

"You think this might be related to our case?"

"Well, if it isn't, it still gives us a whole lot to work with."

He hung up and looked at Lance. "I gotta get back to Mobile. You comin'?"

"What's up?"

Edge shared with her the particulars of the theft of the emerald from Fred Keyes' house and Waltham's discovery. She didn't seem hugely impressed.

"No, I've got some things to do here. I'll get back over there in a couple'a days. Then I'll call you."

She either had to service her old man, or go to see her therapist, Edge thought. In the front of his mind, he was contemptuous; in the back, envious.

"I think you can handle it. Besides, I'm just supposed to be with you to observe, right?"

"Right."

"Right?"

"Right."

CHAPTER 23

Edge arrived back in Mobile at six that evening. He parked at his office and checked his machine again. JoAnn Ward had called. He called her back.

"Hey," he said. "What's up?"

"Nothing. I, I just wanted to see how you were."

"I'm working. You, on the other hand, are apparently in pretty bad shape."

There was silence on the other end of the phone. "My husband didn't take all this too well. He, he's very upset."

"Why? It wasn't your fault you got kidnapped."

"He doesn't see it like that. He wants to know who this 'Mark Hatchett' is; he wants to talk to him."

"What did you tell him?"

"Nothing yet. But I've got to, soon."

"Can he keep a secret?"

"Yes. He'll have to."

He paused. "How's your face?"

She chuckled. "It feels a little like my arm did. I've got a broken tooth, and my eye may have some damage, but . . . I'll heal. I'm still young. You heal quick when you're young."

"You still in Mauvilla?"

"No. Me and Dan, that's my husband, are taking a few days, in Florida."

"That'll do ya good."

"It's nice." She paused. "John?"

"Yeah?"

"Thanks again."

"Don't mention it."

The next morning, Edge was up early. He was at Andy Allison's apartment complex shortly after eight, sitting and watching from across the parking lot. Edge was thankful that Lance had stayed in New Orleans. For with what he might have to do today, he was going to need privacy.

At nine, Allison exited the apartment and got in the Caddy. He pulled out onto Azalea Road and started south. Edge didn't know where Allison was going, but he did know that at the first opportunity, he was going to take him for another kind of ride.

Allison stopped at a convenience store at Highway 90 and Azalea Road. Edge pulled over at the shopping center across the street. He watched as Allison walked inside and came out ten minutes later with a grocery sack. Shortly, the Caddy started back toward the apartments.

In five minutes, Allison was pulling into a parking space in front of his building. Edge saw his chance and parked right beside him. The startled Allison froze as Edge walked toward him.

"Hey, Andy. We gotta talk."

Edge took his index finger and put it into Allison's side then began marching him up the steps in the breezeway.

"What's this all about?"

"I told ya, we need to talk. You got your keys?"

Allison handed them to Edge, and at the top of the stairs, Edge used them to open the apartment door. He pushed Allison forward over the threshold and face first onto the floor.

Edge got a surprise when he stepped in behind him. There were two young men in the apartment. One was tall with a big Afro, wearing a red pullover shirt. The other was shorter with an ebony complexion, wearing a white t-shirt and tan shorts. Both wore tennis shoes; nice ones, like those named for that basketball player.

The tall man was on the couch watching television. The shorter one was in the kitchen, immediately to the right, making a sandwich. Edge noticed that he had a knife in his hand.

The men looked up. They seemed to know that there was trouble. Edge stood just inside the doorway.

"Well, well, Andy. What have we here?"

No one said anything. Edge walked up behind Allison and grabbed him by the hair. He pulled him to his feet and back in front of the open door.

"Who are these people, Andy?"

Edge watched both men. Quickly, the tall one next to the couch ran toward them. He pushed

Allison to the floor, out of the way, and was going to overrun Edge also, but Edge sidestepped him, elbowed him in the head and sent him flying onto the concrete outside. He scrambled to his feet and flew down the steps, and was out of sight in seconds.

The man in the kitchen was frozen. He dropped the piece of bread on which he was working and began moving slowly toward the living room, knife in hand. Edge reached behind him and pulled out his forty-five.

"Don't even think about it, Clyde," Edge said.

The man's eyes widened at the sight of the pistol, and he dropped the knife.

"You got two seconds," Edge said, "to get outta here."

The man looked at Edge, then at Allison lying on the floor, then back at Edge. Without another word he started running toward the door. Edge stepped aside, and in an instant the boy was gone.

Allison struggled to his feet. He straightened his shirt and rubbed his arm.

"You ruined a perfectly good party, man," he said.

"Shut up, Andy. You're about to go to jail."

"What are you talking about?"

"I'm talking about a big ole emerald broach up in Montgomery. They know where it came from and who pawned it. You're in some deep shit, my friend."

Allison froze. He wiped his mouth, and his eyes darted around the room. Edge guessed that he was quickly calculating what he could take with him when he took a powder. His eyes stopped on Edge.

"Hey, I didn't know it was stolen. It was them other two; they're the ones you want."

"You mean 'fric and frac' there?" he nodded toward the door. "What do they have to do with it?"

"They're the ones that stole it."

Edge turned around and closed the door. Then he bent down and picked up the paper bag full of beer that Allison had dropped. He nodded toward the kitchen table, and they both sat down.

Edge popped the top on a can and slid it over. Allison looked at it, looked at Edge, then picked it up and took a long swig.

"So, how'd it go down?" Edge said.

He took a deep breath and exhaled. "I got a call from a guy, you know, and he tells me he has some merchandise."

"Who?"

"You know, a guy."

"Stop playin' games, Andy. Was it Lardy?"

He snorted. "Yeah. He gives me stuff, sometimes, and I go pawn it for the money."

"What's the split?"

"I get forty and he gets sixty."

"Nice." Edge paused as Allison took another drink. "So, who were those guys?"

"Ah, you know, just some guys. They come over sometimes and we have a few beers."

Edge looked at him hard. "Bullshit."

Allison took another drink then opened another beer, his second. Edge was patient. He could wait.

Edge got up and walked over to the kitchen. He checked the cabinet over the sink and found a bottle of bourbon. Picking up a shot glass, he walked back to the table, filled it full, and set it in front of Allison.

"Tell me about Chuck."

"Chuck?"

He drank the whiskey. Edge refilled the glass.

"You know, the guy that killed Bootsie."

"Oh, yeah, Chuck." He took another drink, and Edge opened another can of beer.

"You talked to him?"

"No, man. I told you that I got his name off the wall."

"Bullshit."

Allison laughed. "Yeah, you're right. It is. Hey, you're a pretty smart dude."

"Hey, Andy, did you ever call your mother?"

He stopped. "My mother?"

"Yeah. You know, the first night I talked to you, I told you to call your mother."

His bottom lip stuck out. "My mother." He looked as if he was about to start crying.

He took another long pull thereby draining that can. Edge opened up another can and refilled the shot glass.

"So, who were those two guys?"

"Them guys? Oh, that was Demetrius and Tyrone."

"Which one works at the alarm company?"

"Ha, ha, ha. You thought you had me, hunh. You thought I'd tell you that Demetrius was the one." He laughed.

"No. I knew you wouldn't do it. What was the short guy's name?"

"Oh, well, I can tell you his name. He don't mean nothin' to me. That's Tyrone Woodson."

"Were they here today to make the split?"

Allison reached in his pocket and pulled out a roll. "Yep. I pay 'em outta my part."

"Well, okay." Edge nodded. "Andy, I wish you'd tell me who killed Bootsie."

"Man, I told you, it was Chuck."

"You talked to Chuck at The Lunatic, right?"

"Sure did."

"What's he look like?"

"He's got, uh, he's got, uh." He looked up and smiled. "I don't remember." Then he chuckled drunkenly.

"Andy, you ever heard of a guy named Chuck Latimer?"

Andy threw his head back and laughed out loud. "That's him. That's the Chuck, on the wall." He leaned in close to whisper. "He's a queer that hangs out at The Lunatic. Nobody knows he's queer, though." Andy made the 'shhh' sign with his finger to his lips. "He's got a twelve inch dick."

Edge smiled and shook his head. Allison laid his head down on the table. He was drunk; good and drunk. And now he was passed out. Edge had only helped him do what he had wanted to do anyway.

But, before he left, Edge wanted one more answer. He grabbed Allison by the hair and lifted up his head.

"Wake up, Andy, wake up." He slapped him until his eyes opened.

"What? What?" he said slurring his words badly.

"The other day, I followed you. You met Bobby Wyatt at a café out west then you went to Lazy Man's Pawn Shop. What did you get outta that truck?"

His head swayed back and forth. "I didn't get nothin'. I lef' some money."

"For who?"

"For Chuck."

"Not Chuck the queer."

He shook his head. "No, no. Chuck, uh, Chuck the killer."

Allison laid his head back down on the table and fell asleep again. Edge shook his head. If only they'd been patient and watched the truck, they'd have gotten a look at the real Chuck, the killer Chuck, and then they'd've been able to connect all three of them to Wyatt. He silently cursed himself.

He poured Allison another drink – a hair of the dog for when he woke up. Then he rose from the table and walked out the front door.

At noon Edge was back at his office making notes for a report for the police. Demetrius was the inside man at the alarm company, and Tyrone Woodson and Lardy McLain and Andy Allison were the other links in the chain of a burglary/stolen property ring. They made up the route that the emerald took from Mobile to Montgomery. He wondered how much they'd gotten for the stone.

When he finished he sat back in his chair and closed his eyes. He could see Allison knocking back drinks and looking at him with his thin face.

His mind then shifted to Bootsie Wyatt and the scene photograph of her face; the blood pooled around her head and on her clothes. Edge had seen mangled bodies before, and each one took a little out of him; each one looked like someone he knew. Bootsie was about the same age and around the same physical appearance of an aunt that lived in Florida. He squinted tightly and tried to think of something else. In minutes he was asleep.

He awoke with the sound of the telephone. It was Victor Riley.

"Edge? Is that you?"

"Yeah."

"I need you to get down here."

"What's up?"

"I think you know."

Edge paused. "I don't think I do."

"Andy Allison's dead."

In thirty minutes Edge was sitting in Riley's office at the Police Department's Detective Division annex.

Also present was Albert Mayhall, another of Riley's homicide detectives. Mayhall was a bull of man, over six feet tall with huge hands and a massive head topped with jet black hair. He stood over Edge who was seated in a wooden chair across from Riley.

"Now, you have the right to remain silent. If you give up . . ."

Edge cut Mayhall short. "What is this?"

"This is murder, Edge," Mayhall said.

"You think I killed Allison?"

"You were at his apartment this morning. You had the opportunity. We got your prints all over the place. You're trying to hang the Wyatt murder on him . . ."

Edge shook his head. "No, no. You guys have got this all wrong. I don't think he killed Bootsie. But I do think he knows, uh, knew who did it."

"So you tried to beat the truth out of him?"

"No, no, come on." Edge wasn't afraid, he was incredulous.

Riley spoke up. "Edge, why don't you start from the beginning."

"Okay, but you need to get somebody from burglary down to hear this."

Riley nodded. "Okay."

He picked up the phone and dialed a three digit number. In two minutes, James Williamson, from the Crimes Against Property unit, a tall man with a short Afro, was standing in the corner with a notepad.

"Okay, Edge," Riley said. "Spill it."

Edge took a deep breath. "About a week ago, I went out to Brighton Place off Japonica to deliver some papers for a lawyer. The place I went to, the Keyes' residence, had just been broken into." He turned to Williamson. "Were you there?"

Williamson nodded. "They had some jewelry taken."

"Right. And one of the pieces was a big emerald. Well, I put the insurance people on it, and they found the rock at a pawn shop in Montgomery; a place called Zips. My contact told me that Allison pawned it. I went over there this morning to confront him with it. I was gonna use it as leverage to get him to hunt for the Wyatt woman's jewelry."

"What makes you think he knows where it is?" Mayhall said.

"'Cause, the rocks are the only way we're gonna be able to connect anybody back to the Wyatt killing." He looked at Riley.

"So, when I got to his apartment, we went inside and there were these two guys – kids, really – waitin' for'im. When we came through the door, they both took off. One of'em tried to bowl me over, and the other threatened me with a knife." Edge looked at everyone. No one spoke.

"Anyway, after they were gone, I sat down with Andy at the table, and he drank until he was shitfaced. Then he spilled it about the Keyes' heist."

Williamson stood up straight.

"He said that the tall black guy, Demetrius, the one that ran out first, worked for Keyes' alarm company. The other guy, Tyrone Woodson, was the one who hit the house. They left the stuff with Lardy McLain, down at Alabama Point, and Andy took it from him to sell upstate."

"You got him drunk? On what?"

"Boilermakers." Edge smiled. "Didn't take long either."

"So you didn't hit him?" Riley said.

"Listen, if that's what it would have taken, I'd've probably done it. But I didn't have to. Really, it was too easy."

"What did he say about the Wyatt killing?" Riley said.

"He denied doing anything more than what I told you the other day," Edge said looking at the Lieutenant, "that he got the name of 'Chuck' off the bathroom wall and gave it to Bobby Wyatt. Today he told me that this 'Chuck' is a queer named Chuck Latimer who hangs out at The Lunatic. That part was all a big joke." Edge paused. "He did tell me that he made a money drop for Bobby Wyatt, for the real Chuck. He said there are two Chucks." He paused again and looked around. "Andy Allison was in good health when I left him."

Riley looked at Mayhall. Then he turned to Edge. "What clothes were you wearin' today?"

Edge looked down at his shirt and pants. "These."

"We'll need to search your apartment," Mayhall said.

"Sure. Get your warrant." He paused. "You say he was beat to death?"

"Yes."

"With what?"

"Don't know yet."

Edge held out his knuckles. "Clean as a whistle."

"What about your alibi?" Mayhall said.

"You mean, where was I when he was killed?"

"I think you know what an alibi is."

"I was at my office." He paused. "Alone."

"That's not an alibi."

"You wanted to know where I was. That's it."

"This doesn't eliminate you," Riley said.

"Well, I didn't kill him. He was my only link to Bootsie's killer."

"We're gonna have to go through your house."

Edge shrugged. "Alright. But if you break it, you bought it," he said using Riley's own words against him.

Riley nodded. "Sure." He paused. "You know, Edge, I did some checking on you. The state says that you were in the French Foreign Legion."

"That's right."

"How long?"

"Eight years."

Riley paused. "Comment vous applez-vous?"

Edge smiled. "Please. 'What's your name?'" He paused and looked at all three of them. "You can be a little tougher than that."

"How much of the language do you know?"

"Just enough to keep from gettin' thrown in the stockade. I learned, 'dig that hole,' 'attencion,' 'manger,' that means chow. That's the most important one." He looked at Riley. "Look, Lieutenant, I'm on your side. All I'm tryin' to do is hang this Bootsie Wyatt thing on her old man. He's involved, I know it."

At that point Mayhall exited the room, probably to get a search warrant. Edge wasn't worried, but he didn't want his home trashed.

"Okay," Riley said, "tell me again about the two black kids."

CHAPTER 24

In two days, Lucy Lance was back in Mobile. She looked rested and when Edge picked her up at the hotel, she couldn't stop talking.

"So, when we finished with Morton back home, I went down to the Police Department and did some checking. Seems he did some time for ADW."

"Yeah, we knew that. What were the circumstances?"

"You're not going to believe this. He beat up a guy at a music concert, for money."

"This is too easy. Where?"

"Tupelo."

"Let's go."

They left for Tupelo, Mississippi, that afternoon at one. It was an easy drive straight up Highway 45.

"I heard about Andy Allison," Lance said.

"How?"

She looked away, out the passenger window. "I have my sources."

"He was a scumbag. Good riddance."

"John. He was someone's son." She looked away. "So much death."

"I never picture these hoods having lives; no parents, siblings, nothing. In my mind they've forfeited their right to a normal existence." He paused. "Besides, I've met his mother. She ain't no prize."

She looked straight ahead. "Do the Police have a suspect?"

"Yeah. Me."

Her face shot toward him. "You?"

"I was the last person to see him alive. They searched my house two days ago. Until they lay hands on someone else, I'm the only name on the list."

She said nothing, no doubt contemplating the possibility that the man with whom she was riding through the warm Mississippi afternoon was a murderer.

"I hope you don't take this the wrong way, but . . . did you kill him?" she said.

He laughed. "Well, I think I'm insulted. We've worked and slaved together, driven across the south, even been in an unarmed confrontation, and you don't think you know me?"

She looked at him again.

"No. I didn't kill Andy Allison." He paused. "But if I had, it wouldn't have bothered me a bit.

"Besides, the police don't have a case. I was at the office when he was killed. They went over my house and couldn't find anything. They'll run across the two black kids that were there when me and Andy got to his house, and I think they'll find out they killed him because they thought he snitched on'em. And, they were right."

She said nothing for two miles. Then, "Look. If you need an alibi, I'll tell them you were with me. I'll tell them that we're having an affair."

Edge smiled. "Really? You'd lie for me?" He paused. "I'm flattered; not only that you'd lie, but for the lie itself."

She stopped to think. "Well, you do have some value as an investigator; I mean you know more about this case than anyone. And, if I clear it, there's a bonus in it for me; a bonus that I and my family can use. You can't do me much good from inside a jail cell."

"Wow, what an endorsement."

"Well, you're innocent, I need an investigator. Everybody wins."

He laughed out loud. "Well, as tempting as it sounds, I've already told'em I was alone. Besides, if I told them you were there how would you ever explain it to your husband?"

She looked out, through the windshield, apparently not having thought her plan through.

"Oh, he wouldn't believe it."

"Ha, ha. Well, if he wouldn't believe it, what makes you think the cops would? Anyway, thanks, but, no thanks." He smiled and shook his head. "I'll find out who did it."

They made it to Tupelo in four hours and pulled

into a Microtel just off the four lane right at five o'clock. Lance got them two non-adjoining rooms, and Edge slept the whole night.

The next morning, they located the Police Department downtown, off old Highway 45. They found a parking space out front and they were with the Detective Division commander in ten minutes.

"How you folks doin'?" Arthur Compton said.

He was a stocky man with coal black hair that was greased heavily. A large semi-automatic pistol rested in a shoulder holster under his left arm.

"Fine, sir. We're John Edge and Lucy Lance representing the Manhattan Mutual Insurance Company, and we're looking into a case of homicide down in Mobile, Alabama. You guys sent one of our suspects away a few years ago, for ADW."

"And now he's killed somebody and you want to keep from payin' his claim, is that it?" He smiled broadly.

"Well, he may have killed somebody, and it's not his claim."

"So, how can I help you?"

"We'd like to take a look at your file and if the bull that sent him up is around, we'd like to talk to him."

He nodded. "When's your case supposed to have happened?"

"It would have been about six months ago, in Mobile."

"Who's the suspect?"

"Charles E. Morton."

Compton threw back his head and laughed out loud. "Charlie Morton. You think he murdered somebody?"

"That's what we're tryin' to figure out."

"Charlie Morton couldn't kill a flea. He'd be too drunk to stand up and do it."

"So what about this ADW thing?"

"Well, first of all, I worked that case. Charlie was here in town with a couple'a friends for some country music show over at the auditorium. I think they drove up from someplace down in Webster County."

"Winona."

"Is that where he's from?"

"Yeah."

"That's not in Webster County, but, okay, Winona. Anyway, 'bout halfway through the show, Charlie was havin' a beer up in the balcony with his buddies. He was drinkin' a long neck and one of his friends said he didn't think Charlie could hit the stage with an empty beer bottle; it looked like it was about forty or so yards away, but it was downhill, so it prob'ly wasn't quite that far. He said he'd bet Charlie a hundred bucks that he couldn't do it. Anyway, Charlie reared back and heaved it as far as he could and hit the fiddle player right in the noggin; knocked him out cold. He's lucky to be alive, really."

Edge smiled. Lance looked shocked. "How'd you know it was Charlie?" he said.

"A half a dozen people right around his seat jumped him and worked on'im 'til the police got there. If we hadn't had an officer in the building, they might'a beat the shit out of him.

"When we got him to the station house, we ran the breathalyzer on him and he blew a .17. The DA said to charge him with Assault with a Deadly Weapon instead of Attempted Murder, 'cause he just heaved it an didn't really know where it was gonna go."

"That musta' been some bad band," Edge said.

"Actually, they was pretty good; from up in Nashville. We hadn't had a concert down here in quite a while. The last mayor we had hated drugs. He made us search all the kids comin' into the auditorium to see them rock and roll acts. The kids complained, and pretty soon nobody wanted to come here no more."

· Edge nodded. "Let me ask you this, reckon one'a them boys that was with him would talk to us?"

Compton knitted his brow. "I don't know." He sat back in his chair. "I don't remember but one of'em. His name's Tiny Garrison. I remember he testified at the trial."

"He must notta been scared'a Morton."

"Oh, Tiny ain't scared'a nobody. He weighs about three fifty. Charlie wadn't gonna intimidate him."

"Think we could give him a call?"

"No use callin'. He's right down the street, at the hardware store. Just go on down there and ask him. It's Garrison's Hardware. His daddy owns it, but Tiny usually works the counter." He paused while Lance wrote. "But listen, now if he don't wanna talk, don't try to make'im. He might not like it too much."

Edge nodded and looked at Lance. "It'll go smooth as silk, Lieutenant."

It took them five minutes to find Garrison's Hardware. It was one of those musty old storefronts on the town square one block over from the PD. When Edge opened the door, a small bell tinkled and a hound dog seated on the floor near the cash register lifted his head and struggled to his feet.

Lance led the way and turned toward the counter. A huge man, who could only have been 'Tiny,' was standing there separating nails by size and putting each into one of three plastic buckets.

"Mr. Garrison?" Lance said.

Tiny looked up. "Yes, ma'am. Can I help ya?"

"Yes. My name is Lance, and this is Mr. Edge, and we represent Manhattan Mutual Insurance Company."

"Well, I don't need no insurance."

"Oh, no, we're not here to sell you a policy. We'd like to talk to you about Charlie Morton."

He smiled and chuckled as he turned back to the nails. Then he shook his head.

"Charlie Morton. I ain't thought about that moron in a while. Not since he hit that fiddler with the bottle. What's he done now?"

"Well, we don't know. Have you got time to talk?"

"Sure. What'chu wanna know?"

Lance looked around. The store seemed deserted.

"Have you seen or talked to him since he got out?"

Garrison looked at Edge, no doubt wondering why he wasn't asking the questions. He looked back at Lance.

"Yeah, he called me once, about six or eight months ago; said he was in New Orleans, wanted me to come down."

"Did he say what for?"

"It don't matter. I wadn't gonna go, anyway."

"Ambush?" Edge said.

He chuckled and shook his head. "He ain't that crazy. No, he said he had a deal cookin' with an old Army buddy. Said he needed some muscle, and I was the biggest guy he could think of. I told him I had a job, and he needed to sober up. He said he was clean, which was a lie, I could tell by how he talked."

"He say what he wanted?"

Garrison shook his head. "He just said he was ready to let bygones be bygones and could we get together and talk about this deal."

"Why didn't you say, yes?"

Garrison looked at Edge. "She do all your talkin'?"

"She's doin' alright, for now."

He smiled. "I didn't say yes 'cause Charlie's a screwup. Everything he touches turns to shit. Like that thing at the show. Can you imagine anybody flingin' a bottle toward the stage, and hittin' somebody? On a bet? That could only happen to Charlie. If he was involved in it, it had to be trouble."

Edge spoke up. "Where'd you meet Charlie?"

"I met him about six or eight years ago, down in Winona, at a ballgame. My brother was playin' football for Tupelo. Charlie was there with his boy, uh, uh, Leo, or Leon, or somethin', watchin' the game. He was drunk and just walked up and started talkin' to me at the concession stand."

"You met his son?"

"Yeah. He brung him over here a couple'a times. Seemed like an okay kid."

"You guys talked after meeting?"

"Yeah. After he found out about my daddy's store, he said he wanted to open up a store." He paused and looked back at Lance. "I don't know what you guys are investigatin' but, well, Charlie's harmless."

Edge nodded. "Well, I can think of one fiddle player that would disagree, but thank you for your time." They turned toward the door. "By the way, did Charlie ever get the hundred dollars? You know, for throwin' the bottle."

Garrison smiled. "Yep. I pay my debts."

They dined at Mama Lou's Soul Food Café downtown, not far from the turnoff to Elvis Presley's home. Edge ordered pork chops, and Lance got a vegetable plate.

"Well, I'm convinced of it, now. Morton's involved," Lance said.

"How do you know?"

"Well, he contacted Garrison, before the murder, looking for a hit man."

"You sure that's what he was doin?"

"What else? He had a project going with an old Army buddy; he needed some muscle. Sounds like he was calling everyone he knew."

Edge lifted his brows as he cut a piece of pork chop.

"I suppose . . ."

They ate silently. Edge wanted to go over it all, but he wanted Lance to listen, not offer opinions.

"I don't know if I told you, but we had a connection between Wyatt and the killer."

Then her brows went up. "Really?"

"Yeah. Remember the day we followed Andy Allison from the café to the pawn shop? Well, he picked up money from Wyatt at the cafe and was making a money drop to 'Chuck.' All we had to do was wait, and we'd've had him."

"Now, Allison's dead, and we can't verify it."

"Right. We've got to keep looking; looking for that connection to 'Chuck.'"

They looked at each other and ate in silence.

"What we need is another angle," Edge said. "We've been trying to connect the killer to Bobby Wyatt by way of the jewelry, and through Charlie Morton. So far, nothing's turned up." He paused. "Can you think of another way?"

Lance looked down. "Well, one way is to follow the money."

Edge stopped. "Do we have access to Bobby's bank records?"

"We could try. Shelia can get a lot of information. She's got contacts everywhere; insurance companies, stockbrokers, banks.

The entire financial world is pretty incestuous; everybody knows everybody else's business."

Edge nodded. "Why don't you contact Shelia and take a look at that."

Lance nodded. "Okay, but I don't know what it would prove. A man in Wyatt's position probably moves money around pretty often. And, in this case, he would've paid in cash."

"I know, but let's look anyway. This is moving way too slow. We've got to do something to break things up."

"Like what?"

"Like a visit to our favorite fence, Lardy McLain."

CHAPTER 25

The next day they left Tupelo and were in Mobile by noon. Edge dropped Lance off at the hotel and then went back to his office. He checked his messages. There was one from Tommy Dickens and one from Vic Riley. Edge called Riley first.

"What can I do for you Lieutenant?"

"I just wanted to let you know we picked up Demetrius and the other guy, what was his name?"

"Uh, Tyrone."

"Yeah, Tyrone. They've both got alibis. In fact, they tell a little different story than you."

"Oh?"

"They said they were there when you beat Allison to death."

"And you believe'em?"

"Well, yes and no. They're lowlifes that are goin' up for burglary, but they're both tellin' the same tale. I can't ignore that."

"They had plenty of chances to get their stories straight."

"I know, but . . ."

Edge didn't want to have to take time off from the Wyatt case just to clear himself of the Allison murder. There were too many other things to do.

Edge took a deep breath and exhaled. "Lieutenant, you once said that if I walk into your office with a man in handcuffs, you were gonna throw me in jail. If I go out and find out who killed Andy Allison, is that what you're gonna do?"

"Edge, you find out who killed Allison and bring him in, I'll take him, and you can walk right out the door."

In an hour, Edge was Andy Allison's apartment complex. He was going to do what he knew that police had not done, or what they had not taken the time to do: canvass the neighborhood.

After hitting every apartment in Allison's building and in the four buildings right around it, he did what he should have done immediately: find the maintenance man.

He located Eric, a middle aged man with white hair, a dark tan, and a paunch, working on a stubborn door hinge at Building G. He wore a green uniform shirt with his name stitched over the pocket.

"Eric, did you see any vehicles over near the Building G three days ago? Any cars or trucks that didn't belong there?"

"Three days ago? Well, let me see?" He scratched his head.

"Could'a been anywhere around E, F, G, H . . ."

"Yeah, seems like there was one truck over there, about one or two that afternoon; looked kinda outta place."

"What kinda truck?"

"Just an old beater; rusty with some fish traps in the bed."

"What color?"

"I don't really remember. Might'a been faded red. It was a Ford, I think. Like I said, just an old beater."

"Where was it parked?"

"Over in front of J. I remember 'cause I was checkin' an air conditioner over in J-6."

"Did you see anyone with it? You know any more about it?"

"No. Never did." He took a Phillips head out of his toolbox and started to work on a stubborn screw. "But you know who would know something, though? Ms Whitfield. She's got eyes like a hawk, and she watches everything that comes in an' outta this complex."

"How can I find her?"

"She lives in A, uh, number 4. It's over there right at the entrance."

Edge jotted the information down on his notepad. Then he thanked Eric and hoofed on over to Building A. He knocked on the door of apartment four and showed his state-issued license to the older woman who answered.

"Ms Whitfield?"

She was in her seventies and wearing a print dress. She also had binoculars hanging by a strap from around her neck.

"Who are you?"

"My name is Edge, John Edge. I'm a private detective, ma'am."

The old woman took glasses out of the pocket of her housedress, put them on, and leaned in to look closely at the credentials.

"What'chu want, I'm busy," she said.

She seemed to be a fractious old woman. Her face was in a permanent scowl, and her mouth was in a tight line.

"I'm looking into a murder that happened over in Building G, ma'am. I'm trying to find someone who got a look at an old Ford pickup, maybe red; kinda faded. It was seen in the complex the day one of the residents was killed."

The old woman froze. "Come on in," she said softly and slowly.

Edge followed her into the living room of her apartment. There was a rocking chair sitting in front of a large sliding glass door that opened onto a balcony. A table sat next to the chair, and there was a glass of water and a notebook on the table. From her vantage point she could see the entrance to the complex from off Azalea Road and any vehicle entering or leaving the area from that direction.

"You sit down."

Her bossy tone was back. Edge took a seat on a clear plastic-covered couch. Whitfield sat down on the rocking chair and picked up the notebook off the table.

"When did this murder happen?"

"Three days ago, ma'am. Over in Building G; about one or two in the afternoon."

Ms Whitfield took off her glasses and wiped them on the hem of her dress before putting them back on. Then she thumbed the pages of the notebook.

"I got broke into about three years ago. Since then, I make it my business to know ever'body that comes and goes from this place." She nodded resolutely.

"Did the police talk to you the other day?"

She shook her head. "No. Nobody told me about a murder, and it wadn't in the paper."

She ran her finger down the page of the spiral notebook. She pursed her lips and rocked back and forth.

"Okay, here. Here's an old red Ford."

"Did you get a license?"

She looked at him and nodded once. "Does a bear shit in the woods?"

Edge, unfazed by her vulgarity, got out his notebook.

Ms Whitfield recited an Alabama license plate that began with a '2A.' Edge copied it then recited it back.

"What was this murder about?" Whitfield said.

"It was a case of too much mouth."

After he left the complex, Edge stopped at a pay phone and called the License Commissioner's office. He gave them his state PI ID number, and he dropped the Manhattan Mutual brand, and they gave him the registration for the plate. As a result, Edge started towards Bayou La Batre, Alabama, a sleepy fishing village at the south end of the county.

The vehicle was registered to a Lester Wright. Edge found his residence on Rock Road in the Bayou. It was a wood frame house, small, with watermarks around the outside up to about three feet off the ground. The faded red Ford was parked in the front yard on a shell driveway.

Edge parked behind the truck and walked up to the front door. He stood aside, and reached in his vest pocket and turned on a small tape recorder. Then he knocked.

"Yeah?" said the man that opened the door.

He was well over six feet and a half feet tall with the huge forearms and the large hands of an oysterman. He wore a red pullover shirt with a tear in it, jeans, and white fishing boots; what the natives called 'Bayou La Batre Reeboks.'

"You Lester Wright?"

"Who wants to know?"

"My name's Edge. I work for an insurance company."

"I don't need no insurance."

"I'm not tryin' to sell you anything. It's about your truck."

He leaned out and looked toward the vehicle. "Somethin' wrong with my truck?"

"It was used in a crime."

His brows narrowed, but he said nothing.

Edge looked all around. "Mind if I come in?"

Wright looked him up and down and reluctantly stepped aside. Edge took three quick steps into the living space and then stepped toward the middle of the room, as far away from the big man as he could. Wright closed the door and turned toward him.

"So what's this about my truck bein' used in a crime."

"That hunk a junk was spotted up in Mobile three days ago; at an apartment complex."

Wright froze, set his jaw, and flared his nostrils. He said nothing.

"Now, I know you didn't just go up there and beat that poor boy to death on your own. Somebody paid you, right? Who was it?"

He still said nothing.

"Was it Lardy?"

Wright's eyes opened wide. "Sounds like you know it all, already."

"Not all. You're a pretty big dude. How'd it feel to take down a drunk who was already half ploughed? Make you feel like a tough guy?"

He chuckled slightly. "It wadn't so hard. Two knocks and he was gone."

"Am I right? Was it Lardy that paid you?"

"Well, since I'm about to squeeze your head like a melon, I guess I can tell you. Yeah. He called and said he had a job; said a boy up in Mobile had a big mouth and couldn't keep it shut."

"How much'd he pay ya?"

"A thousand."

"A grand? For a hit?"

"Oh, I wadn't s'posed to kill him. I was just s'posed to make it hurt a little, and he was s'posed to get the message to keep his pie hole shut."

Edge looked away and exhaled. "Well, that's all well and good, but now they're blamin' it on me."

He smiled. "You? How come?"

"'Cause I was at his apartment before you showed up. They think I beat the poor slob to death. By the way, what'd you use on him?"

Wright lifted both his fists into the air. "Just these; just ma guns." He kissed his biceps. "And, now I'm gonna use'em on you."

"Nope, Lester. I'm gonna hand you over to the police."

He shook his head. "You ain't leavin' this house."

At that, the big man took two steps toward him. Edge knew that if Wright was able to get a hand on him, he was dead. Edge backed up as far as he could to the opposite wall and broke down into a fighting stance.

When Wright was within four feet, Edge turned to the side and kicked him hard in the groin. Wright stopped and grimaced while grabbing his crotch. Edge shifted left, and Wright turned toward him.

Edge was trying to make his way toward the front door. He had the tape – his insurance policy – and he needed to keep it from getting damaged.

Then the thing happened that Edge had feared the most. Wright made a lunge for him and took hold of him by his left arm. His grip was like iron.

Edge reached for the pocket of his vest and took out a sapper. He bopped Wright over the eye with two quick blows that drew blood. The blood sprayed onto Edge and dripped into the strong man's eyes.

But Wright still held tightly onto Edge's upper arm. Edge yanked twice and then swung the sapper in an upper cut at Wright's right elbow. That did it. His radial nerve – or funny bone, as the kids call it – caused his arm to go limp. He let go of Edge's bicep. Edge bolted for the door as the big man leaned over and held his useless limb.

Edge was reaching for the knob when he felt Wright's arm on his shoulder stopping his momentum. Edge ducked and tried to disengage. Wright held on tightly. Edge turned toward him and tried to yank away from his grip.

In times past, in another place, Edge would have pulled his pistol and made short work of someone like Wright. But now, he was trying build a reputation as a PI that did not pound his adversaries into submission. He'd already had to kill Sam Parisi. He didn't want to have to kill this large man, too.

Edge broke down again as he tried to hand fight his way out of Wright's grip. Oysterman, who use their arms to work the tongs back and forth, are freakishly strong.

"Lester, you need to let go."

"Not a chance. You're not leavin'."

Edge gave him two quick strikes with his left hand to the midriff then used the sapper to swing for his face. This time he hit paydirt. The lead filled pouch hit the tall man on the point of his chin and stunned him noticeably. Edge hit him again in almost the exact same spot, and he fell backwards onto the floor, striking his head on the corner of a table in the process. He was out cold.

Edge walked over and checked him for a pulse. When he found a strong one, he turned back to the door. In seconds he was in the Impala and on Rock Road headed toward Bellingrath Gardens.

An hour later Edge was in Victor Riley's office, seated in a metal chair. Riley was behind his desk with earplugs in his ears listening to the tape in Edge's machine. When it was over, he pulled out the plugs.

"So, who is this guy?"

"Lester Wright. He's a fisherman and known knuckle crusher down in the Bayou."

"How'd you find him?"

"Well, I located a witness at Allison's apartment complex." Edge told him about the maintenance man and gave him Whitfield's name and apartment number.

"Pretty good," he said. "You could teach my people a thing or two."

Edge looked around. "Look, Lieutenant, I don't wanna be a party pooper, but don't you think you ought to get down there and pick that guy up? He just might decide to blow town."

Riley pursed his lips and shook his head. "I've got enough here for a warrant. This case is closed. We'll call the PD down there and let them know he's wanted. They'll run across him and pick him up eventually."

"Don't count on it. My guess is Lardy McLain will get him outta town pronto, so he can't spill the beans on'im. Besides, whoever tries to take down Lester Wright will have a fight on his hands."

"It'll be okay."

Edge said nothing for a few seconds while Riley put the cassette tape in an envelope and sealed it up. Then he cleared his throat.

"So, this gets me off the hook, right?" Edge said.

Riley looked at him. "Yeah, Edge." He paused. "You know, there's something about you that I, I, just don't know." He shook a finger at him. "But I'm gonna find out."

"Okay, okay. You're gonna find out. But, about me, am I in the clear?"

"Oh, sure. You were in the clear before. I wasn't going to hold you on the word of those two turds, Tyrone and what's his name. I just wanted you to go and find out who did it."

"How'd you know I'd do it?"

"Like I said. There's something about you. I had confidence in you."

Edge rose from his chair. "Lieutenant, don't ever have confidence in me."

"Get outta here," Riley said.

Edge turned and walked out of the office door assured of the fact that he had an ally at the Police Department.

CHAPTER 26

Edge met Lance for dinner that night. They sat down at the Jolly Ox near the mall on Airport Boulevard. Lance ordered salad and Edge a small steak.

"Wow," Lance said after hearing about the confrontation with Wright. "I bet you wish I'd been there with you."

"You, with no weapon? He'd've killed you."

"I could have taken him down."

"Don't get me wrong, Lucy, I'm sure you've got some skills, but this guy is huge. He'd've squashed you like a bug. Sometimes, you just need a weapon."

"Well, anyway, where do we go from here?"

"We've got to get to Lardy McLain and find out what he knows. My guess is that he has an idea where Bootsie's ring and earrings are, and he can put them in the killer's hand. And, then . . ."

"So how do we get him?"

Edge chewed and thought. If Lance was so eager to be involved in the case, a case that she was just supposed to be observing, well, maybe he could find something for her to do.

"How about a little undercover work?"

"Undercover?"

"Sure."

"Wellll, I don't know."

"I get it. You're all talk."

"No, no. I'll do it."

"Are you sure?"

"Sure. What's the plan?"

"You've never seen McLain, so we send you in with some jewelry to get rid of."

"What if he blows me off?"

"Ordinarily, he might. But, remember, we've got an informant that can introduce you."

"Who you talkin' about?"

"Tommy, the loser."

"You think he knows McLain?"

"Sure he does. I think he's done business with him."

She took a bite of salad and chewed thoughtfully. "So I show up, after a phone call from Tommy Dickens . . ."

"Maybe, we'll even get him to go with you."

". . .and lay out some jewelry. McLain takes it and says he can move it. When we get the money back, . . ."

"We've got him in a trick."

"You think it can work?"

"If we can make him believe that you're a lady burglar who'll take five cents on the dollar for some hot rocks, it can."

At eight the next morning, Lance and Edge knocked on Tommy Dickens' door. Owing to the fact that Dickens was a doper and a thief, Edge correctly assumed that he would not be up before ten or twelve, and he would probably be in his apartment. Edge had to bang on the door hard, and multiple times, but Tommy finally opened it.

"Yeah," Dickens said yawning.

"Come on, Tommy, we gotta talk," Edge said as he pushed past him into the room. Lance followed closely while looking around at the filth.

"Gee whiz, Tommy," Edge said, "when you gonna clean this place up?"

Dickens sat down at the dining table and rubbed his face and head repeatedly. He coughed twice and swirled the resulting phlegm around in his mouth.

Edge sat down at the table across from him. He looked at Dickens' eyes and said nothing. Lance folded her arms across her chest and surveyed the room with a sour look on her face.

"What?" Dickens said.

"You called me, brother. What'chu got?"

He looked at Edge with knitted brows and open mouth. Then he pursed his lips.

"Can't remember, can you," Edge said. "That's 'cause you didn't have nothin', Tommy. You just thought you could sit down and bullshit me out of a twenty, right?"

Dickens said nothing.

"Well, do you have anything, or not?"

Dickens shook his head and looked down.

"I knew it." He looked over at Lance. "Didn't I say that he was dry?"

"You said it," she said.

Dickens looked at the floor.

"Tommy, you can't scam me. I'm too smart for you. You haven't been a snitch long enough to pull one over on me."

He reached and grabbed the thick hair on the young man's head and lifted his head up. Dickens' eyes were half closed.

"Tommy, do want to make some real money?"

Dickens' eyes woke up. He was suddenly more animated.

"Tell me you know Lardy McLain," Edge said.

"Yeah. I know him."

"He ever fenced anything for you?"

Dickens said nothing.

"Oh, come on, Tommy. What'chu think, I'm stupid? You're a thief. You've probably been hittin' houses since you were in grade school. Now, has Lardy ever fenced anything for you?"

"Yeah, once or twice."

"Well, Lucy and I have a little proposition for you." He paused. "You up for it?"

"Like what?"

"I want you to introduce Lucy here to McLain. She's got some stuff she wants to move, and we want you to tell Lardy she's okay."

Dickens looked from Edge to Lance and back again. "He'll never buy it."

"Why not?" Edge said.

"She's too good lookin'. Ain't too many women burglars anyway, and I try to bring somebody that looks like her inside, and he'll know it's a set up."

Edge turned to Lance and smiled.

"I knew you'd screw it up somehow."

"Shut up."

Edge turned back to Dickens. "Okay, so we muss her up a little; put on some fake tattoos, get her some grubby clothes, rat up her hair. What then? Will she fit?"

Dickens looked at her ostensibly trying to imagine her hourglass figure in dirty jeans and flip flops. He shook his head.

"I don't know."

"You don't know what."

"I don't think I can sell it."

Edge looked away and wiped his mouth. "Well, Tommy, you're just gonna have to. See, we need to find out who killed this Wyatt broad right now, and this is the only lead we have. Now, you sell it, sell it for all you're worth, and I'll make it worth your while." He paused. "Or, I'll see if I can't find that piece'a shit revolver that I took outta here, and we'll just take it to the crime lab and see how many bodies we can hang on it."

Edge looked at him hard. Dickens stared back at him with a worried look on his face.

"Or," Tommy said, "we can go see Lardy."

"That's'a time," Edge said smiling broadly. He turned to Lance and nodded his head vigorously.

Two days later, at seven in the evening, Edge and Lance picked Tommy Dickens up in front of his apartment and began to drive south, toward Alabama Port. They were early. The meeting with McLain was not until right before closing, at nine.

Lance was in possession of three diamond rings, actually one diamond ring and two with cubic zirconia stones; a string of very average pearls; and a platinum ring, the most valuable piece in the collection. She had secured the pieces on loan from the ManMut vault of recovered property in Atlanta. They were pieces recovered after homeowner's insurance claims were paid; pieces that were waiting to be sold to help the company recoup its losses.

The transformation that Lance had undergone was impressive. She had gone to the Sheriff's Office and had taken a look at some mugshots in order to try to get the right look. Afterwards, she used makeup to create dark circles under her eyes, highlighted her hair white with baby powder to age up her appearance, and blackened one of her front teeth. In the interim since meeting with Dickens she had gone without washing her hair, and she'd trimmed her nails and removed all of the polish. She was wearing dirty jeans, flip flops, and a tight fitting, maroon t-shirt with the words 'Hot Mama' written in glitter across the chest.

On the way south, the three stopped at the Oyster Shucker, a red neck dive on Dauphin Island Parkway. It was a weather-beaten, wood frame building on the bayside of the road just before Alabama Port.

Inside, Lance ordered a beer to calm her nerves. Dickens ordered something stronger.

"Okay," Edge said, "here's the plan. You two enter the front door. Tommy, you give Lardy the high sign and then wait 'til everybody else leaves the store."

Tommy nodded as he sipped his whiskey.

"After that you make the pitch." He turned to Lance. "You got the rocks?"

She patted the front pocket of her jeans. "Right here."

"Okay. I'll find a way to get on the back side of the store, up next to the glass door right behind the counter. I'll be listening."

He looked at Dickens. "All you do is make the introduction, then get out of the way. If he asks how you know her, tell him you met at T-Bob's; tell him you been tryin' to fuck her, that'll impress him." He turned to Lance whose brows were up. "If Lardy asks you where the stuff came from, you can either tell him you stole it yourself, you can lay it off on your ole man, or else you can clam up and just tell him to mind his own business. The important thing with this guy is attitude."

"What if he tells me to get lost?" she said.

"Then you turn and walk out, and we'll come up with plan B. The important thing is to get the stuff in his hands and find out when to come back for the money."

"What if he asks how we got there? About a car?"

"Just tell'im you caught a ride and they let you off at the corner; at Alabama Port. You walked the rest of the way."

Lance smiled. "You think up these lies pretty easily, don't you."

"Hey, all the world's a stage." He paused. "You nervous?"

She rubbed her hands together. "Yeah. Well, a little."

"Your ole man know what you're doin'?"

"Are you kidding? He'd skin me alive." She paused. "Edge, what if things go bad?"

"I'll be there. You guys just head for cover, and I'll try to take him down."

"You'll be there, right?" Dickens said.

He smirked. "Yes, Tommy. I'll be there."

In an hour, Edge parked near the highway, and away from the front door of McLain's Fish Camp.

"You guys give me two minutes then walk in the front door," Edge said. Lance nodded.

He waited until Lance and Dickens left the car before he got out and walked quickly down the boardwalk on the side of the building and found his way up the platform to the glass door that opened into the store, right behind the counter. From his vantage point he could see Lardy's expansive backside, and he could hear everything.

McLain was seated on his stool, his butt cheeks spilling over the edges, counting money when Lance and Tommy walked in. Edge could see Tommy looking around the store as the two of them walked to the counter and stopped. The sound was muffled, but Edge could make out every word.

"Hey, Tommy. What'chu got? I gotta close up."

"Hey. What's goin' on, Lardy?"

Edge could hear the nervousness in his voice.

"I told you, I'm tryin' to close up. What do you want?"

"She's got some stuff to get rid of." Tommy nodded toward Lance.

McLain looked Lance up and down. Lance stood with her arms folded in front of her chest.

"Who are you?"

"Melissa," Lance said. Her voice shook also.

"Where you know Tommy from?"

"Uh, uh, T-Bob's, downtown."

McLain was skeptical. He finished counting out the money and put it into a zippered bank bag.

"I ain't makin' no promises, but let me see what'cha got."

Lance stepped directly up and pulled a plastic sandwich bag out of her pocket. She opened it and poured the pieces out onto the counter in front of McLain. He looked down and picked up the diamond ring first.

Using a jeweler's loupe he took from the pocket of his overalls, he examined the stone. He laid the ring down then picked up the earrings and the platinum. When he was finished, he put everything down and looked up.

"Where'd you get this shit?"

"I, my boyfriend hit a couple'a houses. This is the best of it."

A Penny for Your Murder

"Well, your boyfriend's a dumb ass. This stuff is a pile'a shit, all except this platinum ring, maybe. The rest of it . . ."

It looked like everything was going nowhere. Edge was concentrating on what was going on inside and almost didn't hear anyone walk up behind him. At the last minute he turned to see a snaggle-toothed man with gray hair wearing a plaid shirt and overalls, standing, pointing a revolver at him.

"Okay, mister, step inside," the old man said.

Edge nodded, turned, and pulled open the glass door. A surprised McLain turned quickly.

"What the f- . . .?" he said as he reached for a sawed off shotgun under the counter. "Who's that, Ernest?"

Snaggle-tooth, now identified as Ernest, followed Edge inside. "I caught this bird listenin' in outside. I was out tyin' up the skiff, and I seen him skulkin' around the door. You know'im?"

McLain used the shotgun to motion Edge around in front of the counter next to Lance and Tommy.

"Let me see. What the fuck? Yeah, it's that dude from a couple of weeks ago askin' about . . ." He paused and looked at Tommy.

"You son of a bitch," McLain said. "What are you tryin' to pull? What'd'ju bring them here for?"

Dickens began to back up. McLain pointed the shotgun at him and without warning fired one barrel at his knees. Dickens fell to the floor while grabbing his shattered joints. He moaned loudly.

Edge wasn't happy that Tommy got tagged, however the shooting had accomplished what they had set out to do and that was to get leverage on Lardy – that is, if they all lived through it.

While all eyes were on Tommy, Edge slipped his hand behind his back to the .45 in the holster. He pulled the pistol and held the weapon down, behind his leg. He knew McLain meant business, and he was ready.

Lance leaned forward and grabbed the counter to steady herself. Edge saw that the color had left her face. Clearly, she was stunned. He was surprised.

Looking at Lance, McLain cracked open the shotgun, took out one spent shell, and slid a live round into the breech. He locked it in place and pointed it at her. Ernest lowered his revolver and stepped back from around behind McLain and walked over and stood in front of Tommy.

"You done good work, Ernest. These birds was tryin' to get me into a trick bag; bringin' that shit in here and tryin' to get me to unload it for'em."

"I don't know if I'd'a shot him, Lardy." He looked down at Tommy and shook his head. "He don't look so good."

"Call me a doctor," Dickens said with a grunt.

"Look, Lardy," Edge said. "If you'll just talk to me about Chuck, we can put a bow on this whole thing and go home. You don't have to shoot anybody else, and who knows, maybe we even talk Tommy outta goin' to the police."

"What would you say if I told you I never met Chuck."

"I'd believe you. But I'd also say that you moved some of Bobby Wyatt's dead ole lady's merchandise. All I'm lookin' for is a name, the name of the man you got it from."

Lardy said nothing and seemed to be thinking. He pointed the shotgun, first at Edge, then at Lance. If he killed Edge, he'd have to kill Lance, Dickens, and maybe even Ernest.

It was clear that he had shot Dickens out of anger and frustration and getting him some help and taking care of him monetarily would be the price for Tommy's silence. For their part, Edge and Lance had witnessed Tommy's shooting, but if Tommy refused to file a complaint, or testify, it would all be moot.

Edge had to think fast. His plan was unraveling quickly.

"Lardy, I gotta proposition for you," Edge said. McLain looked up.

"You tell me what you know about Chuck, Bobby Wyatt, and his ole lady's murder," Edge raised his .45 and pointed it at McLain's head, "and I won't shoot you in the head in an obvious attempt to save the life of Tommy Dickens."

McLain was stunned. He looked as if didn't know what to do. Edge saw his trigger finger twitch.

"Unh, unh, Lardy. Don't make it easy for me."

Lance reached and took the shotgun out of his hand. She stepped away from the counter.

"See, Melissa here understands. She'll be able to tell the police just exactly what happened."

Ernest, who was watching everything from his vantage point over by Dickens, suddenly dropped his revolver and took off for the front door at a run; a fast run for a man of his apparent age.

McLain looked toward the door, took a deep breath, and exhaled. "Well, it looks like you got me over a barrel.'

"I sure do, Lardy. Now, tell me what I want to know, and let's get Tommy some help over there. I imagine he's in a little pain."

McLain wiped his mouth and looked toward Dickens who was writhing on the floor. He cleared his throat, a sure sign of deception. McLain was going to tell something, but probably not everything.

"Okay, look, Marty came to me and brought some stuff to get rid of."

"Marty? From Lazy Man's Pawn?"

"Yeah. It was a diamond, some earrings, and a string of pearls."

"Go ahead."

"I told him I didn't want'em, for him to take'em to a shop over in Pensacola and dump'em."

"How much'd he get?"

"I don't know. I never heard. If it was me, I'd'a paid him about two grand. I think that's what John usually pays over there."

"They're worth twenty times that."

"So what. They're not mine. I just move'em and get the best price I can."

"So, Marty took'em. Where?"

"I don't know. I told him to go to John's Pawn. I don't know where he went."

There was the lie, Edge thought. His expression told McLain that he didn't believe him.

"I don't know, I tell ya. Marty brought the stuff to me, I told him where to go, and he took off."

"You passed on it?"

"Yeah, I got a feelin' about it."

"What kinda feelin'?"

"A feelin' like the stuff came from somewhere a little too hot for me."

"I can't imagine any place bein' too hot for you. What'd Marty tell you? What'd he tell you about Chuck? Where'd he tell you the rocks came from?"

"He didn't tell me nothin'. I just gotta feelin'. I read about the Wyatt broad. This stuff was too nice, I figured it came from there."

"Could ya'll get me some help?" Dickens said loudly.

"Just a minute, Tommy," Edge said. He nodded at Lance who reached for the phone.

"So, why'd Marty bring the stuff to you in the first place?"

"'Cause it all comes to me. I get it first. I either move it, or if I don't want it, whoever has it can do whatever they want. Sometimes, I make suggestions."

Edge nodded. And if things didn't come to him first, guys like Lester Wright swung into action. It was a miserable way to make a living.

CHAPTER 27

The next morning, on his way to see Tommy Dickens, Edge picked up a newspaper in the lobby of the hospital and scanned the headlines. A double murder had happened overnight. The police speculated that it was possibly over drug activity. He read the story as he rode the elevator up to the fourth floor.

When Edge walked into Dickens' room, Arthur McLemore from the Sheriff's Office Detective Division was standing at his bedside taking notes. McLemore was a thick man with a receding hairline and glasses on the end of his nose. He looked up from his notepad at Edge.

"Hey, Tommy, how ya feeling?" Edge said.

McLemore turned his direction. "Uh, and you are?"

"I'm John Edge."

"Oh, right. You're that PI that was out at McLain's last night. I saw your name on the report." He paused and looked back at Dickens. "Tommy here tells me he was shot as a result of an accidental discharge. That the way you see it?"

Edge nodded. "Yes, sir. That's what happened; whatever Tommy says."

McLemore nodded and closed his notebook. "Well, I don't believe none'a'ya. But, no complainant, no case." He walked past Edge and stopped at the door.

"By the way, McLain's already made bond on that sawed off shotgun charge." He paused. "Just so you know."

McLemore left the room. Edge walked to Tommy's bedside.

"How you feelin'?"

"Better. They cut out a bunch'a pellets and left two or three in there. They said they was too close to some nerve to get out; said there was a artery that they didn't want to damage."

"So, when will you be up and around?"

"They said two or three days. I'm goin' home tomorrow afternoon. I'm gonna be on crutches for a while."

"That's good, Tommy. That's good."

Edge looked around then reached in the inside pocket of his vest. He took out a plain envelope and handed it to Tommy.

"Here's a little something for you. Thanks for helping us get information outta Lardy."

"Think Lardy's gonna come back on me?"

"I don't, but it don't matter. He's got bigger things to worry about than shootin' you."

Edge was hoping that Lester Wright would put the finger on Lardy for Allison's murder, if he hadn't already.

Dickens took the envelope and lifted up the flap. There were ten, brand new, crisp, fifty dollar bills within. He counted them, and his eyes lit up.

"Fuck me. It's five hundred bucks." He was genuinely enthused.

"I hope it helps." Edge figured that it was more money than Tommy had ever seen at one time.

"Yeah. Yeah, it will."

Edge thought it was little enough to buy Tommy's cooperation in what had happened the night before; a small price to pay for a man that would never again walk normally. The money had come out of a discretionary fund that the insurance company kept for just such situations.

"How long's that gonna last you, Tommy?"

"Oh, this is gonna go a long way. I'm gonna invest this."

Edge smiled. If Tommy invested it in anything more than a few cases of beer or a marijuana stalk, he'd be surprised.

"Well don't be showin' it around. The hospital will want you to use it to pay your bill."

Dickens looked left and right then put the bills back in the envelope. "Oh, yeah. You're right." He slid the envelope under the sheets.

"What can you tell me about Marty?"

"Marty? Oh, I don't know. He runs the pawn shop over on Halls Mill."

"Well, I know that. What about him? Has he got a record?"

"A record? I don't know. I think he might'a been in for DUI or somethin'."

"He ever been to prison?"

"I don't think so."

"He into anything else except stolen property?"

"I don't think so. He told me one time he wanted to do what Lardy does."

"What's that?"

"He wants to be the dude, you know? If you got hot shit, he wants to see it first. He wants to get a cut from everybody's action."

"So if Lardy goes up, he gets the job, right?"

"Maybe. I don't know."

That revelation got Edge to thinking. It could be that the Wyatt jewelry never made it to Lardy. Maybe Marty only told him about it, or Lardy found out about it some other way.

Edge took a deep breath and exhaled. He figured he'd done enough damage to Tommy Dickens.

"Okay, Tommy. You get well soon."

"I will, John. Hey, I'll find out some stuff for you just as quick as I get outta here."

Edge shook his head. The poor dumb schmuck didn't even know that he'd never find out anything more than the time of day from now on.

Edge met Lance for lunch at the hotel. It was good to see that she'd transformed herself from dope whore thief back to attractive insurance investigator.

"Did you go by to see Tommy?" she said.

"I did. I gave him the money. He seemed proud to get it; said he was going to 'invest' it." Edge smiled. "Have you talked with Shelia? Is she still keeping an eye out for Wyatt's jewelry?"

"I talked to her today. She wasn't too happy about our undercover fiasco, but I told her it was necessary." She paused and took a sip of water. "She trusts me."

Edge nodded. "It's a good thing, because when Tommy wakes up and realizes he sold two good legs for five hundred bucks, he's gonna hate himself."

"Tommy doesn't strike me as a man that can figure that out."

"Maybe not right now; but maybe twenty years from now, after he talks to a lawyer."

"When the statute of limitations has run out." Lance paused. "Okay, now that's over. Where do we go from here?"

Edge chewed on a roll. "Well, our next step is Marty. Tommy told me that when it comes to stolen property in this town, Marty wants to be the big cheese. Maybe we can use that in our favor somehow."

"I don't see how. I mean, who's gonna walk up and confess to moving stolen property in a capital murder case."

"Oh, he won't do that, you're right. But he knows about this case. He sent the rocks to Lardy; his lot and truck were used for the money drop for 'Chuck'; and there's a good possibility he might have put Wyatt in touch with 'Chuck.'"

"So, how do we get at him?"

Edge looked her in the eye, hard. "Maybe you should take a little vacation. Let me see what I can find out."

That afternoon, late, after five, Edge sat in his Impala across the street from the Lazy Man's Pawn Shop and watched the parking lot. The truck that Allison had used for Chuck's payoff was still there. It still had the 'For Sale' sign in the back window, and it appeared as if it hadn't moved.

The sign out front said that the business closed at six. Edge's plan was to wait until five forty five, and then walk in and browse, maybe buy something.

As he watched, he thought about what he was going to say to Marty Morningside, a two time loser for felony drugs, who had barely done six months in the prison system. He would try to reason with him first, but if he couldn't . . .

At a quarter to six, Edge drove into the parking lot of the pawn shop and put his car on the side next the truck. There was one other car in the lot; one that Edge guessed was Marty's.

The bell on the door frame sounded as he entered the store and began to walk down the aisles. There was no one at the counter. He picked up a car stereo from a shelf and wondered from what poor unfortunate person it had been pilfered.

A waif-like woman in a tube top, not more than five feet tall with sandy hair and freckles on her face and shoulders, walked through a curtain behind the counter. She saw Edge and smiled.

"Hey. Can I help you?"

"Yeah," he said walking toward the counter. "I was looking for Marty."

"Oh, Marty ain't here. He took a couple'a days off and went outta town."

Edge bit his lip and nodded. "You must be Ms Morningside."

"Anita. How'd you know?" she smiled.

"I heard Marty's wife was a real looker."

She blushed. "Well, ain't you sweet. Are you comin' onto me? 'Cause if ya are, now, I'm married." She smoothed out her hair.

He wasn't. He was just buying time. Then he had a thought.

"No, no. I was just joshin'. I really come in here to get something."

"What's that?"

"Well," he said slowly, "you know a guy named Chuck?"

She knitted her brow. "Chuck? I don't think so."

"A friend'a Marty's."

She shook her head slowly. "No, I can't say as I do."

"Well, he told me he'd pawned a gun and a knife down here."

"Ohhhhh. Right. Chuck. I forgot. Yeah, Marty mentioned him. He didn't say nobody was comin' for his stuff, though."

"Well, Chuck, I mean, I owe him some money, so I just told him I'd get his stuff back for him and then we'd be square. He said this stuff had sentimental value."

"Well, okay. I guess. I think it's back here in the safe. I'll go see."

Edge's heart was pounding as he considered the possibility that he was about to lay his hands on the murder weapons that killed Bootsie Wyatt.

It was three or four minutes before Anita Morningside reappeared from behind the curtain. She was carrying a paper bag that was crumpled and looked as if it had been opened and closed many times.

"Is this it?"

She laid the bag on the counter and unrolled the top. From inside she removed a Smith and Wesson, Model 10 revolver and a K-Bar knife in a scabbard, and put them on a velour display pad.

Edge could hardly contain himself. "Yep, that's it. Just like Chuck said."

Using two fingers, he picked up the gun by its checkered grips and looked it over. It looked as if it had recently been cleaned.

"It's okay. You can handle it."

Edge looked at her and smiled. "I don't like guns. They make me nervous."

He laid the revolver down and picked up the knife by the handle. It was devoid of any noticeable blood.

"Yep, this looks like it." He put the knife down. "How much will it take to redeem 'em?"

"Well. Let me see. I don't see a ticket in here for it. Maybe he don't want to let it go."

Edge frowned. "Oh, no. I come a long way. I'd sure like to get this back to Chuck and get out from under what I owe him."

"Let me look back in the office."

She disappeared through the curtain again, and Edge toyed with the idea grabbing everything up and running out. He resisted the urge so that if he had to, he might come in again.

She walked back through the curtain. "I sure don't see it. That's so unusual. He never takes in nothin' without a ticket."

"Well, I tell you what. You name a price and if it's more than my debt, you can keep it. If it's not, I'll buy'em and give you somethin' for your trouble."

She looked thoughtful. "Well, Marty usually gives'em a fifty or a hundred on a gun, and . . . I guess the knife's probably worth about twenty." She paused. "Can you give me a hundred and twenty five?"

Edge reached for his wallet. He opened it and pulled out a hundred, two twenties, and a ten.

"How about I give you a hundred and fifty. That's what I owe Chuck." He held out the cash.

The woman smiled broadly as she took the money. "Well, that's right nice'a you."

"Hey, you were more than fair." He paused. "By the way, was there any ammunition with it?"

She picked up the bag and poured it out. Five live rounds and one spent shell fell out onto the velour.

"None but what was in this bag. You're welcome to it."

Edge put the revolver, the knife, and the rounds back in the bag, picked it up, and held out his right hand.

"It was a pleasure doin' business with you, ma'am."

She smiled and shook his hand, no doubt thinking how proud her husband would be of her when he learned that she had gotten a hundred and fifty dollars for a knife and leather scabbard, a beat up gun, and five bullets.

"You're certainly welcome. Come again."

Edge turned and almost ran out the front door. He got in the Impala, and it wasn't until five miles down the road that his heart stopped pounding.

CHAPTER 28

The next morning, Lance met Edge in his office to examine the gun and knife that he had purchased from Anita Morningside. He had left them locked in his desk drawer overnight, the only secure place he had. Edge told her the story of how he came to be in possession of the weapons.

"I bet you about wet yourself when she said she had them," Lance said.

"I got a little excited. But the police are gonna have another murder on their hands when her old man gets back and finds out she sold these things."

"That would sure be a shame." She paused. "What are we gonna do with'em?"

"Well, let's just think a minute. What do these things tell you?"

"Well, the knife looks like a military knife. That and the name 'Chuck' would indicate that Charlie Morton owns them."

Edge shook his head. "Not really. Anyone can get one of these K-Bars at an Army-Navy store, gun shop, anyplace. No, we're better off trying to find the owner through the serial number of that gun."

"What about the gun?"

"Well, that .38 calibre Smith was popular with pilots during Vietnam. I think it might have been government-issue. They didn't carry forty-fives."

"Another point in the Charlie Morton column."

"You're right. But for some reason, I don't think he did it."

He paused and looked down at the instruments of death. The gun shot Bootsie Wyatt in the head, and the knife cut her throat and stabbed her in the heart. Dead three times. He'd seen these instruments used in war, and had even used them himself, but here at home, on a private citizen, for no other reason than that she was in the way, it was wrong.

"By the way," Edge said, "have you heard any more from Wyatt about the payoff?"

"He's called Shelia."

"He wants to hurry up and get the money before we get onto him. My guess is that either Allison, before he died, Marty, or maybe even Charlie Morton, one of them has given him a heads up about where we're headin'. If we get real close, I bet he makes some kind'a move."

Lance looked down at the gun. "So, we turn this over to the police, or what?"

"Well, I certainly don't want to get a reputation for withholding evidence." He put the gun and knife in the bag. "Let's go."

In Victor Riley's office, Edge laid out the bag and its contents on the desk. Then he took a seat next to Lance.

"What are these?" Riley said.

"We think they're what killed Bootsie Wyatt."

"Where'd you get'em?"

"I bought them at the Lazy Man's Pawn on Halls Mill Road."

"And they just sold'em to you?"

"Well, the owner's wife did. I don't think she knew what she had."

Riley nodded. "You think Marty Morningside is involved."

"You know him?"

"Yeah. Busted him for dope about ten years ago. Once upon a time, he was a snitch of mine."

"I think he hired Chuck to kill Bootsie, and he may have even supplied him the weapons."

"And you can prove this how?"

"I can't, just yet."

Riley nodded. "Okay, we'll see if this gun matches the one that killed Ms Wyatt. The knife, as I'm sure you know, we can't match back."

"Can you just let me know who the gun was purchased by?"

"I can do that, but it takes a while."

"I can wait."

"Are you getting close, Edge?"

"Maybe yes, maybe no."

"We've actually gotten in a couple of leads on this thing."

"Anything we can use?"

"I don't think so. They take the case in a whole other direction; like with jealous lovers and all. Your motives all deal with a screwball husband, am I right?"

"That's about the size of it."

"We'll work ours out, and if I they begin to intersect with yours, I'll let you know."

Edge nodded. "By the way, what happened with Lester Wright?"

"Oh, yeah. Well, we picked him up and searched his house. He had bloody clothes in a laundry bag in the back."

"Were you able to put it back on Lardy McLain?"

"We're still workin' on that. McLain paid him in cash and we're waiting on phone records to show they had contact, but there's really nothing else to tie him back to Lester." He paused. "And, by the way, I had a talk with my guys about your witness at the apartment complex."

"Oh?"

"Yeah. I laid into'em good for not finding her." Riley paused and looked at him. "That was some good detective work."

"Thanks. I was lucky."

"You're lucky a lot. That's the sign of a good detective."

Later, at a Chinese buffet on Airport Boulevard, Edge went straight for the Moo Goo Gai Pan, and

Lance for the fried rice. They ate and discussed the case.

"We're missing something. I don't know what," Edge said.

"Well, you know how *I* feel. I like Charlie Morton for it."

"I understand. Chuck, the same as Charlie; the military style weapons; doing a favor for an Army buddy; needs money. I get it." He paused. "I don't know. But I make this a young man's crime; mostly, because of the wounds."

"Three fatal wounds."

"Right. Charlie's killed before. He'd be much more confident. He wouldn't feel the need to spill so much blood."

"You're forgetting the screw up factor."

Edge shook his head. "Maybe not on something like this. He's been to war. He'd've done it right." He paused. "Killing comes back to you."

"You sound like you know a lot about killing."

Edge said nothing.

"Were you in Vietnam?"

"I was in the French Foreign Legion."

"And you went to war?"

"I went a lot of places."

"Mysterious." She paused. "Where are you from, Mr. Edge?"

Edge chuckled. "You don't trust me."

"Sure I do. But I think, for the sake of the company, we have the right to know a little something about your background."

He chuckled again. "Okay, I was born in a log cabin in Kentucky. I learned to read by the fire light and learned to write with charcoal on the back of a shovel. I walked five miles to the nearest town to borrow books from the library. I was self-educated. When I got old enough, I moved to Springfield, Illinois, and read law. I didn't become a lawyer because I got drafted. I went . . ."

"Okay, okay, okay. I get it, Mr. Lincoln. You don't want to talk about yourself." She looked at him. "Just don't cause the company any embarrassment."

"I'm a private detective. Is there anything more embarrassing than that?"

Lance went back to her hotel in order to spend some time with her husband who was visiting from New Orleans. She made plans to rendez-vous with Edge the next day.

Marty Morningside being his only lead to the killer, Edge went back out to surveil the Lazy Man's Pawn Shop. He parked down the street and got out his binoculars.

At about two o'clock Edge looked up to find a new Cadillac Coupe de Ville pulling into the parking lot. He put the glasses on the vehicle and saw Bobby Wyatt getting out.

Wyatt went inside, was inside for five minutes, and came back out. Edge made a note of the date and time and decided not to follow him when he left. It was another connection between Marty and Wyatt. Edge also made a note of the license number of the money drop truck.

He spent from one to five watching the store. There was no sign that Marty was back. The same truck was in the lot, along with the wife's vehicle. When he gets back, it'll all surely hit the fan, he thought.

Edge wanted to protect Anita Morningside. She had done what she thought was right, and had no idea that she was selling evidence of a murder to anyone. She certainly had no idea she was turning it over to the police. And, as a matter of fact, unless someone had told him, Marty probably had no idea who Edge was. For all he knew, the man who walked into his store a couple of weeks ago was just as shady as he was.

The next morning Edge once again set up across the street from Lazy Man's Pawn. It was a long shot, but Anita Morningside had said that her husband would be back in a couple of days. That would put him back in town that morning.

It was shortly after ten o'clock when a blue pickup truck pulled into the parking lot. Edge used field glasses to identify the occupant.

He gave Marty twenty minutes to get himself situated inside, then he started the Impala. Edge didn't know exactly what he was going to say to him; though winging it had been a good strategy up until then. He intended to start by bringing up Chuck's name and then dropping in the fact that he had the gun and knife. If Morningside hadn't put two and two together by then, . . .

Edge parked next to Marty's truck. The tinkling bell announced his presence, and he took four steps inside and started looking at an electric guitar leaning against an amplifier in the corner.

No one was at the front counter. Edge thumbed the strings on the guitar and waited.

"You sold it!" a man's voice said from the back room. "You stupid bitch!"

Edge listened closely. Then he heard the unmistakable sound of a hand striking flesh. He walked toward the counter.

"Oh!" a female voice said; then he heard the sound of another slap, then three more.

Edge walked around the counter into the back room. Anita Morningside was standing in a corner with her hands shielding her face. Marty was three steps away with his arm upraised.

"Hold on, Marty. No need for that," Edge said.

Marty turned his direction. "Who are you?"

"That's the man I sold the gun to," Anita said through a sob.

"You?" Marty furrowed his brows and took a step toward Edge. "I know you. I seen you before."

"Right. I'm a friend of Chuck's. I came in here looking for somebody to move some stolen rocks. You gave me Lardy's name."

"Who are you?"

"You can call me, John."

"Yeah. Yeah, okay, John. Well, look, I'm gonna have to get that gun and knife back. See, it's pretty valuable."

"Marty, that ain't gonna be possible."

"Why not?"

"'Cause I don't have'em anymore."

Marty's face got hard. "Well, that's too bad, 'cause you're just gonna have to go get'em."

"Marty, I just came back here to see who was beatin' your wife's ass; and low and behold it was you. I didn't come back here to argue about a purchase."

"I gotta right to slap my ole lady if she does somethin' stupid." He looked at the woman menacingly. "Just tell me where the gun is, and I'll go get it myself."

"Marty, I just can't do it."

Morningside moved toward him as his wife cowered in the corner. Edge readied for battle.

"Wait a minute, Marty. Don't be stupid."

Morningside got within three feet and swung wide with his right hand. Edge ducked then countered with a short right to Marty's ribs. Marty bent double, and Edge hit him again with a rabbit punch to the left side of his head, then a left jab square on his mouth.

Marty sat down hard on the floor, but began immediately trying to struggle to his feet. Edge waited until he stood up straight and then hit him again under the chin. Marty fell backwards.

"Stay down, Marty."

Morningside raised himself to one elbow and then fell back, gasping for breath. He groaned.

Edge knelt next to him. "Where can I find Chuck?"

"I don't know," he sputtered.

"Tell me where he is. I gotta give him some money."

"I don't know where he is."

"How do you get in touch with him?"

Silence.

"Come on, Marty."

"Why should I tell you?"

"I think you know?"

Silence.

"You're in it pretty deep, Marty. When it crashes, it's gonna fall on you too, unless you get in front of it now."

"What's he talkin' about, Marty?" Anita said. She was still in the corner.

Marty looked at her. "Nothin'. Shut up."

Edge looked at Anita. "It's murder, Anita. Marty's up to his neck in it. He's goin' away for a long time."

Silence.

"How can I find Chuck?"

"Who are you?"

"I'm the jawbone of an ass, and if you don't talk, I can come down hard on you."

Silence.

"Are you the fuzz?"

"No." Edge paused. "Look, Marty, you tell me what you know, and we'll just let the police take care of themselves. All I want to know is where Chuck is and how Bobby Wyatt figures in all of this."

Silence.

"Come on, Marty. Use your head. I know Bobby made a money drop here, at your business. I know that you had the murder weapons. I know that you fenced Wyatt's ole lady's jewels. If I go to the cops now, you don't come out smellin' so good; and this is a capital case. Accessory before and after the fact just might get you life."

Marty Morningside was still lying on the floor, supine. Blood trickled from the corner of his mouth, and he wiped it away.

"Tell him, Marty. Tell him," Anita said.

He looked at her first, then back at Edge. "Okay, okay. But I want a deal."

"What kinda deal?"

"With the cops, the DA; immunity."

"Look, you tell me what I wanna know. After that, you work out your own deal. I'm not the cops. I just want Chuck, and Bobby Wyatt."

Silence again. This time Marty took a deep breath and exhaled.

"I called Bobby Wyatt, and he told me he had a guy he wanted me to contact about takin' out his old lady. He said he didn't want his prints on it."

"How'd you know he was in the market?"

"Andy Allison told me."

"How much'd Bobby give you?"

"Fifteen grand."

"Marty, no," Anita said.

She put her hand over her mouth and looked genuinely surprised. Edge looked at her and could see the beginnings of a mouse under her right eye.

"Who was this guy?"

"Some dude named Charlie, over in New Orleans." Morningside struggled to his feet.

Edge stopped and looked away. Charlie was the killer?

"What happened then?"

"So, I called him, and he said he wouldn't do it his self, but he'd get somebody to do it. So, I shot Charlie a few bucks."

"What's Charlie's last name?"

Marty looked at him like he was crazy. "No last names."

"What happened then?"

"A few days later, this guy Chuck shows up in town. Me an' Andy show him around and a couple of days later he, you know . . ."

"Did you get him the gun and the knife?"

Marty shook his head. "No. He brought'em. I asked him if he needed a piece, and he said no."

"So, what were you doing with'em?"

"Chuck give'em to me. He told me to get rid of'em."

"So you hid'em in your safe?"

"I was just holdin'em, 'til the heat died down."

Edge shook his head. He looked at Anita, then at Marty. He shook his head again. Then he drew back and hit Marty square on the jaw knocking him out cold. Anita yelped.

CHAPTER 29

Edge believed he had enough to show that Bobby Wyatt was behind the killing of his wife; not physical evidence-wise, mind you, but enough anecdotal evidence to get the police involved with both feet.

But he didn't want to go to the police until he had the thing wrapped up, and as yet, he still hadn't identified Chuck. Chuck was the key. If Chuck was looking at the death chair, he might just give up Bobby Wyatt in exchange for his life, and Edge's work would be over.

Lance met Edge for lunch at a small bistro on Dauphin Street across from Cathedral Square. It was hot, but there was a breeze, so they decided to eat on the sidewalk.

"So Marty Morningside spilled it all about Bobby Wyatt's involvement."

"Yeah. Marty said he was the go between that lined it up. He said he went to New Orleans to see Charlie."

"Charlie's the killer?"

"That's what I thought. But no, Charlie didn't do it, he only located someone. The description of Chuck doesn't match Charlie."

"But we can put Marty with Bobby?" Lance said.

"Only by Marty's confession; well, and by the weapons, if they match."

"And he paid him money."

"Only by Marty's confession." Edge took a bite. "If we try to go to court with what we have, it won't fly. Allison would have been enough. He knew everything, but now he's dead."

"So you're thinkin' that we need to get Charlie to tell who Chuck is."

"Right, then we can squeeze him to make him implicate Wyatt."

"Or, we could go to the police with what we have now, and they can pick up Marty and sweat him."

"They could, but he'll clam up without a deal, and I'm not sure the police want to give him one; not one that doesn't include jail time."

"So, what's your plan?"

"I don't know, just yet. But I'm thinking it may take us back to New Orleans."

The next morning, Edge and Lance were back on the road, down I-10, to the Crescent City. They arrived at ten and immediately made their way to

Telemachus Street, and the halfway house where Charlie Morton lived.

At the door, the same fat man, who appeared a bit fatter than before, told them that Morton had gone to the store to get milk but that he was expected back shortly. Edge said that they would wait, and he and Lance repaired to the Impala to talk and listen to the radio.

"What do you guys hear from Bobby Wyatt?" Edge said.

"He's still calling Shelia. She told me that he calls about three times a week."

"Oh. How is he?"

"As you might expect. He's angry and demanding his money. Shelia told him that we were getting close to a solution and for him to be patient. She's trying to palm him off on me. He's called me a couple'a times, wanting a meeting." She paused. "She also told me that she had done some checking."

"And?"

"Well, the Bean and Dream is not in as good a financial shape as I'm sure Wyatt would like."

"Another motive for murder."

"Right." She paused. "And she also said that Wyatt wanted to get an audience with us."

"What for?"

"He didn't say."

"Okay, well, when we get back to town, let's give him a call."

"What are we going to say?"

"Nothing. It's not what we're gonna say to him, it's what he's gonna say to us."

They both looked up at the same time to see Charlie Morton ambling toward them carrying a full grocery bag in his left arm. He had a blank look on his face, and the slowness of his gait told them that he was depressed, or high. This might be a good time to talk to him, Edge thought.

Edge and Lance got out of the Impala and met him just as he was about to turn off the sidewalk and into the small yard in front of the house. The cur was nowhere to be seen.

"Hey, Charlie," Edge said.

Morton looked up and his mask told them that he didn't immediately know who they were. After a second, the light of recognition went off, and instead of a smile, his visage took on a defensive air; by that it is meant that his jaw tightened, his eyes narrowed, and his shoulders went up.

"Can we talk to you for a minute?" Edge said.

"What about?"

He had no doubt heard from back in Mobile that the two investigators were making progress. Edge walked up and stood in front of him.

"We've just got a couple of questions to ask you, Charlie." He paused and looked him in the eye. "I know you'll want to make the time to answer 'em."

Morton took a deep breath and exhaled. "Okay. But let me put up the milk first."

They followed Morton inside and waited for him in the parlor while he walked to the back of the house. It took him nearly five minutes to return. When he did, he took a seat in a chair in the corner, as far away from Edge and Lance as he could.

"Charlie, we got some disturbing news the other night," Edge said.

Morton crossed his arms and leaned far back into the chair. "Like what?"

"Well, like maybe you know a little more about what happened to Bobby Wyatt's wife than what you told us."

"No, no. I been up front with you guys. I, I haven't talked to Bobby in two years."

"Are you sure?"

"Of course."

"How about Marty?"

It was as if he'd been shot. His eyes opened wide, he grabbed the chair arms, and his shoulders went up to his neck.

"I, uh, I don't know what you're talking about," Morton said. Edge noticed he said 'what' and not 'who.'

"Well, he sure knows you. He said you found a hit man to kill Bobby's wife."

"Now, that's not right; that's not right. He called me, but I told him I wanted no part of it." His tone was frantic, and he moved to the edge of his chair.

"Come on, Charlie. It's over. Go ahead and tell it. It'll make you feel better."

He talked fast. "No, no, now, I haven't done anything. This Marty you're talkin' about, whoever he is, he called me about this fool idea, and I told'im straight up, no way, no how, no nothing. I said Bobby's a friend of mine, and I ain't gonna be a party to this."

Edge looked at him. "I can see you're reluctant to open up. Maybe when the police come you'll be a bit more forthcoming."

"Now, look here . . ."

"No, no, don't worry about it. We've got enough to go to the law, and they can handle it from here."

"Oh, shit." Morton put his hands over his face and bent over.

Edge stared at him, then turned to Lance and nodded. He thought a female voice at that vulnerable moment might do the trick.

"Charlie, look. We're not the police. We're insurance people. We just want to keep from payin' out a lot of money to somebody who doesn't deserve it. The police, they do their thing, and we do ours." She paused. "Now, just tell us what happened, and then we'll know, and you can go about your business."

Morton looked up at them both. His eyes told the story of a man that was whipped by his past, both distant and near.

"You don't understand. I done a really bad thing."

"Did you kill her?"

"No, no. But . . ."

"I understand, an old buddy needed some help and you helped. Things just gotta little outta hand, right?"

"No, it's worse than that."

"What could be worse?"

Morton said nothing. Edge looked at him.

"Charlie, who is 'Chuck'?"

275

The words struck him like lightning. He sat up straight. "You guys gotta go. You gotta go, now."

Morton stood up and marched out of the room. Lance looked at Edge and smiled.

"You sure said the wrong thing."

"Or, the right thing."

After Edge dropped Lance off at her office, downtown, near the Superdome, he drove back to Mobile. He hit town at about two and went directly to the Police Department. It was time to fill in Victor Riley on what he had learned.

Riley wasn't in a good mood. He had another murder on his hands and it was beginning to show.

"What do you want, Edge?" Riley was chewing a Tums and washing it down with coffee.

"I just came by to see how the Lester Wright thing turned out."

"Wright?"

"You know, he beat Andy Allison to death at the apartments on Azalea Road. Did he roll on Lardy McLain?"

"Oh, yeah," he said nodding. "Yeah, he told it all. Allison was a regular makin' stolen property runs for McLain. The two kids told him how that Allison was working with you and was goin' to spill it all to us. Lester said he went over there just to put the fear'a God in him, but Andy fought back a little; he was drunk, you know. Lester said he hit him once too often, he went down, and didn't wake up."

"What'd he hit him with?"

"His fists."

Edge nodded. "So were you able to make a case on McLain?"

"Actually, no. The money was in cash, the phone call between the two was from a payphone, and there was nothing else to hang on Lardy; the uncorroborated testimony and all that."

Edge shook his head and thought of Tommy Dickens. He had suddenly become the only way to put Lardy McLain in the penitentiary. Edge was certain that Dickens had no idea what a powerful position – or a dangerous one – he was in.

"Is that all you wanted? 'Cause I got work to do," Riley said. He nodded at the stacks of reports on his desk.

"Well, if you've got time, I wanted to fill you in on where you are on the Wyatt case."

"Wyatt? Oh, yeah." He took a drink and coughed hard when some of the liquid went down the wrong pipe.

"So, Marty Morningside acted as the go between for Wyatt and his old Army buddy Charlie Morton. We think Morton hired Chuck to kill Bootsie."

"Do you know who 'Chuck' is?"

"Not yet. But we're getting close."

"Come back when you have him."

"It must be nice to have all this free labor."

Riley smiled and leaned back in his chair. "It's question of priorities, Edge. Your case is cold, while I've got about five hot ones on my hands. These cases are like hot potatoes. I had one, it was hot, but it cooled off. You picked it up, now it's hot again. You can't give it back to me. You have

to wait 'til it cools off again; then I'll take it back."
He paused. "Besides, in your hands, this Wyatt
thing'll be solved in no time."

Edge smiled as he rose and turned toward the
door. "You know, Lieutenant, burned hands are
painful, no matter whose they are."

At his office, that afternoon, Edge checked his
service. There was one surprising call. He returned
it immediately.

"I need to see you." It was the voice of Bobby
Wyatt. His tone was agitated.

"Where?"

"Make it the dead end of Old Bay Front Road,
near the runway, at six."

"I'll be there."

It took Edge until six fifteen to get to the gate that
separated the Brookley Airfield from the local
University that owned about a mile and a half
of bay front property that once belonged to the
US Air Force. It being summer, the area would
be deserted. There was a sea breeze, and the
sounds of private aircraft taking off and landing
intermittently provided a soundtrack.

A half dozen empty homes that formerly
housed military officers lined the last block of the
asphalt road that led up to a gate in the chain link
fence at the end of the street. Wyatt's Cadillac was
parked in the driveway of the last house on the
side opposite the bay. He was standing next to the
car. Edge parked and walked toward him, his head
on swivel. The word 'ambush' crossed his mind.

"You're late," Wyatt said.

"I had to take a dump; and there was traffic."

Wyatt looked around. He took a deep breath and talked slow.

"Look, Edge, you and me, we're a lot alike."

"How so?"

"We're both guys who're used to getting what we want. We also have a healthy affection for money."

"We've only met once. What do you know about me? About the money thing, I mean?"

"I read people pretty well. You wouldn't be working for an insurance company if you didn't want to make big money. Everybody knows the insurance people have all the coin."

Edge smiled. "Go on."

"So, how about a deal?"

"A deal? What kind'a deal?"

"A deal, deal. You get the insurance people off my back, and get'em to pay off this claim, and I'll increase your net worth by fifty thousand dollars."

Edge looked away toward Mobile Bay. He rubbed his mouth and lifted his eyebrows.

"Fifty grand. Wow."

"Wow, is right."

"But, you killed her."

"No, I didn't."

"Or, you had her killed."

"Or, so it may seem. But you and I both know that's just the insurance company talkin'. They think they know what happened, and that's what they want you to prove so they won't have to pay me." He paused. "My wife's gone. We all need to move on."

"So, who killed her?"

"How should I know?"

"Who do you think killed her?"

"Once again, how should I know?"

"Bobby – can I call you Bobby? I've got a contract with ManMut. I'm afraid I couldn't sell out for just fifty grand."

"Okay, so name your price."

Edge stared at his face. It was surprisingly smooth for a man his age. His silver hair provided a contrast to his olive skin and made it appear as if he'd just come back from vacation. His animal white teeth flashed in the twilight.

"I don't think you've got enough. Because I'd be cutting my throat professionally, I'd have to be taken care of for the rest of my life. I'm afraid I couldn't settle for less than half. Fifty/fifty."

"One million?"

"That would just about cover it."

"You're outta your mind."

"Like I said, if I play it your way, I got no place to go."

It was Wyatt's turn to look toward the bay. The breeze caused the hairs in his widow's peak to dance lightly. He took a deep breath and exhaled.

"Edge, you know I can't do it. I need almost all of that money to keep my business afloat." He paused and looked up. "I'd do anything to get it."

It was a stark admission. Did he mean, even murder, Edge thought?

"That's my price," Edge said.

"Well, I guess we don't have anything else to talk about."

"Just a question or two."

Wyatt said nothing.

Edge wanted so badly to drop the whole load on Wyatt; Marty, Morton, the money drops, everything. But he knew it wasn't the right time.

"Bobby, you know that since you've tried to buy me off, you've just made yourself more of a suspect. Why'd you do it?"

"All I want is my money, Edge. You're the one person that I thought would understand; that would help me."

"Now that you know I won't, what are you gonna do?"

He paused. "I, I'll just have to think of another way."

Edge nodded and started to turn toward his car. "By the way, when's the last time you talked to Charlie Morton?"

He chuckled. "Ha, Charlie? I haven't seen or heard from that alky since we got home from Vietnam. I haven't thought about'im in years."

Edge nodded. He wanted to say more, but he knew it would do no good. He'd have to get someone on the inside to finger Wyatt or there'd be no case.

"No, Bobby, I guess you're right. You're gonna have to do what you gotta do." He paused. "And I gotta do what I gotta do."

Edge walked back to his car, got in, and started the engine. He left Wyatt standing on the driveway watching as he drove away.

CHAPTER 30

Edge spent the next morning in his office. He was thinking; a time consuming process that almost always caused him to fall asleep. A doctor had once told him that when the brain is confronted with a problem that it can't solve, it almost always shuts the body down in sleep so it can work on the problem exclusively, without having to think about doing anything else. True to form, Edge dropped off in about twenty minutes, though he had only gotten out of bed a couple of hours earlier.

He awoke to the sound of the telephone. It was the answering service. An older woman named Nora told him to call the Police Department. In two minutes, Riley was on the line.

"What's up?"

"We took a look at the revolver you brought in." He paused. "It's the gun that killed Bootsie Wyatt."

Edge's heart jumped. "Fantastic. Have you picked up Marty Morningside yet?"

"Not yet. He wasn't at his store, or at home. We thought you might know where he is."

"I don't."

"Okay. If you see him, call us."

"You know he'll roll on Bobby Wyatt."

"If Bobby's involved."

"He is."

"I hope for your sake he is."

"My sake has nothing to do with it. I'm getting paid no matter what."

"Just call me if you find him."

Edge hung up and closed his eyes. Several things were rolling around in his head. One was Charlie Morton and his demeanor when they saw him last, when he mentioned the name of 'Chuck.' Morton almost broke a leg getting out of the room. Second, was Morningside and his admitted relationship with Morton. The weapons, as Lance had surmised, both pointed to Morton, and now that Edge knew that the revolver was a hit, it only made her theory seem more likely.

But Morton didn't fit the description of the 'Chuck' that was seen at The Lunatic; and Wyatt's characterization of Morton as an alky or a drug head was correct. Could he be trusted to pull off this murder? There was only one other person who came to mind as a likely suspect. Edge picked up the telephone.

The next day, Edge was in Eupora, Mississippi, by ten o'clock. It was a hard drive in hot weather but it had to be made. He parked his car in front of a trailer in a park on Highway 82, east of the country club. It was Tuesday. The yards of the mobile homes were deserted except for a couple of older women hanging laundry on makeshift clotheslines.

This particular home was a seventy-two foot, double wide, white with green trim. There were three wooden steps inside a metal frame that led up to the front door. Edge knocked three times and waited.

The woman that answered was young, barely in her twenties with dishwater blonde hair and blue eyes. She had underlying good looks: fair skin, a small nose, and an hourglass figure that showed through her faded housedress.

Had she been a woman of means, she would no doubt have had her hair colored blonde, and be wearing polyester pants and a print blouse in the middle of the day, but, the double wide home notwithstanding, Edge could tell by her frock and personal maintenance that she was low income, if not poor.

"You Marilyn? Marilyn McGrath?"

"Yes, sir. Who are you?" Her accent was soft but deeply southern.

"My name is Edge." He showed her his Alabama credentials. "I'm a private investigator from Mobile." He paused. "Did Leon or his Aunt Polly mention me?"

She shook her head. "No."

"Well, can we talk?"

She looked him up and down. Finally, she nodded. "Let me turn off the stove. We can sit in the backyard under the tree."

Edge nodded reluctantly. He was hoping to get a look inside the trailer.

"I'll walk around to the back."

In five minutes, Marilyn McGrath had slipped into thong sandals and exited the back door. She sat down in one of the two metal lawn chairs that were within five feet of the trunk of a large oak tree toward the back of the lot. A breeze blew and the partly cloudy skies kept the temperature a bit more pleasant than it might normally have been.

"Whew. I had to get them peas off the stove or they'd'a burnt." She swatted a fly in front of her face. "What can I do for you, Mr., Edge was it?"

"Right. Leon's Aunt Polly gave me your name. She thought that you might could help."

"I'll do what I can."

"Well, ma'am, I'm doing some work for an insurance company in Mobile and unfortunately Leon's father's name has come up in our investigation."

"Well, that don't surprise me none. He ain't the brightest bulb in the box."

"You've met him?"

"I knew him growin' up. He was forever raisin' sand all the time; gettin' in trouble for drinkin' and such. What's he done?"

"We think he knows something about a murder that happened in Mobile."

She appeared stunned. "Whoa. That don't sound like him. I mean, he raised cain for as long as I can remember, but I never knowed him to hurt nobody, outside'a just fightin'."

"Tell me something. Does Leon live here?"

She shook her head. "No. We been goin' together for three years, but he don't stay here. I told him, he don't move in 'til I getta ring."

"Does he have any of his things here?"

She looked suspicious. "Just a few. Like, what'chu talkin' about?"

"I thought maybe some letters from his daddy; maybe he mentioned something about the case."

"Oh, no. The only thing he's got here is a couple'a shirts he brought over for me to mend, some pants to wash, and a box'a bullets."

"Bullets?"

"Yeah, for his pistol."

"Wonder why he'd bring'em over here?"

"He come in from a trip one night and had'em in his hand. He laid'em down, and I guess he just forgot to pick'em up and take'em home."

"You think he coulda' got'em from his daddy?"

"I don't think so. He ain't seen his daddy in a while, that I know about."

Edge paused and looked toward the street as the wind blew in his face.

"You think maybe I could look at'em for just a minute?"

"I don't see why not. They're just some bullets."

She rose from her chair and was in and out of the trailer in two minutes. She handed Edge a box of .38 calibre, SureShot ammunition; an off brand that he didn't recognize. He opened it.

It was a fifty round container, but six rounds were missing. Edge pulled one of the cartridges out of the box while McGrath watched.

In any investigation, fortuitous incidents must occur. At that moment one happened. The telephone rang and Marilyn McGrath rose to go inside to answer it. While she was gone, Edge took the tray of bullets completely out of the box. He took three rounds out of the back end and then slid the tray back into the box with the end with only the missing six rounds showing. He took the three rounds and dropped them into his pants pocket.

McGrath was back in five minutes. She sat back down in the chair, this time her look was not friendly.

"That was Leon. He said I shouldn't talk to you. You're gonna have to go."

"Did he say why?"

"He said ya'll are tryin' to hang a murder on his daddy that he didn't commit. You're gonna have to go."

Edge handed her back the closed box of bullets, with three missing, and McGrath none the wiser. Then he rose from the chair.

"Oh, by the way, Marilyn. One more thing. What is Leon's full name?"

Edge asked the question knowing that Marilyn had recited her wedding vows a thousand times in her head, and they included: 'do you Marilyn McGrath take . . .

"Oh, it's Charles Leon Morton."

That night, back in Mobile, Edge locked the bullets in the desk drawer in his office and got on the phone to Lance.

"I've found Chuck."

"Really, who is it."

"It's Charlie's son."

"Really?"

"You sound surprised. You don't think Charlie would pimp out his son as a hit man for Bobby Wyatt?" He paused.

"I guess."

"Sure he would. Now, we just have to prove it."

The next day, Edge set out looking for Marty Morningside. As he drove to that part of town, he thought of all the people who'd know where he was. There were only two: his wife, Anita, and Lardy McLain.

If Marty intended to have a business to come back to, he would have to put his wife in charge of running the store until he got back from wherever it was he went. Edge went to the Lazy Man's Pawn Shop first.

As he came through the front door, the bell tinkled. Edge looked up as the curtains moved and Anita Morningside slipped through them to take her place behind the counter. She was not a pretty sight.

He could see that one eye was swollen shut and there were bruises on both cheeks. A tooth was missing in front and her bottom lip was swollen.

She looked at him hard. "What are *you* doin' here?"

"I'm lookin' for Marty. Where is he?"

"Why should I tell you?" She spoke with a lisp.

Edge looked at both sides of her face. "Yeah, I can see why you'd want to cover for'im."

"It's 'cause'a you that he done this."

"Me? All I did was buy a gun. By the way, you spent that hundred and fifty bucks yet?"

She looked down. "I had to use it at the doctor."

"Of course you did. Now, where is Marty?"

She was silent.

"The police want him, Anita. If you hide him you could go to jail yourself."

She looked away and wiped a tear from her eye, no doubt wondering how she had fallen in love with a man who could beat her so badly, why she felt compelled to shield him from justice, and why her whole world was suddenly falling apart.

"He's in Biloxi."

"Where?"

"I don't know. He wouldn't tell me. He told me that it was better if I didn't know. He just said he was gonna go over there an' lay low for a while.

"It'll have to be a long while."

She smirked.

"Who'd know?" he said.

She shrugged her shoulders. "Louis, maybe; or Lardy."

"How can I find Louis?"

"He works at the fillin' station on Highway 90; the Shell near Demetropolis Road."

Edge nodded. "Okay. I'll find it." He paused and looked at her. "You know he's no good, right? You're gonna have to get shed of him."

She shook her head. "But I love him."

It took fifteen minutes to get to the Shell. Edge parked on the side and walked in the front door. It appeared as if the station was one of the last in the city where actual mechanic work was done.

"Is Louis here?"

The man behind the counter, an older gentleman with a ball cap sitting cockeyed on his gray head, wearing grease-stained coveralls, looked up.

"Who wants to know?"

"Me, John. Marty told me Louis could fix the rattle in my car."

"Marty?" He shook his head. "That boy ain't no good. He bad news."

"Hey, it's just a rattle."

The old man looked at him. "Louis out in de garage." He nodded that direction.

"Thanks."

Edge walked into the service area and found a tall man with dark skin working under a red Mustang that was up on the lift. Oil streamed down from the crankcase of the Ford into a bowl on top of a tall stand.

"Louis?" Edge said.

"Yeah."

"My name's John. I need to find Marty."

"Marty?"

"Yeah. Where is he?"

"I don't know. He ain't tole me 'fore he took off."

"You know he's gone, though, right?"

"Who is you, man?"

"I told you, my name is John. Marty moved some stuff for me. I need to find him to get paid."

Louis took the bolt and screwed it into the hole in the bottom of the crankcase. He wiped off the underside of the part and began to move the bowl from under the car.

"Look, man, I heard he had to take off, that the police was lookin' fo' him. I thank he went to Biloxi. I don't know."

"Who knows?"

Louis looked at him. "Lardy know."

CHAPTER 31

Edge knew it would eventually come down to this. He knew that he would at some point have to confront Lardy McLain. The trick would be getting what he needed from the fat man without being hurt in the process.

That night, at nine, Edge parked in a wooded picnic area two hundred yards north of the McLain's Fish Camp and began walking toward the business. He was wearing dark pants and a black shirt, boots, and he was armed with his forty five and a knife. Edge stayed between the shoulder of the road and Heron Bay, and the sound of the water as it lapped to shore, as well as the multitude of crickets, masked his approach.

In ten minutes he was in the woods twenty yards from the building using a small ocular to watch the business. There was no one around. Ernest, the stooge that waylaid Edge the night of the Tommy Dickens shooting, was no longer working there, he having ultimately become afraid for his safety.

Edge put the glass in his pants pocket and crept toward the back door, the one that opened onto the boardwalk and the pier. The small waves continued to mask the sound of his movements. He reached the glass entrance and peeped around the corner. McLain and his four hundred pounds were sitting on a tall stool with his back to the door. Edge took a long leather thong out of his back pocket and unrolled it.

He caught the fat man completely by surprise. Edge threw the strap over his head and before McLain could move, Edge had looped it around his throat and pulled it as tight as he could.

The big man fell off his stool, and Edge guided him face down to the floor while both Lardy's hands clawed at the thin leather lace. Edge stood, straddling him, and spoke.

"Okay, okay, calm down, Lardy. Calm down." His tone was soothing. "I'm gonna take a little pressure off, now. Just calm down."

Edge loosened the thong slightly as Lardy tried to fit his fat fingers into the space between it and his neck. Edge wasn't going to let that happen. He pulled it tighter and spoke again.

"Get your hands down by your side. Then I'll loosen it some."

The fat man complied, and Edge loosened the strap. Lardy could be heard gasping for breath. Edge spoke softly.

"Now, I could kill you and nobody would ever find out, Lardy. But I'm not, although you deserve it. You paid to have that Allison boy killed and there was no sense in it. But, I'm gonna let the police take care of you on that; that and all the hot property you been movin' outta here. What I want to know is: where is Marty?"

"Marty?" he gurgled.

"That's right. They tell me you know where he is. Now, I'm gonna loosen this thing up a little, and you better talk."

Edge gave him a little slack. Lardy grunted. "Okay, okay. I'll talk. Just take this thing off me."

Edge yanked as hard as he could. "That's not what I want to hear, Lardy." He paused. "Shit, maybe I should just kill you right now."

"Nnnnnnnn," he gurgled again.

Edge loosened the leather thong before the big man went unconscious. "Now, tell me what I want to know."

"Okay, okay. He's in Biloxi." He grunted out the words.

"Where?"

"In a house on the back bay."

"What's the address?"

"Uh, Hengen Lane; uh, uh, 9200."

"Are you lying to me?"

"No, no. Please don't kill me." His voice was almost a whimper.

Edge was still straddling him, bent at the waist so he could hear what he was saying. He didn't know whether to believe the fat man or not, so he reached and pulled handcuffs out of his back pocket.

"Put your hands behind your back, Lardy."

The fat man tried but couldn't get them both to the small of his back, so Edge held the thong with one hand and handcuffed Lardy's right hand to the hammer loop on the side of his overalls. Then he took both ends of the thong and tied them to his left hand. Only then, with McLain's hands immobilized, could Edge relax.

Edge picked up the phone. He dialed the Police Department's dispatch line. They connected him to the Homicide Squad, to a detective, Abel Hanks.

"You guys looking for Marty Morningside, right?"

"Who is this?"

"This is John Edge. Riley told me to call when I found out where Marty Morningside is. Can you copy?"

There was a pause on the other end of the line, then, "Go ahead."

Edge recited the address provided by Lardy McLain. "Get somebody over there fast, he's on the move."

"I'll have to check with the Lieutenant. What's your number?"

"I'll call you." Edge didn't want to tell the police where he was or who he was with.

"Okay. Call me back in fifteen minutes."

Edge hung up and heard McLain cough. "You okay, there, Lardy?"

The fat man coughed again. "Yeah. Let me go."

"Not yet. Not until the police have Marty. And, that better be the right address."

"I'm gonna kill you, Edge."

"Well, stand in line, brother. You got about a dozen people ahead'a ya."

Edge's mind raced back through the last eight years, in his other life, people that he had worked over to get information or cooperation.

"Lardy, when you get out of prison, if I'm alive, you come after me. We'll give it a go and see who the better man is. Maybe you'll have dropped a few pounds by then."

Edge turned and locked the back door that he'd entered, then walked quickly and locked the front door. He found the light switch, and when he flipped it, the room turned almost pitch.

When he got back to the counter, he picked up the phone and called the police again. Hanks answered.

"Yeah, I checked with the Looey. He said to get the PD over there, in Biloxi, to check it out. We should be hearing from'em in just a few minutes."

"I'll call you back." Edge hung up the phone.

He looked down at McLain, still prone on the floor. "What makes you such an ass, Lardy? I mean, you're involved in a lotta shit. Plus, I bet you've even killed a couple of people."

McLain had bent his right leg at the knee taking some of the pressure off his diaphragm. As a result, his speech was not as labored and was much plainer.

"I'm gonna kill you."

"Who else have you killed?"

"Fuck you."

"How about Wyatt's wife; you kill her?" Edge asked knowing that it wasn't true, that of all the murders that he'd been involved in, he probably hadn't had anything to do with Bootsie Wyatt's.

They sat quietly. Edge looked at his watch and read the newspaper by flashlight as he waited for twenty minutes to elapse. Finally, he picked up the phone and dialed. Hanks answered once again.

"They got him," Hanks said. "It was some rental house over there. They said it looked like a sty. He was sleepin' off a drunk in the bedroom, on a mattress on the floor."

"Okay, good news," Edge said. "Leave a note for the Lieutenant that I'll see him tomorrow."

Edge looked down at McLain. "Well, Lardy, ya done good."

He reached and unlocked the handcuff then cut the very end of the leather strap with a knife he carried in his pocket. Then, without another word, Edge slipped out the back door. McLain was struggling to his feet as Edge ran quickly into the woods.

CHAPTER 32

Edge was at the Police Department at ten the next morning when officers from the fugitive unit of the Sheriff's Office brought Marty Morningside, who had waived extradition in Mississippi, into the Church Street station wearing belly chains and leg irons. There was a confident look on Morningside's face; a look that said that he had some cards to play.

In the corner, near the coffee pot, Edge stood with Riley and Vaughn, and watched as Marty shuffled past them and into one of three interrogation rooms on the second floor. Marty's wife, who had been picked up earlier that morning out of her sleeping bed, was in the next room.

"You think he'll talk?" Vaughn said to no one in particular.

Riley looked at Edge. "You know him better than anyone."

"Sure he will; for a deal. He's not crazy. He'll want immunity for the murder. Is the DA on his way?"

"John Walton's coming," Riley said. "I put in a call for him about an hour ago."

Edge, too, had put in a call that morning, for Lucy Lance. He wanted her to be there when Marty spilled it all, so that she could report to Manhattan Mutual that everything had come together. Lance said she was coming from New Orleans and would be there right around ten.

When Marty got situated, Riley, Edge, and Vaughn all trooped into the plain, bare room where suspects were questioned. It had three chairs, a metal table, and was outfitted with a tape recording system. Vaughn and Riley took the chairs across from Marty. Edge stood in the corner.

Vaughn read the handcuffed man his constitutional rights. Marty said he understood and leaned back in his chair.

"Marty, I guess you know that because of Mr. Edge here," Riley nodded in Edge's direction, "we've got you over a barrel. The gun he bought from your wife killed Bobby Wyatt's wife."

Marty leaned forward. "You may think you got me, but that guy there bought the gun from my wife, not me. And she don't have to testify against me, so really, you don't have me as tight as you think you do."

"Don't count on your wife hangin' with you, Marty. The last time I saw her face, she had a couple of reasons to turn on you. Besides, the privilege lies with her, not you. She can testify if *she* wants," Riley said.

Marty's face tightened. Apparently, he didn't know as much jailhouse law as he thought he did. Edge stood, deadpan, and thought of the woman in the next room, her closed eye and missing tooth. Marty Morningside was a son of a bitch.

"You'd hang your wife out to dry, Marty?" Vaughn said.

Marty leaned back. "No, I wouldn't. But, I'm not goin' up for a murder I didn't commit." He leaned forward again, this time shaking his index finger at Vaughn. "I can lay it all for ya', and I mean, all out. But, I want a deal."

Riley looked at him. "Call your lawyer."

Arthur Martin was the most expensive and arguably the best defense attorney in town. He wore expensive suits, alligator shoes, and silk ties, and because he'd bested the DA's office in a couple of high profile cases in the past five years, he'd been able to take control of over five hundred acres of prime real estate in the south part of the county, land that was rumored to sit on top of one of the largest and richest gas reserves in south Alabama. His bald head was shiny and his pencil thin mustache gave him an air of sophistication that he did not actually possess. As he would say, he was just a poor but honest country solicitor.

After talking to Marty Morningside for fifteen minutes, Martin stepped out of the interrogation room and stood in front of John Walton, the chief assistant DA. Edge listened closely. Lance who had arrived thirty minutes earlier, stood at his side.

"My client, while not guilty of any crimes, would like to set the record straight and thereby assist you in bringing the killer of Dorothy Wyatt to justice."

"That's big of him," Walton said. He was bald also, but thin with large hands.

Martin smirked. "In return, he would like immunity from prosecution in Ms Wyatt's murder, and would like a minimal sentence for tampering with evidence."

"He gets five years for conspiracy to commit murder, two years for evidence tampering, and two years for whatever we can prove is stolen out at that pawn shop; and in return he testifies truthfully and cooperates fully against Bobby Wyatt in the murder of his wife, against whoever actually killed Dorothy Wyatt, and Wayne McLain in the murder of Andy Allison."

Martin looked away, but spoke quickly. "Five plus two, plus two. Concurrent?"

"Right."

"Sold."

Walton nodded toward the door and he, Riley, Vaughn, and Martin stepped inside. Edge and Lance repaired to the observation room that adjoined Interrogation 1. Edge turned on the intercom.

"This is exciting," Lance said.

They caught Walton in mid-sentence. "So, just tell me what happened," Walton said, "and remember, if you lie about anything, the deal's off, and I walk in there and convince your longsuffering wife to roll all over you. That and everything Edge can say about you makes you good for the actual killing."

Morningside nodded. "About seven or eight months ago," he began, "Andy Allison called me, said he had a live one on the line, and he thought we could maybe make some real money. He said a friend of his had an old man who wanted to off his wife. He said he'd already taken him for about ten grand, but the dude was rich, and he thought we could get more. I told him sure, what was his number?

"The next day, I called Bobby Wyatt. I said I heard he needed a job done. He said, yeah, and wanted to know if I could help him. I said, what kind'a job, and he said he wanted somebody to take his wife outta the pichure."

"What did you think he meant when he said he wanted her 'outta the picture?'"

"I knew what he wanted. He wanted her killed."

"Did he ask how you got his number?"

"Yeah. I told him I got it from Lardy McLain. He didn't ask no questions."

"Go on."

"Wyatt said he'd been jerked around and was already out about twenty grand. He said time was running out, and he needed it done pretty quick."

"He say why?"

"No, and I didn't ask him."

"What else?"

"He said he knew a guy that could help, but that he wanted me to contact him – he wanted to keep his fingerprints off of it. I said sure, for the right price."

"How much?"

"I told him that with expenses, it'd cost him twenty five thousand. He said he'd been worked over by some kids, Allison and some wetback, and he wanted to make sure it was done this time. I told him, it was guaranteed."

"Who'd he say to call?"

"Some guy named Charlie. He give me his number. Bobby said Charlie was in the Army with'im, and he'd murdered somebody over in Vietnam; threw a girl out of his helicopter, I think. I said fine, but if he didn't want to do it, or if I didn't feel like he was up to the job, I'd use my own people and no questions asked. He said okay.

"So, I met Charlie over in New Orleans, but I could tell pretty quick he was a dope head, or an alky, or somethin'. I told him I didn't think he was the right guy for the job, and he ought'a bow out. He said to wait, let him get hold of his son. He said that he thought he could do it, or knew somebody who could."

"Who's his son?"

"His name's Leon, that's what everybody calls him; but Charlie said to call him Chuck, that Charles was his first name, and that way when people were lookin' for'im, they wouldn't know it was him."

Walton looked at Riley. "Do we know this guy?"

"Edge knows him. We can get him."

Walton looked back at Marty. "Go on."

"So, anyway, Chuck comes to town, and I met him at The Lunatic over on McVay Drive. He got a couple'a drinks in'im and got to talkin' with Andy Allison – Andy was bartendin' – and 'fore I knew it, he was sayin' what he was in town to do. I shoulda' shut down everything and bowed out of it right there, but, well, the money was too good."

"What was your cut?"

Marty paused and chuckled. "Fifteen. Charlie got two, Allison got one as a finder's fee, and Chuck, or Leon, got seven. Five before and two afterward. Andy was one of the ones that had ripped off Bobby, and that was how he got that Caddy."

"Well, you're just a prince, aren't you."

"Hey, it's a dog eat dog world."

"Did you know Allison before then?"

"Yeah, he'd brought in some hot stuff for me to get rid of a couple'a times before."

Walton nodded.

"So, we set it up. Chuck got the gun and the knife from his old man, and Bobby give me directions on how it was to be done; and, Chuck, ... he just did it. Afterwards, on his way outta town, he stopped at the shop and give me the gun and knife and told me to get rid of'em for him. He said he didn't want to be drivin' around with'em in the car. I said okay, but then I decided to hang on to'em, for insurance. I took'em and cleaned'em up, and put'em in my safe. They been there ever since," he paused, "'til my wife sold'em to that guy, Edge." He paused. "He a detective or somethin'?"

"PI," Riley said.

"I shoulda' known. My ole lady never could spot the fuzz."

You couldn't either, Edge thought.

"Anyway, about six months later, Andy picked up the rest of the payoff from Wyatt and brought it over to my shop and put it in a old pickup truck I got for sale out there, and Chuck come and got it a day later. It was under the seat." Morningside paused. "That's it."

"How about the jewelry?"

"I took it over to a shop in Pensacola. I got fifteen hundred for all of it and mailed two fifty to Chuck and told'im that was a bonus."

"What about Allison? What got him killed?"

"Oh, well, Lardy called me a week or so ago and said that Andy Allison was runnin' his mouth to somebody about everything. He said a couple'a guys in his operation overheard Andy tell some white guy how everything worked. Lardy said Andy needed to be shut up. I said, what do you want me to do about it? He said, who could do the job? And I said, Lester Wright, from down in the Bayou. I'd heard he'd killed some boat people who'd been muscling in on some shrimpin' territory." He paused. "Lardy knew him and said, 'oh, yeah, I didn't think about him. I'll call him.'"

"Back to Bobby Wyatt," Riley said. "You talk to him since?"

"A couple'a times. He said that the insurance company had sent a man and a woman out to try to tie all of it to him so he couldn't get his money.

He wanted to make sure I was locked up tight. I said no problem."

"Famous last words."

"Hey, a man's gotta do, right?"

"Yeah," Riley said.

Martin looked at Walton. "That enough?"

"I guess. He's gotta give us names, dates, places, all that. But, yeah . . . if it's all true."

Edge reached and turned off the intercom. "That enough for you?"

Lance smiled. "I'll call Shelia, but, yeah. I think you've earned your fee, and a healthy bonus."

"By the way, I gotta call from Bobby Wyatt the other night. He tried to buy me off for fifty grand."

"What'd you say?"

Edge raised his brows. "I'm here, aren't I?"

"That was a silly question, I guess."

"Has he made contact with you?"

"Oh, several times." She paused. "He never offered me money, though."

Vic Riley opened the door and stepped into the observation room. He looked ragged, but he was smiling.

"Well, I guess you two are to be thanked. That was a good bit'a detective work."

"It was Mr. Edge. He handled it all."

"Edge, good job."

"I didn't do anything, Lieutenant, that you wouldn't've done if you'd had the manpower."

"What's next?" Lance said.

"We'll get men in route to pick up Lardy and start the ball rollin' on getting Leon back to

Alabama." Riley looked at Edge. "You know where he's at?"

"Yeah. I can take you right to him." He reached in his pocket. "Oh, by the way, I got these from his girlfriend." He handed Riley the three rounds of .38 calibre ammunition he had taken from the box shown to him by Marilyn McGrath, the box that she had taken from her trailer. He explained their significance.

Riley took the rounds. "You wanna go up and be there when we pick him up?"

"If we can do it before he and his old man get word we're looking for'im."

"Vaughn's on the line with the Highway Patrol as we speak."

"I'll have a bag packed in an hour."

CHAPTER 33

Leon Morton was taken into custody by the Mississippi Bureau of Investigation and was brought to the Starkville office of the Highway Patrol at eleven o'clock that same morning.

Edge drove himself, and Vaughn and Hanks followed in a city car, and all three were in Starkville by four that afternoon. They were met in the lobby of the trooper post by Agent Randy Robinson, a short, thin, thirty-year old with jet black hair and a black mustache, and a forty five in a cross draw holster on his left hip.

"He was laid up in the bed with his girlfriend, ah," he consulted his notes, "Marilyn McGrath. We brought her in, but we didn't have anything on her, so we let her go. She was goin' to get Leon a lawyer."

"You get the bullets?" Edge said.

"Yeah; a box of .38s?"

"Right."

"Yeah, we got'em." He nodded over his shoulder. "We got him in a holdin' cell here. I didn't want to put him in the county jail." He paused. "He looks like he might try to kill his self."

"Maybe he wants to get something off his chest," Vaughn said.

"We'll bring him out," Robinson said.

Robinson walked out of the lobby after directing Edge and the others to an interrogation room. Edge looked at Vaughn.

"You want me to wait out here?" he said.

"No. Come on in." His tone was reluctant but conciliatory. "You had as much to do with breaking this thing as anybody. You talk to him."

Edge nodded. It seemed hard for Vaughn to make that admission. They walked into the sparse room and were waiting when Robinson brought in Leon Morton. When he was seated, Edge began by reciting the rights waiver.

"Do you understand your rights?"

Morton nodded. "Yeah."

"Leon, I understand that some people know you as Chuck, is that right?"

"Charles is my first name. Mama wanted me to be named after my daddy, kinda for tradition, but she wanted me to have my own identity. She said she didn't want to call him and have me come, you know. So ever'body's always called me Leon."

"I understand. And, your father, when's the last time you talked to him?"

"Oh, gosh, it's been four or five months ago. He . . ."

"He what?"

"He, well, me and him hadn't got too much to talk about."

"He got you into a bad deal, didn't he?"

"You might say that. Turned out he wasn't that great a father." Leon looked away wistfully.

"Chuck, we picked up Marty Morningside." Edge paused. "He told it all."

Morton said nothing.

"The police are in the process of drawing warrants on your father and a couple of others." He paused again. "Now's the time for you to get in front of this and do the best for yourself."

"You mean tell my side of it?"

"Yeah. No one can help you better than you. It's a cinch your father won't."

Morton nodded his head and chuckled slightly. "You know when I was a kid, before he and mama split up, he used to take me for walks in the woods up near the house. We'd look at butterflies and lizards and such, and then we'd go fishin' at the pond on Aunt Polly's place. I caught my first fish when I was about five; it wadn't but about six or eight inches long. I don't remember much about it, but I remember catchin' that fish. I was so proud; Daddy, too." He paused. "He took me huntin' too, when I was older. I shot my first deer with him. He showed me how to skin it and, you know, butcher it. But after ever'thing we'd do, he'd come home and get sloppy-assed drunk, and him and mama'd get into it, and he'd slap her around. Mama said that when he was younger he was a really good man, but after he come home from overseas, well, he just didn't know how to leave it all behind. In a way, I think he liked havin' somethin' wrong with him; he liked feedin' that bad side.

"Anyway, when him and mama split, I went to live with her in Memphis. After that, I'd only see him ever' so often. It seemed like as long as he had his family with him, and a job ever' now and then, he thought he could drink and smoke dope all he wanted, and he felt like he was holdin' it together. After we left, he knew that he wadn't, and he just seemed to go downhill a lot faster. Whenever I'd see him, like when I was in high school and around that time, I couldn't hardly stand to be around'im. He'd try to take me out to drink with him, and I went, 'cause I wanted to be like him, but, you know, my heart wadn't in it." He paused and looked Edge in the eye. "Mama quit lettin' me see him 'cause he wadn't a real good influence. I still love'im, though. I'd do anything in the world for'im, and I think he'd do anything for me, that he could. That's when . . ."

"When what?"

"You know me'an Marilyn are gonna get married."

"I know. She told me."

Morton nodded. "Yeah, we was gonna get married."

"You needed some money?"

Morton said nothing.

"You might as well tell it, Chuck."

Morton chuckled. "I guess ever'body'll be callin' me that from now on. I been Leon for as long as I can remember. Marilyn calls me Leon."

Morton was dancing around it and wanted to let it go, but he was saavy enough to believe that if he confessed, a trial, and therefore a sympathetic jury, would be useless to him. They'd have to convict him even if they felt something for him.

"What about the ammunition in Marilyn's trailer. Is that yours?"

Morton thought for a minute, wondering how exactly they could connect the box of .38s to the murder of the Wyatt woman. He decided to be careful.

"I don't really know about them shells. I saw'em in the house, but I don't know where they come from."

Edge nodded. At least he had admitted to knowing they were there.

"When's the last time you were in Mobile, Chuck?"

Morton looked up. "You know, I don't know. I just don't remember. Seems like I been down there to the beach sometime back, a few years ago, maybe; but I really don't remember when."

"You ever been a bar called The Lunatic Lounge, in Mobile?"

"Man, I been in so many bars over the years. Whoever looks at the name over the door? As long as they got a drink inside, they're good enough for me."

"Do you know Marty Morningside?"

"Marty who?"

"Runs a pawn shop in Mobile."

"The name don't ring a bell."

"How about Andy Allison?"

"Who?"

"You know him? Andy Allison?"

Morton paused. "Not that I know of."

Edge looked at him hard. He had brought up most of the players in the case, and Morton had been deft at denying knowing any of them. In addition, he had not confirmed ever being in The Lunatic Lounge, or even being in Mobile. But, Edge was willing to talk as long as Morton was.

"Man, I can't believe it," Edge said.

"What's that?"

"That you're gonna let Bobby Wyatt screw you like this and then just walk away. He's gonna get off, Chuck, and you're gonna let him. He got what he wanted and all it cost him was a few thousand dollars. It's gonna cost you many, many years . . . maybe even the rest of your life."

The look on Chuck's face told Edge and the others that it was a scenario that had not occurred to him. Wyatt had been such a remote player in the whole affair that it had apparently not crossed his mind that someone had wanted Dorothy Wyatt dead and that she was dead for some reason. He looked up at Edge.

"I want a lawyer."

Edge got back to Mobile at midnight. Vaughn and Hanks had stayed behind to see and meet with the Webster County DA, and make arrangements for Leon 'Chuck' Morton's extradition.

Edge stopped in at his office before going home. The message light was blinking on his answering machine. Edge sat down and pushed the button.

"Mr. Edge, call Bobby Wyatt as soon as possible." The operator recited a number.

Edge picked up the phone and called the number. It was Wyatt's answering service. A female answered.

"Can I help you?"

"My name is Edge."

"Oh, yes, Mr. Edge. Mr. Wyatt wants to talk to you."

"Tell him, I'll call him tomorrow."

"He said to tell you it was very urgent, that no matter what time you called back, that you were to get the message to meet him. He said to tell you that Lucy would be there."

Edge stopped. It was happening again. Wyatt was making a last stand, and he had Lance.

"Where?"

"He said to come to the last house on the right, on Old Bay Front Road, near the airport. He said you'd been there before."

"I'm on my way."

CHAPTER 34

When Edge parked his Impala on the street, fifty feet from what was later determined to be 100 Old Bay Front Road, he could see Bobby Wyatt's Cadillac parked in the driveway next to the house. Edge took a minute to look around to try to assess the danger. He assumed that he'd be dealing with Wyatt alone; he couldn't imagine that anyone would be willing to help him do what Edge thought he was about to try.

Edge walked onto the grass and then slowly toward the perimeter of the building. It was at that moment that he realized just exactly how tired he was. His legs and arms both ached, and his head hurt.

As he moved down the side of the house, he stopped to look in each window of the mostly dark home. Through a dirty pane near the front he could see a light on in the living space near the front door. He could also see Lance seated on a beat up couch.

Her hands were behind her back and she was leaned over to her side. Even in the dim light he could see that she was bleeding and there were bruises on her face. Her hair was disheveled and her button-up blouse was torn. Wyatt was not in view.

"Son of a bitch," he said lightly and to no one.

Anger welled within him. He resisted the urge to storm the front door. Instead, Edge started toward the back. The rear of the property was dark and the leaves of several oak and pecan trees in the backyard rustled in the wind off the bay.

When he reached the rear corner of the house, he pulled his .45. He looked around and saw no one. He could see that the back door was slightly ajar. He put his foot on the bottom step of three leading up to the threshold.

The noise of the wind masked the movement behind him and the first indication that something was wrong was when he felt hard metal on his back.

"Stop right there, Edge."

Edge recognized the voice of Bobby Wyatt. He froze.

"Is she dead?" Edge said.

"Just drop the gun."

Edge purposely tossed the weapon toward the opposite side of the steps. Surprisingly, Wyatt made no attempt at any further search.

"Now, up the steps and into the house."

Edge walked slowly up the concrete and pushed the door open. Wyatt was right behind him, within two feet. Edge knew that he could use that fact to his advantage.

It was a shotgun house; by that it is meant that there was a kitchen just inside the back door, and a long hall up one side of the structure. A couple of bedrooms and a bath led off the hall to the right.

They walked down the north side hall of the home and in seconds were into the dimly lit living room. Edge stopped and looked at Lance. Wyatt stepped by him and to his right and took a vantage point where he could see and cover both of them. Edge identified the weapon in his hand as one of the new Glock brand semi-auto pistols. Edge gritted his teeth.

He had not known Lucy Lance long, nor were the two especially close, but she was his partner. And for that reason, and that reason alone, he made up his mind that at the first opportunity he would kill Bobby Wyatt.

"You two have caused me a lotta trouble," Wyatt said.

Wyatt was standing with his back to the corner of the room. Edge studied his face. It was red with rage.

"That money is mine. I paid the premiums on it for twenty fuckin' years. She never worked, I did it all. Now, you're gonna keep it from me?" He took several deep breaths.

"You killed your wife, Bobby. Nobody's gonna pay you for that."

"I did not kill my wife!" he roared.

Edge studied Lance's face. She had not moved since the two had walked into the room.

"Is she alive?" He nodded toward Lance.

"Who gives a shit. I'm about to lose my business, my freedom, my whole life."

Edge looked back at Wyatt. "Well, you're not gonna save any of it like this. You need to leave crime to the criminals, Bobby. You don't really know what you're doin'." He paused and nodded toward Lance. "Let me get her outta here, and get her some help, and you can call your mouthpiece. He'll think up some way for you to weasel out of all it."

"Are you kidding? You two aren't leaving this room alive."

"Don't do it, Bobby."

"Why not?"

"Think of your kids. You'll be in the penitentiary and they won't have anybody. Think of your girlfriend."

"Who cares. They never loved me. She poisoned them against me." He paused. "Arianna is gonna marry me, now. I need that money to make it happen, and to keep my business together."

Edge shifted left and took a position between Wyatt and Lance. Bobby would have to shoot through him to hit her.

"You made too many mistakes, Bobby. You never should'a trusted the low lifes that you threw in with."

His anger began to rise up again. "Who I should I have trusted? The fuckin' insurance people?

They're the ones screwin' me." He paused. "Well, not anymore."

With that Wyatt raised his gun to point shoulder; aimed directly at Edge's face. Edge dropped to a crouch, lowered his shoulder, and charged him. The gun went off over his head, and the two tumbled to the floor.

Anger rose in Edge, and he struck like a snake. He pushed Wyatt's gun arm down with his left hand, then he head butted Wyatt. He gave him a right to the face; then another, and another. Wyatt went limp and the pistol dropped from his hand. Edge picked up the weapon and then stood up.

With Wyatt semi-conscious, Edge continued his blitz. He stomped him three times in the ribcage, once in the abdomen, twice in the nose; and he kicked him in the left temple. Wyatt's motionless body belonged to Edge and his rage, and he intended to use it to satisfy his lust. He took out his switchblade, pushed the button that extended the blade, and knelt by the motionless man's body.

Edge grabbed Wyatt by his silver hair and pulled his head back thereby exposing his neck. He was just about to cut into Wyatt's flesh when something arrested his attack.

"Edge, don't."

The whispered voice was that of Lucy Lance. Edge froze. He had almost forgotten her. He turned toward the couch, knelt next to her, and raised her up. Blood issued from a wound to her abdomen. He put his ear to her lips and listened.

"Don't kill him." Her breathy voice was almost a sigh.

"What?"

"No more killing."

Edge reached behind her and used his switchblade to cut the ropes that held her wrists together. Then he repositioned her supine on the couch. He checked her pulse. It was weak.

He knew he had to get her help as soon as possible. He took Lance's bindings and tied Wyatt's hands and feet, though there was no reason to do so. Wyatt was out cold, and he appeared to be in mortal danger himself.

Edge exited the front door and squeezed off three rounds into the air in an effort to attract attention. Then he noticed the whip antenna on Wyatt's car. Edge entered the unlocked vehicle and used his Motorola brick phone, and the CB radio, to call for help.

At the University Medical Center's Teaching Hospital, Lucy Lance was rushed into emergency surgery. Bobby Wyatt followed close behind. Edge sat in the Emergency Department waiting area and was there when Victor Riley arrived. Edge sat with his head in his hands and his eyes shut while listening to hospital sounds over the loudspeaker.

"Edge?" Riley said.

Edge looked up. "Lieutenant."

Riley looked tired and beaten himself. "What happened?"

Edge shook his head. "When I got back from Mississippi, I had a message to meet Wyatt on Old Bay Front Road. When I got there, he got the drop on me. He'd worked Lance over, and was gonna kill me. I rushed him, and the gun went off. I think he shot her in the belly. I was gonna kill'im, but . . ."

"But what?"

"She stopped me. She said there'd been enough killing."

Riley nodded his head. "How bad was she hurt?"

"Not half as bad as I wanted to hurt him. They're both in surgery."

He exhaled loudly and looked around. "Okay. Well, we'll just wait and see."

They both sat in silence for the next two hours. Riley leaned back and closed his eyes, and Edge just held his face in his hands. They were in those positions when a doctor in bloody green scrubs entered the waiting room.

CHAPTER 35

Wyatt was in the hospital six weeks. He suffered a concussion, several broken ribs, a broken pelvis, a punctured lung, a broken nose, and several lost teeth. But he lived. He was arrested immediately upon his discharge.

Lucy Lance deceased in surgery.

Two weeks later Charles Leon Morton turned state's evidence and gave a statement implicating Marty Morningside and the now deceased Andy Allison. His testimony completed the chain and enabled the police to get a warrant for Wyatt's arrest.

After Wyatt's incarceration, Edge prepared a final bill for Manhattan Mutual Insurance, and Shelia Waltham came down from Atlanta to pay it in person. She joined Edge for lunch at the General Jackson.

"I take it you were at the funeral?" Edge said.

"I was. It was . . . well, just sad. Lucy's daughter came from Massachusetts." She paused. "Her husband took it all very, very hard."

Edge said nothing.

"The autopsy report said that she died from a skull fracture. So, I guess, she was effectively dead when you got there. The gunshot wound was just . . . well, it just helped it all along."

"Maybe if I'd called the police, they could've gotten there quicker. Maybe if I hadn't left town." he said. He shook his head and looked away. "I don't know."

"Sounds as if it was just a matter of time. The police tell me that she was abducted from the hotel, they think around seven, after dinner. He had four or five hours to work her over before you got there. Don't . . . ." She started to say, 'beat yourself up,' but caught herself.

Edge said nothing. He thought of Lance's face as she lay in the couch. Her words of mercy for Wyatt were still in his ears. He wished he'd ignored them.

"So, Wyatt's in jail and the company saved his claim. Was his motive greed?" Waltham said.

Edge cleared his throat. "No. I think he just didn't want his wife around anymore. He's got, or had, a new girlfriend, and he wanted to save his business from the financial trouble that it was in. If he'd lost his business, he surely would have lost the woman. He had to do something to keep his world the way he wanted it."

Waltham nodded. She looked him in the eyes and then reached and patted his hand.

"I know it doesn't help, but you did a good job for the company. There'll be a bonus."

He nodded. "Should I reach out to her husband?"

Waltham looked away for a minute. "Not right now. We gave him all the reports. He knows what happened."

"Does he hold it against me?"

"Probably. He's angry at the world, right now. But he'll get over it."

CHAPTER 36

Seven months later, Edge was in his office when the phone rang. It was a voice he recognized.

"Mr. Edge, I need to see you."

"I thought all of our business had been concluded."

"If you could just give me five minutes, in the park."

Edge was silent. His old life did not need to be intruding into his new life anymore.

"Okay, I'll be there in thirty minutes."

Edge sat down on a park bench on the southeast corner of Beinville Square at six o'clock and waited. There was a cold breeze off the waterfront, and he pulled the lapels of his coat together with his right hand. The area was deserted.

Five minutes later he noticed as a man and a woman walked toward the bench. The woman was JoAnn Ward. She was carrying a bundle in her arms. The man was tall, thin, and distinguished, wearing a camel's hair overcoat over a suit. His hair was black as were his horn rimmed glasses. Edge sat up straight.

When they got close, Ward spoke. "Thanks for seeing us."

Edge nodded. He slid to one end of the bench. Ward sat down on the other. The man stood next to her. Edge could see Ward was carrying a baby.

"This is my husband, John. Dr. Daniel Atchison."

Edge nodded. "What can I do for you folks?"

Atchison spoke up. "Mr. Edge, I just wanted to meet you and thank you for all you've done for my wife and myself." He paused. "JoAnn has told me the entire story," he emphasized the word 'entire,' "and I want you to know that your secret is safe with me. If it weren't for you, our daughter wouldn't be here." He nodded to the baby.

She smiled. "John Edge, meet Molly Denise Atchison."

Edge looked at the child and nodded, and sniffed. "Congratulations," was all he could say.

When Edge stood up, he extended his hand to Atchison. "Thanks. I know you must be a little sore at me . . . I'm sorry."

"Nonsense. You've saved my wife's life two times. There's nothing to apologize for."

Edge nodded. "Thanks." He turned and looked down at the sleeping infant.

Atchison cleared his throat. "Well, we'll leave you to your work. I know it's probably something very, uh, . . . interesting."

He reached in his pocket. "Anyway," he handed a business card to Edge, "if I can ever be of help. Please call me."

"I will." He paused and looked at the card. "You guys take care."

With that Edge turned and walked away. He needed a drink, badly.

The End

EPILOGUE

Marty Morningside testified against Charles Leon Morton as well as Bobby Wyatt and with his plea arrangement ended up being paroled after serving thirty six months in prison. Edge didn't think it was enough, but it was the most he could have hoped for.

With his testimony in the Bobby Wyatt case, Leon, or 'Chuck,' avoided the death penalty and was sentenced to life in prison without the possibility of parole. He does his time at the facility in Atmore, Alabama, and every year, like clockwork, John Edge receives a Christmas card from him.

Lardy McLain was given a ten year sentence for soliciting the murder of Andy Allison. The leniency was due to the fact that it came out in trial that he had only wanted Allison roughed up a bit, not killed, and because the jury found out what a ne'er do well Allison was. McLain got five more concurrent years for about twenty cases of receiving and concealing stolen property that the Police were able to hang on him. Lester Wright got life.

Charlie Morton was not charged. In the end, all the state had was the word of Morningside and Leon that Charlie was a part of it all. Leon wouldn't testify against his father, and the police couldn't tie the weapons back to him.

Bobby Wyatt took his chances in front of a jury in Dothan, Alabama, after having asked for and gotten a change of venue. He was convicted of conspiracy to commit murder and given a thirty year sentence in Bootsie's case. He received life without parole in the case of the death of Lucy Lance.

Wyatt did his time at Atmore for the first five years. Afterwards he was able to wangle a transfer to the McFarland Work Farm, a new facility built by a new governor who was trying to make prisons self-sustaining. They grew vegetables, wheat, and even raised cattle.

Wyatt was assigned to ride the herds and did so with gusto, until one day he turned his back on a bull that, for reasons known only to God, charged and gored him. The horn went right through his heart, and he was killed instantly.

Edge got the news from Victor Riley by telephone. At his office he thought for the hundredth time about Lance's words as she lay dying. Then he thought about how to forget them.

Fin

Printed in the United States
By Bookmasters